Father John
vs the Zombies

Book One
of the *Father John* Trilogy

KARL EL-KOURA

Father John
vs the Zombies

Father John vs the Zombies
© 2012 by Karl El-Koura

ISBN: 978-0-9881558-2-4
Cover design by the author.

For more information, visit:
www.ootersplace.com/FatherJohn

To Kirsten

Chapters

Chapter 1

THE zombies attacked their home late at night on a Monday. Johnny and his wife were in bed, their young daughter sleeping between them. He'd been staring at the ceiling in the nearly pitch-dark room when he heard glass shatter. He jumped out of bed, instinctively grabbing the steel bat. The one he leaned against the wall every night before turning in; the one he prayed he'd never have to use.

"The boards will hold them," his wife said to him, whispering so she wouldn't wake Izzy.

He stood in front of their bedroom door, the bat slung over his right shoulder. He was suddenly aware of every sound—his own breathing, his wife's, Izzy's; the ever-present howling outside, the noise he couldn't get used to, the noise that had kept him from having a good night's sleep for the last nine days. More glass breaking.

You've left us alone for over a week, he thought. *Why are you coming here now?*

Howls and yells. Thumping and banging, as their arms and feet and heads hit and kicked and butted against the plywood he'd used to board up the patio door in the guest bedroom. Rebekah had convinced him to cut a hole through their home to put in the sliding glass door last summer, to increase the value of the house and give them access to a backyard deck. They hadn't built the deck yet; he'd planned to, this summer. He'd already requested the time off at work.

It's a strange thing to be thinking about at a time like this.

He felt a hand on his arm and almost jumped. Or swung.

"It's okay," Rebekah said. "It's me."

"Stay with Izzy," he whispered, his voice betraying him by breaking.

The banging against the wood grew louder, more insistent. *Thump! Thump! Thump!*

Are you banging to be let in? Johnny thought. *As if you have a right to this house? This is our home, and you won't enter it. Father, don't let them; don't let them break through that wood, Lord. In the name of your Holy Son, in the power of Your Holy Spirit, keep our house safe and secure as You've done since all of this started, Holy Father. Have mercy on me and my family, Lord, according to Your great mercy.*

Izzy stirred in bed. She sat up. "Mommy?" Her voice was soft and scared.

I'm scared too, little one.

Rebekah walked back to their daughter and whispered that everything was going to be okay.

Izzy refused to sleep in her coat, so she'd been sleeping on it. As Rebekah slipped Izzy's hands through its sleeves, she said, "I want you to play silent monk now, darling." Then Johnny saw his wife pull their daughter into an embrace and, for a mad moment, he wanted to drop the bat and go to his family and wrap both of them in his arms.

He started. They'd broken through. He hadn't heard it break, but the plywood had given. The howling was loud and getting louder, as loud as someone standing in the hallway outside their bedroom.

Something hard hit the door and jostled it with a loud bang. A second hit, followed by another. *Bang! Bang!* He took a step back with his right leg, gripped the bat tighter. *Bang!* and the door looked like it might fly off its hinges.

"I'm here," Rebekah said from beside him. She held her own bat, though hers was made of wood. He only had the one steel bat, and by the time he thought to buy a second, they'd all been sold out.

"Stay with Izzy," he said again.

Rebekah didn't move.

"There's a lot of them," he said, raising his voice a little to be heard over the assault on their bedroom door.

Rebekah looked back at Izzy. "We meet at the church?"

He nodded. Outside the door, the howls of the zombies became even more frenzied. "Wait until I draw them away, but don't wait too long, okay?"

She didn't say anything; they'd already gone over this and he knew she didn't like the idea.

"Okay, honey?" he said.

The door flew open, the lock breaking, the top hinge ripped right out of the wall. Johnny swung without thought or discrimination, aiming for whatever was convenient. He connected with the head of the first zombie, cracking its skull and sending it to the ground. He broke the arm of another, then smashed his bat so hard against its face that he heard its neck snap. His third target was a tall zombie in a dirty business suit, and the bat cracked its short ribs and maybe punctured its lungs; whatever happened, that zombie fell too. Something warm and wet suddenly splashed across his face—blood; guts too, maybe. Rebekah had swung with her own bat, although the plan was for her to hide in the attached bathroom.

More zombies were stepping over their fallen comrades and entering the bedroom. Johnny raised his bat over his head, then brought it slamming down on one of their heads; the zombie stumbled backward and made a strange, sad gurgling sound before it dropped. Momentarily distracted, Johnny paused; a zombie grabbed the bat and tried to wrench it out of his hands. Johnny kicked the zombie in the leg, then let go of the handle and threw a punch at the side of the zombie's head. The zombie dropped the bat and Johnny bent down to grab it off the floor.

Rebekah continued to grunt and swing, dropping her own share of zombies. He was proud of her. "I'm not a delicate flower, you know?" she said to him once when they were still dating—he couldn't remember why. No, she wasn't a delicate flower—she just looked like one.

Zombie bodies were filling the narrow passageway just inside their bedroom door. He felt vomit rise into his throat; the smell was overpowering, the stink of human bodies that haven't been washed in weeks, the stench of feces and urine, of blood dried and crusted on dirt-stained flesh and clothes.

He stood. From the bed, he heard Izzy start to cry. She'd kept quiet longer than he'd expected, even after all the games of "silent monk" they'd played in the last week to help her practice.

"Please," he said to his wife. "Now."

Without waiting to see or hear if she'd listen, he attacked another zombie, having to swing the bat twice before the large creature dropped. He heard movement behind him, but didn't turn to look.

"I love you," his wife said, then he heard the bathroom door close.

"I love you, too!" he yelled; then, "I love you, little one!"

He climbed onto their bed, tried to open the curtains but tore them off in his ferocity. "Come on, you freaks!" He swung the bat against the large window above the headboard; he hit it a second and a third time, then used the bat to clear a path, sweeping away the broken shards that still clung to the frame.

The light of a full moon streamed through the opening and cast a bluish glow on the garish scene. Bodies filled their bedroom floor, as if he and his wife were over-achieving serial killers amassing trophies. He couldn't help but think that the bodies on the ground looked as human as any other body, if only dirtier and bloodier. It was the walking zombies—the howling, crazed creatures trying to bite or bash with their fists whatever was in their way—that were obvious for the monsters they were.

A few of those zombies were banging against the bathroom door, and Johnny knew it wouldn't take much for it to give. "Over here!" he yelled. He tried to swing at a zombie who had climbed onto the bed, but the mattress and swirled piles of covers were too soft and he was too unsteady to give it any real power. He used the bat to push the zombie off the bed instead.

He couldn't stay there, but he wasn't jumping out the window with zombies clamoring to get into the small bathroom where his wife and daughter were hiding. Taking a deep breath, he played his Hail Mary card, in the hope that the pastor from Alabama was right. He tried it: "In the name of Jesus Christ," he said, "the Son of God—"

He didn't need to finish; at the name of Jesus, he sensed as much as heard or saw the zombies stop and turn to face him as if with one will. He climbed out of the window, sticking out his right leg. Their house was a bungalow and he was less than ten feet from the ground. The night air was cold; he was dressed in jeans and a sweater and even had running shoes on, but no jacket. His jacket was in the bedroom closet; they'd gotten a bit lax after a few days.

Someone grabbed his left leg; he kicked reflexively and made contact with something (a shoulder? a face?), but the zombie didn't let go. He kicked again, then again, striking something each time. Still the zombie held on, and started pulling him back in. Fighting against the rising sense of panic, Johnny dropped the bat out the window, grabbed the sill from outside and launched himself away from the house. His plan had been to land on his feet and roll, but he stumbled backward instead and fell down without a chance to brace himself. Winded, he pushed himself on his side with effort, then up to his knees. He looked around, trying to control his coughing and to focus. The bat. . . he couldn't see it. As his desperate gaze swept their backyard, his heart drummed against his chest, louder and harder. The bat had to be there, he'd just tossed it—

Something metallic glinted in the moonlight. He scrambled over and grabbed the bat, then rose to his feet.

A zombie fell out of his bedroom window head-first and broke its neck. A pang of sadness swept through him, and he almost reached out to—what? help? straighten out its neck so the body didn't look so mangled and pathetic?

Johnny forced his gaze to the zombies trying to jam themselves through the patio door and into his home. He yelled at them and they turned to look at him. "What are you waiting for?" he yelled again. "Come on!"

Another zombie followed the first through the bedroom window; it landed on its legs and seemed to break or sprain something. Still it hobbled toward Johnny and he swung his bat to drop it.

"Come on!" he yelled again, then checked over his shoulder to make sure the way was clear. He ran backward to an unbroken part of the large wooden fence that separated his backyard from their neighbors to the east. "Come on!"

As long as they didn't swarm him all at once, Johnny knew he'd be okay. Most of the zombies weren't a big threat on their own; many had banged their heads against so many locked doors, or tore at them with their bare hands, that they'd dislodged most of their teeth or ripped off their own fingernails. Some zombies were missing one or both eyes. So long as he kept the fights one-on-one, and he had a bat and they didn't, Johnny wasn't worried about any individual zombie. It was when they came at you together, with one grabbing your hands while another tore at you... he'd seen the same image played out countless times in videos on the internet and on the news, when all of this had first happened. It was when they came at you together that... he pushed the images away.

Again he swung and almost took off the head of the fastest zombie coming after him; then swung again and took care of the runner-up. Johnny kept one eye on his bedroom window; it was dark and empty with no more zombies coming through. Finally he thought he saw a small bundle get lowered down, then a bigger one landing softly behind it. His wife picked up their daughter and began to run around the side of the house. She was supposed to wave at him to let him know she and Izzy were okay. But maybe she forgot, or maybe she felt, now that everything was actually happening, the second that action would take was a second they couldn't spare.

Johnny followed at a distance, knocking down zombies when they came too close. Throughout he tried to keep one eye on the shadow about a dozen strides ahead of him now. She seemed to be carrying Izzy with both hands. Had she lost her bat at some point? For a moment he considered heading back to look for it. They could always come back later, though; the priority now was to get his family safely to the church.

Rebekah turned the corner at the end of their street and headed west. He followed, scanning the driveways and homes to either side and the way ahead. It was clear for the most part. The zombies he saw were keeping their distance and didn't seem that interested in him or Rebekah. A quick glance over his shoulder confirmed his suspicion; some of the zombies who'd attacked their home were still giving chase, but they were slow and lumbering and were falling behind.

Johnny returned his gaze to his wife and daughter; he was ready at a moment's notice to race up to them if he felt they needed his help. But they turned north on Main Street without trouble. Two more blocks and they'd be in sight of the church.

He tripped, his foot catching on something, and he let go of the bat as he put out his hands to stop the fall. He'd been so focused on making sure the way was clear for his wife and daughter that he'd neglected to check his own immediate surroundings.

A growl drew his attention. A zombie's face, inches from his own. Johnny scrambled away, but bumped into something hard and suddenly a sharp, hard pinch on his right calf made him yell out in pain.

I've been bitten, he thought, in a strange mixture of sadness and acceptance. He wondered what that meant for him, how long he had. He put aside that thought for the moment and mule-kicked with his unhurt leg at the head of the zombie he'd tripped over, whose mouth was still wrapped around Johnny's leg, the zombie's teeth still digging into his flesh and drawing blood.

The first zombie, a female, shrieked with an ear-piercing yell. She tried to reach for Johnny's neck, but he pushed her hands away even as he tried to dislodge with kicks the zombie behind him. Blood was pouring down his leg now, and he felt himself start to go faint. *I've been bitten*, he thought again.

For some reason he looked up the street, searching for his wife and daughter. Was there any point in calling for help? Would he even want to call them back? But they were gone, and the largest part of him was glad for it.

His gaze locked with the female zombie's. Her eyes were listless and droopy, but he sensed a degree of intelligence behind her gaze that he hadn't expected to find. Even as he stared at her, though, she clawed at him, tore a small chunk of flesh from his cheek, and barely missed taking out one of his eyes.

Johnny gathered his remaining strength in his right arm, made a fist, then punched her in the face; her head snapped to the side, but her arms kept trying to reach for his own face or neck. He grabbed her right arm with one hand, her elbow with the other, and snapped. The crack was loud. She never yelled out in pain, though, and still tried to attack him with her other arm and was now trying to crawl on top of him, maybe to pin him back to the ground. Repulsed, he pushed her away hard, then drove his heel into the other zombie's head; that zombie stripped off more skin from his leg, and Johnny cried out again. But at least he'd gotten loose of the zombie's bite.

Johnny felt around for the bat without allowing his gaze to leave the female zombie's. He found it, picked it up and swung just as she lunged at him. Without a chance to brace the swing, though, it was only powerful enough to daze her. Johnny took the opportunity to rise to his feet despite the burning pain from his right leg.

He held the bat in both arms. "Get out of here!" he yelled, expecting his tone to have more effect than his words, the way one might yell at a pair of dangerous dogs.

The female zombie's right arm hung at a weird angle by her side. He thought he saw her smile. Somehow that simple little twitch of her lips, more than anything that had happened that night, sent shivers down his spine.

The male zombie stood too. In the moonlight, Johnny thought he saw his own blood like dark ink smeared around the zombie's mouth.

The shivers multiplied, and a cold sweat broke out over his body. Or was that more than shivers? Was this simply fear he felt, or was it the first step and symptom of his own transformation into one of them? He tried to push the thought away. Maybe the bite, bad as it was, wasn't enough to transmit whatever needed to be transmitted to turn him into a zombie. Maybe the carrier had to be cut and bleeding in its own mouth too, which Johnny couldn't be sure was the case for the male zombie. Tears welled into his eyes, but he tried to force them away. Whatever else the cold shivers meant, he definitely recognized fear inside of him. He didn't want to turn into one of these monsters, didn't want to lose himself, didn't want to attack other people and claw at them and bite them and maybe devour them if he could. He was afraid; afraid of all of that and afraid of never seeing or at least never recognizing his daughter again, of never kissing his wife again or making her laugh, of—

Please God, don't turn me into a zombie, he thought, looking up at the sky reflexively. A long shadow covered the full moon in part, as if even it wished to pull an arm across its face to shield itself from the horrors below. The moon could shield its eyes, Johnny thought, but he'd prayed to God—and God didn't shield His eyes from any horror, did He? Far more than that, He took the horrors of the world onto Himself, to save it. *And what's come of your world now?* Johnny couldn't help thinking the thought, but he chased it away quickly as he'd chased away so many other dark thoughts lately. *You know what fear is*, he thought. *You were afraid once too. Help me overcome this fear as You overcame Yours. Help me be strong as You are strong. Be my refuge, be my shield.*

The female and male zombies were inching closer to him, their wary gaze fixed on his bat. "Leave!" he yelled again, and spoke with such authority that they stopped moving at least. But the commotion had attracted the attention of others. Two zombies he could probably handle, even with the fire burning in his leg. But more than that and he was at risk of being overwhelmed.

He walked away backwards, favoring his left leg. The pair followed, and more were approaching from all around. He gripped his bat tighter.

"If you come any closer," he said to the two as he continued to retreat, "I'll bash in your heads."

They snarled or laughed at him, he wasn't sure. Then, as if responding to an unseen and unspoken command, in one instant they both launched themselves at him. But he was ready and swung at the nearest zombie, then pivoted and swung again. It was enough; the first wasn't moving on the ground, and the other was down and twitching at his feet.

Something grabbed him from behind, wrapped its arms around him, lifted him up and seemed set on crushing him to death. He kicked backward with his good leg and hit the zombie in the shins, but had to elbow it in the face twice, blood gushing out of its nose and onto him, before it let go.

He half-ran, half-hobbled down the street, trying to outpace the zombies that had zeroed in on him, and to avoid the zombies ahead. One block. Another. The streets were bordered by abandoned cars that had been pushed off to the sides. Some of the houses had been burned down; others were still or newly on fire. The blaze lit up the macabre scene on most of the front lawns. Dead and decaying bodies were strewn about, like Halloween lawn decorations taken to a morbid extreme.

Johnny wondered if the fires were accidental or the work of the zombies. Or even if they were set by surviving humans, perhaps as a way to control disease by burning up dead bodies. Or control the real disease by burning up living zombies.

He pushed himself to run in spite of the pain, the church looming into view when he passed the apartment buildings that towered over the corner of Down and Main. The three domes of the church were like dark beacons, the sight of the large golden cross glinting in the moonlight at the top of the largest dome filling him with relief for the first time that night.

A zombie sat on the curb, leaning against the pole of a bus stop sign, backlit by the burning two-story house behind him. He seemed to be the only zombie around. Although his leg screamed in pain, Johnny refused to give it any attention but forced himself to keep going. The zombie's head was slouched down, and he was either sleeping or dead.

He arrived at the church without encountering any other zombies. He'd come up on its northern side, from Down Street, but went around to the front entrance off River.

The church, St. George, was actually a cathedral. Half-moon marble steps led up to the main double doors set in the center of the western face of the church. The doors were large oak ones, each ten feet high and carved with a simple bordered pattern of squares and rectangles.

He climbed the steps and almost collapsed at the doors, but leaned against the bat to hold himself up. His leg throbbed. He was still bleeding from there and from his cheek. He used the sleeve of his sweater to wipe away the blood on his face.

With the fleshy part of his left fist he knocked on the large wooden doors, creating a deep, reverberating sound. He remembered Easter midnight services, which he and his parents attended every year when he was a kid. The priest and the entire congregation stood outside in the cold midnight air, protecting the vulnerable flames of their candles with cupped hands, and the priest knocked on the doors. "Lift up your heads, ye gates!" the priest called out. "Be ye lifted up, ye everlasting doors, and the King of glory shall come in." Then the doors would come open and the lights in the church would come on. Christ had broken down the gates of death, trampling them down by His own death. The Lord strong and mighty, the Lord mighty in battle. Christos Anesti!

Christ is Risen!

It had been a long time since he'd attended Easter matins service.

He knocked again, then tried to listen for any sounds inside. What if the church were empty? But it couldn't be. If no one was inside, Rebekah would've waited for him here—there were no zombies around to scare her away.

"Hello?" he yelled, dropping the bat and knocking with both fists this time, over and over again. "Is anyone in there?"

He allowed his forehead to drop to the door and rest against it. What if the church were empty after all? What if Rebekah had been chased away by zombies and was hiding somewhere else for the moment? Where could they go? This church was supposed to be their Plan B. They didn't have a Plan C.

"Is anyone inside?" he yelled again, his voice sounding in his own ears as ragged and worn-out as he felt.

Before he could knock another time, he heard a voice from the other side of the doors. "Who are you?" The voice belonged to a young man, Johnny thought, and it betrayed a large degree of reservation or fear. He didn't recognize it.

"My name is Johnny Salibi," he said. "I'm Rebekah's husband. Please open the door."

There was only silence on the other side. Johnny couldn't understand; he obviously wasn't a zombie (*yet*, he couldn't help but think). Why wasn't this man opening the door?

"If you have any love for Christ our Lord," Johnny said, pain and weariness forcing a note of desperation into his voice, "you will let me in."

"Stand back," the man said, then Johnny heard a lock being flipped and he stumbled away a step as the large door swung out.

Subdeacon Michael held it open; Johnny could place the voice now. The subdeacon was several years older, of course, probably in his mid-twenties now. At six-foot-three, Johnny considered himself tall, but Michael had a few inches even on him. Much fewer pounds, though. And where Johnny's face was usually clean-shaven (because hair grew on his face unevenly, evidenced now by a week's worth of growth), Michael had a full thick black beard that reached down to his chest, as if in harmony with his black tunic that stretched to the ground.

"Get in, quickly," Michael said, then closed and locked the door behind him. He held a cross and an unlighted flashlight in his left hand. His eyebrows went up at the sight of Johnny's cheek.

Relief swept through Johnny and an overwhelming sense of joy almost sent his feet dancing even as he felt he wanted his leg to be amputated and the pain with it. Subdeacon Michael was obviously healthy, even if the dark fleshy circles under his eyes betrayed that he'd been getting about as much sleep as Johnny himself. But he wasn't a zombie; the church was safe, as they'd hoped.

The doors separating the narthex from the nave were open; large windows ran along the sides of the church, and let in enough moonlight that Johnny could see it was empty. Two candles set at the entrances to the nave were lit, their flames flickering and sending dark shadows to dance on the walls and across the faces of the Theotokos holding the Christ-Child and of St. George slaying the dragon.

"Is everyone in the basement?" He didn't hear any sounds coming from below, but the door leading down there was closed.

Michael had been staring at Johnny's leg. He nodded, then he said, "You're hurt."

A momentary temptation to lie passed. He didn't want to be kicked out of the church (or killed on the spot by Michael), but if he were turning into a zombie, he even more didn't want to endanger a churchful of people, including his own wife and daughter. "I was bit," he said. "Hard."

Michael nodded again. Whatever fear his voice had betrayed before was now strangely gone, although he continued to look at Johnny with a mild apprehension, as if half-expecting him to turn into a zombie at any moment. "We have bandages in the office," he said. "We should get you cleaned up before we go downstairs."

Johnny wasn't sure he understood, but his nerves were so frayed that he didn't want to argue. Mostly he just wanted to sit down and press something against his leg until the bleeding stopped and the throbbing went away. "Whatever you think best," he said, "but can you tell my wife I'm here first?"

The subdeacon brought his right hand to his beard and scratched the bottom of his chin. "Your wife is Rebekah, right?"

Johnny didn't say anything. By the light of the candles, he'd seen the features on Michael's face pull together in a mixture of confusion and concern as he asked the question.

That night had been a long series of frights and attacks of panic, from the moment Johnny first realized the zombies were trying to break into their home until he saw Michael and thought they were safe. But none of it compared to the desperate fear that now gripped his heart. "My wife Rebekah was just ahead of me," he said, speaking deliberately but quickly. "She was just ahead of me, she should be here. With our daughter."

Michael's face had cleared of confusion; only concern remained. He stared at Johnny as if trying to find the words to say what he was thinking, but there was no need. Johnny already knew the truth. Rebekah had never made it to the church.

Chapter 2

THE subdeacon started to say something, but Johnny held up his hand to stop him.

"Can I borrow your flashlight?" he said, the pain in his leg completely forgotten for the moment, the only thought in his mind to get back outside and look for his wife and daughter. But the doubt set in almost immediately: *where should he look for them?* Obviously he'd start by retracing his steps, but he wasn't sure that would help. After they'd been separated, he'd almost subconsciously kept an eye out for them or for anything out of the ordinary. He hadn't seen anything to make him worry, so he'd assumed they'd made it safely.

It didn't matter. He'd go back and check every house between the church and their home, go down each side-street, call out their names at the top of his lungs, even if it meant drawing out every zombie in town.

"Johnny?" He met Michael's gaze; the subdeacon had been saying something, but Johnny hadn't heard a word. "You can't go out there in your condition." Perhaps seeing the look of defiance and anger that seized Johnny's features, he said quickly, "Let me clean and bandage you up first."

Johnny shook his head vigorously. Rebekah and Izzy were still outside, in the dark, likely without a weapon and maybe running from a horde of blood-thirsty zombies bent on catching up to them and—

"Get out of my way." He reached for the latch to unlock the door, but the subdeacon stopped him and pushed him away.

"Don't touch that." The friendly tone had dropped from Michael's voice; it was obvious the subdeacon felt territorial over his doors.

"All right," Johnny said, trying to keep calm. "Please open it and let me out."

"No. I don't care if you don't want your wounds looked after. But unless the bishop says it's okay for you to go out there right now and by yourself, these doors stay closed. Understand?"

In his mind, Johnny saw himself attack the subdeacon, catching him with a surprise right cross to the face that knocked Michael down long enough for Johnny to get the door open.

He pushed the image away, surprised at himself. He'd never struck another human being outside of the karate club, had hardly ever considered it even when provoked. How could such a violent instinct come so quickly to him now? Was it a symptom of his transformation into a zombie, or was it the result of having spent that night bashing zombies with a bat and kicking them in the face? Or was it that the stakes for him had never been so high, and the violent act he contemplated was justified against someone who prevented him from going outside to look for his family?

He didn't know, but he couldn't bring himself to do it even under the circumstances. "Michael, just listen," he said, trying a different tactic. "My wife and daughter mean everything to me. They're out there, and I'm terrified for them. You have no right to hold me here against my will."

The hard look on Michael's face softened. "I get it," he said. "And if the bishop says it's okay, I can help you look, and others will too. Wouldn't that be better than you out there all by yourself hobbling aimlessly in the dark?"

A part of him didn't want to argue; that part felt they were wasting time and just wanted to get outside and start looking for his family already. But another, more rational part saw the wisdom in Michael's words. A search party would be better in every way. And if he were really turning into a zombie, it would be good to know others were looking for Rebekah and Izzy.

He nodded. "Can you take me to him? Bishop Joseph, right?"

"That's right." Michael blew out the candles and turned on his flashlight. "Your face is bleeding."

Almost self-consciously, Johnny wiped at the blood with his sweater again.

Michael shined his light on Johnny's leg. "You're sure you don't want me to take a look at that?"

Suddenly Johnny became aware of the burning again, as if the beam of light were a beam of fire. "I'm fine," he lied.

Michael held open the door and waited for Johnny to go through. Every downward step made him wince, but Johnny pushed himself on. Rebekah was out there, alone with Izzy. Nothing else mattered.

The church basement's windows were small but plentiful; still, they only let in a little of the moonlight.

"The bishop is back there," Michael said, pointing at a dim light in the eastern corner.

Johnny passed through the relative darkness, barely noticing the images the light from Michael's flashlight revealed to him, of cots and tables marking out distinct areas in the church hall. He saw but didn't pay attention to how some people were sleeping in the cots under several layers of blankets so that it looked like just a big bundle of cotton and fabric if not for the exposed heads; or to how others were wearing coats and sleeping while sitting at the tables, hunched over and using their crossed arms for pillows. He hardly noticed the faces that looked up at him as he passed them, peering at him with curious glances; distractedly he wondered if his banging at the door had woken everyone up, or if the current state of the world had turned all the survivors into light sleepers.

The light in the eastern corner was a propane-powered camp lantern, turned low. It threw a grayish glow over an old man, obviously the bishop, and a woman who spoke to him in soft tones. The lamp was placed on the table to the front of the bishop; the woman sat to his left on a cushioned fold-up chair.

The bishop was dressed in black as well, but a shawl or blanket was draped over his shoulders and he wore a black toque with ear flaps, which gave him a slightly comical appearance. His beard was longer than Michael's and grayish-white, like dirty snow. A large golden cross hung from his neck and rested on his chest, while his hands rested with interlocked fingers over the small bulge of his stomach. The bishop had looked up as he and Michael approached, but hadn't said anything.

"Your Eminence," Johnny said to him, wondering if that was the right title, and speaking softly even though the nearest cot was more than a half-dozen paces away. "I came here with my wife to seek refuge."

Bishop Joseph's small black eyes, seeming even smaller underneath his bushy eyebrows, darted around as his gaze searched Johnny's face. "Where is your wife?" he said after a moment.

"We got separated. She's still outside with our daughter. I—"

The bishop immediately turned to the woman at his left. "We'll put together a group of searchers," he said. "Can you ask for volunteers, maybe nine or so?"

The pretty woman nodded. She had short reddish-brown hair and lively blue eyes, although in the dim light the dark purple circles under them were pronounced and gave her face a sense of heaviness, or as of candle wax melting.

"We'll split into three groups," the bishop continued, still speaking to the woman. "You can head one, Isaac another, and—" He turned his head to face Johnny again.

"Johnny," he supplied, relief sweeping through him. He took a deep breath, feeling like he could breathe properly for the first time since he'd discovered his wife hadn't made it to the church. "My name is Johnny Salibi. Thank you, Your Eminence." He turned to the woman seated to the right of the table. "Thank you."

"It's no problem," the bishop said. "We'll split up the groups to make sure we cover as much ground as possible. We have cars too. We'll leave at first light."

Johnny had been nodding along, but he stopped abruptly. "No," he said, the constriction around his lungs returning. "That's too late. We have to leave now."

Bishop Joseph's voice was soft but firm; it didn't seem he was the kind of person who changed his mind just because someone wanted him to. "It's too dark now. Too dangerous." He checked his wristwatch. "Sunrise is in three or four hours."

"I can't wait that long," Johnny said, his voice less soft than the bishop's. He took another deep breath, this one making him feel the exact opposite of the first, then looked to the woman for help and then to Michael. Neither seemed about to contradict the man Johnny took to be the leader of their community.

"I'm sorry," he said, "but I'm leaving right now. Even if it means I have to go alone."

The bishop leaned forward in his chair. "Mr. Salibi," he said, fixing him with his small eyes, "I can only imagine the thoughts going through your head. But you must try and set your fears aside and think dispassionately about this. Our chances of finding your wife and daughter are best in the morning. Come, will you pray with me until then?"

No way I'm leaving them out there for another three or four hours, Johnny thought. And yet, even with his comical hat, the bishop's words conveyed a sense of peace that helped relax Johnny a little, and there was a calm confidence or conviction in the tone of his question that made Johnny want to respond positively; made Johnny want to pray with this man indeed.

Nothing happens without God's permission, Johnny knew. And yet—praying when his wife needed him and it was in his power to do something felt like a cop-out. He'd never doubted the power of prayer—and for him it was an inner conversation he'd held with God for as long as he could remember—but prayer wasn't a substitute for action. Besides, he could pray just as easily while searching for Rebekah as he could in the basement of this church.

If I'm wrong, he thought, *forgive me, Lord.*

"I'm sorry, but no," he said. "I'd be grateful for your help in the morning. I'd be even more grateful if you'd pray for my family tonight. But I can't stay here another minute knowing they're still out there."

Johnny sensed Michael take a step closer to him. He tensed, wondering if the subdeacon planned on grabbing him and forcing him to wait until morning after all.

But Bishop Joseph sat back in his chair and nodded. "You must do as you feel is right," he said, but Johnny felt that it was more of a psychological assessment of Johnny himself than a blessing of his chosen course of action. "We will pray for you and your family."

The words touched Johnny more than he would've expected them to. "Then everything will be okay," he said, and meant it, but realized too late that the bishop might think he was being sarcastic and take offense.

Instead, the bishop turned his hands on his belly so the palms faced up. "God's will be done. That's what we always pray."

Johnny nodded. As he turned to head back to the stairs, he became aware of a commotion at the other end of the room. A small group was gathered at the door to the staircase, holding it open and whispering among themselves.

He ran over to them, having to practically drag his right leg behind him. "What's going on?" he said.

Before they could answer, he heard it: a long, low wailing sound, almost a howling. The sound was wordless but the cry conveyed deep sadness and agony. A thought flashed through his mind: *the sound of a grieving mother who has lost her child.*

Someone started to say something to him. He pushed through the crowd and into the staircase. Ignoring the pain in his leg, he raced up the stairs, aware that Michael was following close behind him.

"Wait," Michael said when they'd reached the top. "Don't open the door."

Johnny unlocked the door and threw it open.

In the moonlight, he saw a figure standing on the lawn across the street, half-hidden by the shadow of a large, leafy tree.

"Rebekah?" he called out, loudly. He felt Michael's hand on his shoulder, restraining him.

The figure kept wailing as if it hadn't heard him, sounding like a whiny police siren, the intensity of its cry dying out as it lost its breath, only to start up again at full force almost immediately afterward.

Was it Rebekah? It was hard to tell; the figure was swallowed up in shadows. But if it was Rebekah, why wasn't she coming any closer? Was she afraid? The way seemed clear. Afraid of the church? Or—had something happened to Izzy that had put Rebekah out of her mind?

Please God, not my little girl.

"Rebekah?" he called out again, panic entering his voice. The grip on his shoulder tightened. "It's Johnny, honey! It's safe here, you can come closer."

The figure didn't move or pause even an extra moment in its up-down cycle of wailing.

Is it possible she can't hear me?

"I don't like this," Michael said.

Johnny turned to face him.

"Something feels wrong. Can I trust you to wait here? I'll go get Bishop Joseph. Don't go outside. Will you wait for him?"

Johnny nodded. Something felt wrong to him too. "I'll wait," he said. "Go."

He'd been honest with Michael; his intention had been to wait. But as he peered out, his eyes began to adjust to the darkness, or the figure swayed and moved outside the shadow of the large tree. Whatever happened, he slowly became convinced that the figure was Rebekah.

She wailed again, and he couldn't stand it anymore, couldn't wait any longer, needed to know what was happening with his wife.

He broke into a run toward her.

Chapter 3

THE figure under the tree was Rebekah. Before his shoes hit the pavement of the street, there could no longer be any doubt about that. But Michael's words rang in Johnny's ears: *something feels wrong here.* His wife had stopped wailing; she stood and stared at him like someone waiting for a complete stranger to get near enough to state their business. She didn't call out to him, or move toward him, or react in any way, except that she had become suddenly and completely silent.

"Rebekah?" he said, coming to a stop a few steps in front of her.

The dark shadow of a bundle slung over her right shoulder had resolved into their little girl. At the sound of his voice, Izzy looked up and over at him. Rebekah let go of her; Izzy fell, but even before Johnny could rush forward to pick her up, Izzy had scrambled to her feet and run toward him and into his arms as Johnny without conscious thought bent down and held them out for her.

Johnny squeezed her, offering silent prayers of thanksgiving to God. But his gaze was locked with his wife's. She stood as still and silent as before.

"Daddy," Izzy said, as if reading his mind, "mommy's sick."

"I'm so happy you're safe, darling," he said, pulling her into a close hug again. "Can I talk to mommy alone for a little while?"

Izzy nodded.

Johnny pointed at the church behind them, intending to ask Izzy to go there and wait, but he saw that the subdeacon was even then coming out of the entrance and running toward them. "That's Michael," he said. "He's a nice man. Can you ask him to take you inside the church and wait for me there?"

She hesitated. Questions and fears whirled in her eyes. "Is mommy going to be okay?" she said, finally deciding which line of thought to pursue. "I think she's sick."

Michael had caught up to them. Rebekah moved finally, taking a step back and making a low growling noise.

"Take my daughter to the church," Johnny said to Michael. "Please. That's all I want from you right now."

Michael took Izzy's hand in his but leaned over to whisper in Johnny's ear. "Do you know why she's standing right there? Because the leaves of the tree hide the cross of the church."

Johnny looked over his shoulder, back at the golden cross on the dome.

"And she can't stand to be near me," Michael continued, still whispering, and holding up the wooden cross in his hand, "because of this. I'm sorry—"

"I know," Johnny said, out loud. "She's sick. Can I talk to her? Will you take care of Izzy for a little while?"

"It's better if you came back with us," Michael said, but his tone betrayed the knowledge that Johnny wasn't about to do that. He pressed the cross into Johnny's hand. "The bishop is coming. You can stay here with your wife, but it would be better if you didn't try to talk to her until he came. Okay?"

Johnny nodded.

"Promise me," Michael said.

"I do—I promise. I'll wait."

He heard Michael ask Izzy if she wanted to race him back to the church.

Rebekah stood deeper in the shadows. He didn't call out to her— what was the point? *The bishop is coming*, he thought. Maybe the bishop would know what to do; Johnny certainly didn't.

Has my wife turned into a zombie? Then: *maybe we can be zombies together.*

It struck him then, as it had many times before in the last few weeks, how quickly the name had come to be used. In zombie lore, zombies were never called that—they were called the infected, the cursed, the plagued; the living dead, the walking dead, even the undead. It was a strange thing, because when the plague actually happened, everyone called the infected exactly what they looked like: zombies.

Of course, they weren't really zombies. These were living human beings who'd had something happen to them (*a virus* was the leading theory) that had turned them into... what? Rabid animals, basically; monsters, even. Vicious, violent, angry, murderous, maniacal, dirty beasts with nothing but destruction on their minds. *If they had minds.* Johnny had thought them basically instinct-driven, the virus having destroyed their higher functions. But that didn't account for the female zombie with the piercing, intelligent eyes.

Because there was another theory, besides the plague being a physical illness. There was a pastor in Alabama who thought the zombies were human beings who had come under the influence of Satan. "That's why they so fear the cross!" Johnny could hear the man's twang, the distinctive way he said "cross,"*the kr-ow-ss.* "That's why they so fear the name of Jesus!" *Gee-ee-zus.*

Maybe they were really zombies, then, in its original sense. Johnny vaguely remembered that the word was a voodoo term referring to someone—alive? dead and reanimated? he wasn't sure—whose body was controlled by another, a zombie master. Was that right? The instinct or temptation to look it up on the internet flashed through his mind momentarily.

When there was still an internet, Johnny had seen that clip of the pastor speaking to his congregation more than a few times. The pastor even claimed he'd exorcised demons from one of the possessed. Many of those who commented under the video thought the guy was a bit of a nut.

But why? The physical illness theory hadn't given anyone any advantage; as far as he knew, governments all over the world had collapsed. Cell phone video footage had come in from every country. Initially these were videos of one or two zombies in a frenzy among a crowd of people, at a shopping mall or an outdoor market. Sometimes the zombies caused a panic, sometimes people just stared at them warily. Sometimes the zombies ran away, the cell phone camera not recording their ultimate fate. Sometimes police or security or someone else put them down. But a few weeks later, the videos were very different—chaotic images of collapsing societies. The zombies and humans had switched roles; now it was crowds of zombies chasing a lone person, often breathlessly recording and uploading their last thoughts and wishes as they ran for their lives. Images flashed through Johnny's mind. Broken windows, cars and buildings on fire. Mangled bodies in the background, tossed haphazardly in the middle of the street. Blood. Lots of blood everywhere.

Johnny had followed the Related Videos chain until very late one night; in fact, until Rebekah came to tell him he was starting to look like a zombie himself and ordered him to bed. The next night, they didn't have electricity, their cell phones couldn't get a signal, and their neighborhood was overrun by zombies.

The plague had happened quickly, and seemed to hit the entire planet at once. Maybe some government somewhere had a stronghold, a protected research facility where scientists were still looking for a cure. But even if there were one to find, Johnny thought, how long before they found it? And how much longer after that before they could get the medicine to everyone? Would there even be enough medicine for everyone?

The bite on his leg still burned. He'd tried to keep his fears at bay so he could focus on ensuring his family was taken care of first. But maybe there was nothing to fear except a bit of pain and discomfort, which he was used to dealing with anyway. Because if the disease wasn't strictly physical, at least it meant he wasn't turning into a zombie.

And if the disease wasn't strictly physical, and Rebekah had come under the influence of the "Evil One," as the pastor from Alabama put it, then maybe the bishop could heal her. But, he corrected himself, even if it were a physical illness, didn't he believe prayer could heal that too?

Please, Lord, he prayed. *One way or another, let him heal her.*

Consumed by his thoughts, Johnny didn't realize that he'd been taking steps forward in an effort to keep an eye on the shadowy figure of his wife, who had been retreating from him slowly. He now noticed with something of a shock that he was a single step from the shadow cast by the large tree.

Something else entered his conscious attention at the same time: the sounds of nasally breathing, of shuffling of feet, of crinkling of clothes and jackets. Soft sounds, easy to miss or discount as the rustling of the leaves of the trees that cast a cover over the long patch of grass-covered land leading to the shores of the river.

It wasn't the rustling of leaves, though. He peered deeper into the dark shadows, took another step forward and saw them: a crowd of zombies, maybe a dozen or more, standing next to and behind his wife. Waiting.

Waiting for what? Johnny wondered. His own mind supplied the answer immediately, and it wasn't a *what* but a *who*. They waited for the bishop.

An avalanche of questions crashed into his thoughts. Was his wife leading an ambush against the bishop? Was Johnny himself the bait?

What would happen when Michael and the bishop got there? Could they hold off over a dozen zombies? And what did it mean to hold them off? Would they hurt his wife, maybe even kill her?

A few seconds earlier, his only interest had been to ensure his wife didn't get scared and run away. He'd kept his gaze fixed on her so that he could chase her if she tried to flee and bring her back to the bishop. But now—he didn't want the bishop to see her now, surrounded by zombies, as if she were some ringleader and they her gang. There were too many of them to expect Michael or the bishop to try to heal any of the zombies; against those numbers, only violence could work, and maybe even violence wouldn't suffice to save their lives. But would Michael even think to bring weapons?

The zombies didn't approach him although he now stood fully in the shadows with them. Perhaps, he thought with a spark of excitement, the wooden cross in his right hand encouraged them to keep their distance.

Later he would wish he'd turned around and walked back to the church. If he'd been able to bring himself to do that, he could've stopped Michael and the bishop from falling into their trap.

Instead, motivated by an instinct deep inside of him that refused to turn his back on his wife and leave her behind, he decided that he would inspire terror in the zombies, banish them away, and hopefully chase and capture his wife.

He raised his right arm so the cross towered over them. "In the name of the Lord Jesus Christ," he said, "I command you to—"

Earlier Rebekah had only moved slowly when she moved at all, as if even simple movements required great effort. Earlier the zombies with her had kept their distance, and kept their voices down and tried as best they could to minimize the noise they were making. All of that changed at the mention of the Lord's name.

Rebekah had sprung into action right away, devouring the distance between them before the next few words were out of Johnny's mouth, knocking the cross from his hand.

He stood speechless, staring up-close for the first time at the woman who was his wife. Her face was contorted with rage, her lips pulled back in an ugly, violent snarl; her breathing hard and ragged, her eyes wide and ferocious. She emitted strange sounds, like the growling of an attack dog about to pounce.

Finally he found his voice. "Honey, I—"

She knocked him to the ground, then jumped on top of him.

He brought up his arms to defend himself. His mind couldn't help making the association to when he and Rebekah play-wrestled. Rebekah on top of him, trying to pin down his arms, he reaching up with his hands to pinch her behind or with his head to kiss her on the neck; she trying to make a serious effort but unable to stop herself from giggling the whole time.

This was nothing like that. Her giggling was growling now; she wasn't using her hands to try and pin his arms now; she was alternatively trying to punch him in the face or tear out his hair. Now when she reached down with her face, it wasn't to kiss him but to bite him.

He tried to hold her off but she was strong, stronger than he'd ever known her. He felt his own strength, whatever of it was still left, going out of him and he struggled within himself not to give up.

His resolve was slipping away from him, though. It was all too much. This was Rebekah growling at him; Rebekah attacking him with a ferocious, mad energy; Rebekah trying to rip off his ear with her teeth. Rebekah, his wife. The mother of his child; his best friend for the last seven years. His love. Rebekah, a zombie.

The frustration and sadness welling up inside of him, he cried out with his own angry yell and hit the sides of her head, boxing her ears to get her to stop trying to bite him. She pulled her head back, shook it, then tried to slash at him with her fingernails.

Rebekah, a zombie. He began to shiver, from fear, despair, or the cold of the ground. Probably all of the above. Rebekah, a zombie. Not dead, that would've been hard enough to deal with. But as good as dead—or worse than dead. For what did his kind, loving, caring wife have to do with this crazed, drooling, snarling creature on top of him?

He heard his name called out. Michael?

"It's a trap!" he yelled, but immediately Rebekah bashed her head into his face to shut him up. Tears blurred his vision, which was already dim from the dark. Blood filled his mouth. Breathing was harder now.

What felt and sounded like a stampede of feet rushed past him. He blinked hard to clear his vision, then arched his neck to see where they were going. But he already knew. Three or four zombies had descended on the subdeacon, brought him to the ground. The rest were headed toward the church. Toward Izzy.

What does my loving wife, he asked himself, *have to do with this snarling, drooling creature?*

She seemed distracted herself by the commotion around the sub-deacon, at least momentarily; perhaps she too thought him more interesting prey than Johnny and wanted to join the fray.

He grabbed her arms quickly, thrust upward with his pelvis, and sent her flying over him. Despite the pain from his torso and face where she'd punched and scratched him, despite the pain from his leg that was still throbbing, despite the tears in his eyes and the blood welling up in his nose, he turned over on his stomach and pushed himself to his knees almost right away. To defend himself, Johnny realized, he couldn't summon up a lot of energy, especially not against his own wife, or the creature that his wife had now become. But to defend Izzy? To defend her and to defend poor Michael, who'd fallen into zombie hands because of him, he found within himself a deep well of energy.

He drew on it. He shut his eyes hard, rubbed them to clear the tears, opened them wide. Where was the cross? Rebekah had knocked it out of his hands. To where? He looked around further afield as his hands and arms searched the area in front of him.

Michael yelled out in pain. Rebekah rose to her feet and approached Johnny.

"I know what you are," Johnny said.

Whatever doubts he had were laid to rest in the next instant. Rebekah spoke, but the voice and words weren't hers. "And we know you," she said, her vocal chords strained, the softness that was so characteristic of her tone completely gone and replaced by a harsh ugliness. "And we know you're frightened, Johnny Salibi. You don't have to be. You don't have to suffer anymore. And you don't have to die. You can join us."

It was the wrong tactic to take with him. At the word frightened, every stubborn fiber of Johnny's being rose up in revolt, refused to acknowledge any fear and risk betraying it in any way to this creature. Ironically, Rebekah would've known that about him and never would've tried that approach.

He rose to his feet. Michael yelled out again.

In an instant, Johnny was by his side. He kicked in the head the zombie that was trying to tear off Michael's beard. Another one of them tried to reach for Johnny, but he stepped back and kicked him hard in the ribs.

Rebekah had been watching with a detached sort of interest. The third zombie grabbed Johnny's neck with both hands and squeezed, but Michael, freed from the assault of three attackers, sat up and wrapped his own large arm around the zombie's neck, holding her in a headlock and turning her body so her kicking feet couldn't connect with Michael or Johnny.

"You okay?" Johnny said, gasping for breath.

"I'm fine," Michael said, but there was enough of an edge to his voice that Johnny felt Michael blamed him for what was happening. With good reason. Michael was still squeezing the zombie's neck, whose violent thrashing was diminishing significantly as she lost consciousness. "We need to get back to the church," he said, pushing the zombie's body away from him finally.

Johnny turned again to look for his wife, but she was gone. So were the other two zombies. A series of loud, frenzied howls were coming from the direction of the church, a sound like a small army of zombies might make.

"Can you walk?" Johnny said.

"I think they broke some ribs." He finally allowed himself to fall back on the ground, and cried out in pain again as he made contact.

The howls from the church were ravenous. A small army of zombies about to feast, their anticipation building into a paroxysm of excitement. If they were demons (could he even doubt that anymore?), the feast would be particularly delicious—nothing less than a bishop for the main course, and a whole churchful of scared families for dessert.

"I need to leave you here for a little while, Michael. It's probably safer here anyway, okay? We will come back for you. You understand what I'm saying?"

Michael nodded and mumbled something. His eyes had glazed over and were drooping shut, opening only a sliver before they closed once more, as if Michael's eyelids were made of steel and the effort to open his eyes, and keep them open the tiniest amount, was beyond him. Michael was either passing out or turning into a zombie himself.

Johnny searched around for the cross again. He couldn't remember doing it, but he'd twisted his ankle somehow, and as he scampered around on all fours, he tried to keep his right foot off the ground, or at least to not put any weight on it.

As the cries from the church increased in intensity suddenly, he considered giving up the search and racing (or hobbling, really) over to them. But to do what? Then again, what could he do against all those zombies even with the cross?

Against the background of the horrific howling, he forced himself to keep looking. Izzy was fine for the moment, he told himself; from the volume of their yells, it seemed the zombies were still outside. Maybe they couldn't even enter the church. Finally he found the cross lying near the trunk of a tree.

Hobbling as fast as he could, with the cross held above his head, he made his way back to the church.

His suspicion was confirmed almost immediately; the large crowd of zombies was outside, practically filling the half-moon stairway, howling like maniacs and banging on the doors. The closed doors.

It took him a moment to process the information, the shock giving way to an acute sense of betrayal. Of course it made sense to close and bar the doors against an invading horde of crazed, murderous creatures. But they'd abandoned him and Michael to those creatures, just to save their own skins.

Could he blame them? *Fear makes people do all sorts of things.* Maybe he would've done the same. But, deep down, he knew that wasn't true; he wouldn't abandon a friend, not while there was a breath left in his lungs. *They don't know me from Adam*, he thought; *but Michael?* Michael was one of their own.

At least Izzy's inside. He looked for his wife in the crowd of zombies, but there were too many and it was too dark for him to tell if she were among them.

Some of the zombies at the back had become aware of his presence, and had turned their heads to snarl at him and the cross he held. The large majority were still banging on the doors, with fists and feet and even with their heads. The sheer pressure of thirty or forty pressing zombies might be enough, he thought. Because sturdy as the doors were, eventually wouldn't they have to give? Certainly before the zombies gave up, now that they'd made it past the view of the three crosses on top of the domes. They'd kept their distance before; but now, for whatever reason, they'd approached. And he felt certain that they wouldn't give up until they'd overrun and destroyed the church, and had killed or scattered everyone inside.

Izzy's inside.

Straightening out his arm so he held the wooden cross even higher, and staring in the eyes of one of the zombies who had turned to low-growl at him, Johnny began to sing.

"Holy God, Holy Mighty, Holy Immortal," he said, as more zombies snapped their heads around to look at him. "Have mercy on us."

Their snarling returned to howling, but it seemed to him that it had intensified, if that were possible. Before their voices were—excited? lustful? Now they were nothing but angry.

"Holy God. Holy Mighty. Holy Immortal."

This was his favorite hymn to sing or to hear. In fact, it was the subject of a long-standing joke in his family. When he was a child, especially on Sunday after the Liturgy, he used to go around the house singing the Trisagion hymn like other children might sing the latest pop song. One of his earliest memories of his father was of him laughing loudly and continuously, as if he'd lost control of himself, when Johnny had first done it, and then, when Johnny had stopped singing, out of hurt or confusion at his father's reaction, his dad had grabbed him and started up the hymn again; and one of his earliest memories of his mother was of her standing and listening to them sing together, a look of delight on her face.

"Have mercy on us," Johnny sang.

Now that so many faces were turned toward him, he scanned them carefully one by one. Still he couldn't find Rebekah's. Their howls rose in intensity as he sang, but they seemed to be held back from attacking him.

His plan, as much as he could be said to have a plan, was to take some steps back, still holding the cross high, and walk or run from the church, leading them away and then doubling back when he had shaken the zombies. It wasn't a perfect plan (what if he couldn't outrun all of them? and even if he could outpace the zombies and make his way back, would those inside even open the door to him? and even if they did, how long before the zombies returned to the church and tried again to break down the doors?) but he pushed away the doubts and fears. "Holy God," he said, taking the first step back.

Whatever force had held the zombies in place suddenly released them, like an invisible restraint snapping and sending them flying at Johnny. He stumbled as the first zombie collided with him, then fell to the ground as the onslaught overwhelmed him. Even as he fell, though, he still looked around for Rebekah.

He couldn't find her, but a voice from inside of him, sounding like his own thoughts, said, *You don't have to die. Simply say "yes" and your life will be spared.*

"Holy Mighty!" he sang, even louder than before.

The fists and legs that had been banging at the doors were now banging against his face, his ribs, his stomach. The cross had been knocked away from him. He pulled his hands to his ears, tried to protect his head with them while his bent arms absorbed most of the kicks aimed at his sides. *You don't have to die*, the voice said. Angry, growling faces flashed through his vision, looking like rabid dogs, as he turned his head this way and that to avoid the biting jaws of the zombies.

He opened his mouth to sing again, to sing for what was likely the last time, to speak his last words—

"Holy Immortal." It wasn't his voice. "Have mercy on us." Multiple voices, and not coming from the church but from the other direction.

The zombies had stopped hitting him to focus on the intruders. Johnny looked up without moving his head but couldn't see anything through the forest of legs in tattered, bloody clothes. He tried to move, to look at what was happening, but his head pounded and the slightest movement of his neck or torso caused him agonizing pain.

"Holy God. Holy Mighty. Holly Immortal." The zombies were screeching, yelling, howling. But they weren't attacking him anymore. "Have mercy on us."

The forest of legs cleared by degrees, the zombies retreating and then fleeing as the small choir kept chanting the hymn.

"He's alive?" someone said softly.

A bright light beamed into his eyes, causing him to squint.

"He's alive," someone else said, with a voice much rougher than the first, and the beam of light was lowered. "Blood all over him though."

What blood? He tried to sit up to look, but his back didn't even make it off the ground; the pain was too much.

"Take it easy," the first voice, a female voice, said.

He managed to turn his head a little and saw them: a group of six or seven, each carrying a cross, now staring over and across him and down the street.

Why aren't you helping me up? he thought, allowing his head to slouch back and closing his eyes again.

"They're not leaving," a third voice said.

"So what do we do?" The rough voice.

"We wait for the bishop." Female voice, same as before, the one who told him to take it easy.

He opened his eyes suddenly. "Michael," he tried to say, but began to cough almost immediately, each spasm sending waves of pain throughout his body.

A face floated into his view—the woman who'd been seated next to the bishop in the basement of the church. So pretty, so peaceful, such a relief to see her face after the faces of the zombies, contorted with hatred and anger. "It's going to be okay, Johnny," she said. "You're going to be fine."

In spite of the pain, he shook his head. "Over there." He tried to point in Michael's direction with his eyes. "Michael."

She looked up, then stood. He thought she was going to go looking for Michael, but she said, reporting to a new arrival, "We managed to drive them away; we sang the Trisagion. But not far enough away—"

"You stay with me, Elizabeth." It was the bishop's voice. "The rest of you, take Michael and Johnny back into the church. Use the front door."

Johnny felt hands grab his feet and grip him underneath his shoulders. He tried to struggle. *Suicide*, he thought; *this is suicide*. He was lifted from the ground, carried forward. The white-painted metal railing of the staircase drifted past him. A tall man with dark skin, relatively short-cropped hair, and a severe, surly look on his face was carrying him from behind.

"No," Johnny said, but his voice was weak and enough blood still filled his mouth that he found it difficult to speak. "Don't leave them."

The man with the angry stare didn't look down. Someone else opened the church door and Johnny was carried inside.

Before the door shut behind them, he could hear the bishop's voice ringing out.

"In the name of Jesus Christ, the Son of God," the bishop said, in a voice so loud and strong that it shocked Johnny it emerged from the same old man who'd spoken to him in the basement, "I command you to leave this holy place." The zombies yelled profanities, their once incoherent howls discernible words now. "We do not fear you here." The bishop's voice rose above all of theirs, as if projected by some invisible megaphone. "We belong to the Almighty God. We worship the Trinity undivided. You won't find any—"

Johnny didn't get to hear what they wouldn't find: the door slammed shut, and presently he was carried through the narthex and into the nave.

"We're going to put you down now," the surly-faced man said to him. "It may hurt a little."

It hurt a lot. His ribs screamed as his body bumped against the back of the pew.

The man pulled out his cross from his belt. He seemed to place himself in the aisle, like someone standing guard, and looked up at the open entryway intently, as if he half-expected zombies to come bursting into the church.

"You just couldn't wait, could you?" he said, but seemed to be speaking more to himself than to Johnny. "Now look what you've done. It'll be a miracle if any of us survive to see the morning."

Chapter 4

"ORTHODOX churches aren't supposed to have pews," he says. Rebekah knows the kind of mood he's in and chooses to ignore him. She stares forward, watching Father Gord prepare for the Liturgy. Rebekah hates to be late, so they always arrive everywhere far in advance.

Usually he would let it go, but this Sunday morning he feels like arguing, feels like making his wife as miserable as he is. "We should be standing, if you want my opinion," he says.

Rebekah turns to face him. "So go stand," she whispers. "There's plenty of room at the back." Her voice is calm; when he's in one of these moods, she is able to tap into a hidden and seemingly inexhaustible reserve of patience.

He snorts, starting to feel a bit better now that he's had time to vent. And vent about what? About having been dragged to this church, even if it is his church more than Rebekah's. At least, he thinks, his parents aren't there—or aren't there yet, anyway.

"Sure," he says, lowering his voice this time, "like I'm going to leave my gorgeous wife's side. Then some fool in a fancy suit will sit beside you and chat you up and you'll forget all about me."

"'Chat me up'?" she says, in that delighted voice she has. Sometimes she liked expressions he used, and repeated them as if to try them out on her own tongue. "Now shush and pay attention," she says, facing the front again.

Johnny smiles, nods. *Maybe it won't be so bad.* He's missed participating in the Liturgy. *It's not the priest that matters but the office.* And Rebekah meant well in bringing him here finally, and he'd given her endless grief the whole walk over, even though it's a beautiful, sunny morning.

He leans in to kiss her cheek as a way to apologize to her or to thank her, or maybe both.

Rebekah turns her body to face him once more, smiles in return,

then quickly grabs his face with both hands and slams his head against
the back of the pew.

Sorry about that."

Johnny's eyes had come open as his head hit the pew. He looked
up at the surly-faced man, whose stern features hadn't softened. A
soft orange glow suffused the church. It took Johnny a moment to
realize the glow was the light from a new dawn, the rays streaming
in through the church's large windows lining the nave and stretching
up toward the ceiling. *It'll be a miracle if any of us survive to see the
morning.*

"What's going on?" he managed to say.

"We're moving you downstairs, if you feel you're able."

"It's okay," Johnny said to the other man who was holding his legs.
His body was sore, but it wasn't any worse than the mornings after
tournaments; and mentally at least, he felt better than he had in over
a week—this was the first night that he'd actually slept for more than
a few hours at a time. "I can walk," he said, returning his gaze to the
stern-faced man.

When they let him go, he sat up with more difficulty and pain than
he expected. "I need to see my daughter," he said finally.

"She's downstairs."

Johnny listened for sounds of howling, but couldn't hear them.
"The bishop chased the zombies away?"

"No." The bishop's voice was weak, in strange and sad contrast
to the night before. He stood at the entrance of the nave. "No, they
haven't left. But they aren't approaching, either."

"So what's the plan?" Johnny said.

The look on the bishop's face turned as hard as the one that seemed
permanently etched in deep grooves on the face of the dark-skinned
man. Johnny read reproof held in check there, and a sudden explosion
of anger sprung up within him. *These are the people who closed the
doors against Michael and me,* he thought, *and he thinks I'm the one
deserving of reproach?*

"Go downstairs and see to your daughter, Mr. Salibi," the bishop
said.

Johnny stood, placing one hand on the back of the pew to help
balance himself. Other people were in the nave, besides the two men

who'd tried to pick him up. The woman from the night before and three others were sitting in pews closer to the front of the church, their heads turned to look at him.

"Where's Michael?" he said, returning his attention to the bishop.

"The subdeacon is recovering."

This is their war room, Johnny thought. *This is where they're going to discuss what to do about the zombies outside. And they don't want me to hear what they have to say.*

"I'd like to stay," Johnny said.

The bishop exchanged looks with the men beside him, who seemed to read an order in his glance. They turned away and walked up the nave to join the others. "Come with me, please."

Johnny used the pews to help him make it to the back of the church. Once in the narthex, the bishop closed the door. Here it was dark again.

"No," the bishop said.

"Why not?"

Bishop Joseph opened the door leading to the basement.

"You have suffered much tonight, Mr. Salibi. So has your daughter."

But that wasn't the reason, Johnny knew. The bishop could stop himself from unleashing an assault of reproach against Johnny for endangering the church and the whole community, he could keep his words polite, but the way he looked at Johnny betrayed everything he was actually thinking.

Under the force of that look, and the reluctant and quiet acknowledgment to himself that things might have turned out better (*could they have turned out worse?*) if he'd listened to the bishop and waited for the morning, Johnny didn't say anything but moved toward the open doorway. He grabbed the railing to steady himself, and the bishop closed the door behind him.

Before he'd taken more than a few steps down, he became aware of a smoky smell, and the sensation sent a word buzzing through his mind: *bacon.* Someone downstairs was cooking breakfast. His stomach growled at him. It had been more than a month since he'd had bacon, because he hadn't known at the time that civilization was about to collapse and the world virtually come to an end. He hadn't known to have his fill before that happened. *Maybe they have eggs too*, he thought.

If they were cooking bacon, that meant they had power of some kind. A stove to cook on. Probably a fridge, maybe even a freezer.

The basement was lined with windows set high on the walls, which let in a fair amount of the dawning sun's light. Although it was still very early, it seemed everyone was awake; linens were being folded up and pillows put away, cots rolled to a back room and replaced with long cafeteria tables and chairs. Amid the stir of activity, Johnny spotted Izzy helping out, carrying plates from the kitchen at the northern end of the room and handing them off to others who were placing them on the tables.

Perhaps sensing that someone was looking at her, she turned her head, then put down the plates she was carrying on the nearest chair, and ran toward him, a look of delight on her face.

He bent down, his knees and back protesting, and held out his arms, then wrapped his little girl in a giant bear hug, all but swallowing her in his arms. It made all of the pain go away.

"Are you feeling better, Daddy?" she said, when he let her go so he could look at her again.

"Yes, honey," he said, gently combing back the blonde hair that had frizzled up on his sweater. "Much better."

She pushed his hand away from her head. "Mommy's sick," she said, moving to the next patient on her mental checklist. "She needs syrup." Syrup was Izzy's word for medicine, probably because she'd never been a very sick baby, and cough syrup was the extent of the treatment besides rest they'd had to give her when she did become ill.

"Yes, she does," he said, then pulled her into another tight embrace.

In his mind, he saw Rebekah grab his face with both hands and slam his head into the back of a pew. It wasn't her fault, he wanted to tell himself. But wasn't it? If it were a physical illness, he couldn't blame her for turning into a zombie. But he no longer believed that. He believed the zombies were demon-possessed human beings, who were driven into a mad frenzy of violence and harm (including self-harm) by their masters. How did one become possessed, though? The night before, his wife, or whatever had taken control of her, asked him to join them. He refused of course—but why hadn't his wife refused? Rebekah's faith had always been strong, stronger than his own often, so why had she given in to the dark spirits?

It was easier to be upset with her than to grieve her loss, he knew; he also knew it made the loss less acute if he could blame Rebekah herself, displace his grief and funnel all of his emotion through anger. Despite all of that, though, the question remained: why had she given in to them?

He became aware that someone was standing by his side, a large man with a bald head and a big belly that stuck out in front of him.

"Mr. Salibi?"

He stood, shook the man's outstretched hand. Johnny had big hands, but they all but disappeared in the other man's.

"My name is Miles Trovener," he said. "I'm in charge of meals around here—and other stuff, too. You can consider me the innkeeper." Without a pause, Miles continued, "Let me ask you—are you Jewish or Muslim?"

Johnny wasn't sure he understood the question. "Christian," he said. "Orthodox."

Miles's face lit up. "Oh, wonderful! So nice to meet another Orthodox. Welcome to our parish!"

This was my parish long before it was yours, Miles, Johnny thought, but didn't say anything.

"The bishop doesn't like us cooking bacon most days," Miles said, looking down at Izzy, who'd been staring up at the two adults and trying to follow their conversation. "Do you like bacon, Izzy?" he said, then laughed when she licked her lips and nodded. He returned his attention to Johnny. "But I figure—who knows how long we'll be able to stay here, you know? So I think to myself, let's use it while we still can. Waste not and want not, am I right?"

Miles spoke quickly and without seeming to stop for breath or to allow for an interjection. If he'd paused, Johnny might've asked what he meant when he said they may not be able to stay there much longer. But he knew.

"Anyway," Miles continued, "for breakfast this morning, I'm getting the Jewish and Muslim families to sit at tables where I know people won't be eating bacon. At least the ones who don't want to be around it. Almost all are very good about this sort of thing, you know?" He leaned in for a conspiratorial whisper. "Tell the truth, most are happy to sneak in a bite or two of bacon themselves." He leaned away again, then chortled, a quick burst of laughter that was a bit infectious. "But it's not what goes into a person, am I right? If it's okay with you," Miles continued, "you and your daughter can sit at the table over there, beside the back column."

"Sure," Johnny said. "Thank you."

"We eat family style here. There's lots of food, so don't be shy."

Johnny and his family had been living on canned goods for the last eight days: beans, mostly, and corn and whatever else could be eaten raw or heated over their portable propane camp stove. Served over crackers, with canned fruit for dessert. He'd stockpiled enough non-perishables that they could've survived for months.

"As long as it doesn't come out of a can," Johnny said, taking advantage of a rare pause in Miles's speech, "I don't think there's much danger of shyness."

"Good man," Miles said, slapping him on the back on his way to something else he spied that needed his attention.

Too late Johnny thought of offering to help. But the buzz of activity was winding down and people were starting to take their seats; and the buzz was so well-organized, like a beehive, that his sudden intrusion would've harmed more than helped. He figured he could lend a hand with clean up.

He led Izzy to their table. Already seated were an elderly couple and three young boys. They looked to be members of the same family and Muslim (the elderly woman wore a hijab). Three empty seats remained.

"Hello," he said, reverting to his overly polite mode, which he did almost subconsciously when he knew Izzy was watching. "My name is—"

"Sit down in your seat," the elderly man said, waving his wrinkled, veiny hand. His tone wasn't exactly rude, but direct, and somewhat unfriendly. "We know you."

Johnny pulled out Izzy's chair and helped her into it, then took off his sweater and sat down beside her.

"Don't be nasty," the woman said; her English seemed better and more natural, but she spoke in a thicker accent than her husband, a Middle Eastern heaviness that weighed down her words and gave her voice a cottonmouth feel. "Mr. Salibi, my name is Fatima. This is my husband Wassim. These young trouble-makers are our grandchildren, Osama, Ahmed, and Mahmoud."

"Pleased to meet you all. This is my daughter, Isabel." Johnny smiled at her. "We mostly call her Izzy."

"Can I go get them this time?" Mahmoud, the youngest of the brothers, said.

Johnny noticed that dishes of food were being placed on the bar countertop of the half-wall that separated the kitchen from the basement hall. When his grandmother said he could, Mahmoud asked Izzy if she'd like to go too. She nodded and had slipped out of her chair before Johnny could help her down. The young ones made several trips to the kitchen and back, needing someone to help them on both ends because they weren't tall enough to adequately reach the bar or the table.

While Izzy was out of ear-shot, Johnny asked the elderly man named Wassim how he knew who he was. The bishop had held a pre-dawn meeting, Wassim said. Everyone was already awake; no one had been able to sleep after the zombies (Wassim called them *hiwanat*, the Arabic word for wild animals) had all but broken down the front doors and had filled the entire church with their violent yells.

"He make good introduction of Izzy to us," Wassim continued. "He make good introduction of you, too, but we"—he glanced over at his wife, who stared back at him with a reproaching look—"maybe we don't speak good English, but we are not stupid. We know you are the one who brought the *hiwanat*."

"That's what the bishop said?" Anger flared up inside of him even though it was true—Johnny had brought the zombies to the church.

Wassim started to answer, but Fatima placed her hand on his arm. "The bishop said you were attacked and recovering," she said, "nothing more. He said we were safe, and we prayed together that we would be safe always under Allah's protection."

Her husband snorted.

Soon the table was full with pitchers of juice and water, with plates and bowls of bacon, of scrambled eggs, of toasted bread and of butter. It all looked and smelled so delicious that Johnny's mouth was watering and he had to stop himself from launching right into the food and shoving it by the handful into his mouth. Even the children were restraining themselves, however. Everyone seemed to be waiting for something, and Johnny thought he knew what it was.

When all the tables were set and loaded down with food and drink, Miles went upstairs and, a few minutes later, the bishop came into the basement, followed by his entourage and then by Miles. The bishop's inner circle split up, everyone breaking off to their assigned place. Johnny found himself slightly embarrassed that the woman from last night—he had a vague recollection that her name was Elizabeth—came to stand by the empty seat at their table.

They'd exchanged glances as she walked over, Johnny quickly shifting his gaze away as soon as they locked together. A rebellious part of him—a part that didn't appreciate being left out of anything, a part that didn't like the way this woman's gaze made him feel intimidated and anxious, a part that cast suspicion over everything he didn't understand—wondered if this table were her normal one, or if she was there to spy on him.

Slowly everyone else had come to their feet, and Johnny had done so more subconsciously than otherwise. Still there was no sign of Michael, and the same suspicious feeling inside of Johnny wondered if what the bishop said about Michael being off somewhere recovering were true.

"O Christ our God," Bishop Joseph said, his loud voice booming throughout the basement as it had outside when directed against the demons, "bless us Your servants, this church, and the food and drink before us. For You are the source of all blessings, now and forever and ever. Amen."

The word was echoed by many, including Johnny. Wassim and Fatima didn't say anything, but their grandchildren repeated the word, as did Izzy in her little voice, and Elizabeth.

Johnny sat down and pulled the chair closer to the table.

Fatima poured orange juice for everyone who wanted some while the plates of food were passed around. Johnny spooned eggs onto his plate and Izzy's, but the slices of bacon had hardly touched his plate before he picked one up with his hands and bit into it.

Izzy, who was too small to reach the table, ate from a plate set between her drawn-up legs. *Your mother would have a fit if she saw you*, Johnny thought, but only winked at Izzy when she caught him staring at her.

When she needed something—like help buttering her piece of toast—Johnny noticed that Izzy seemed to turn to Elizabeth instinctively. He gathered that Elizabeth had been one of the people who had cared for Izzy while he was sleeping, and for a reason he couldn't or didn't want to understand, it made him dislike her even more.

At one point Elizabeth stood to get some coffee and asked if anyone else would like some. Johnny had never been much of a coffee drinker, but the fact that he hadn't been able to have any over the last week, when he could've really used it to clear away the groggy feeling in his head, now made him want some that much more.

He nodded and answered "Milk, two sugars," when she asked him how he took it.

As good as it tasted, though, he barely had enough room in his stomach for more than a few sips. He felt he needed to stop eating for a while, or risk his shrunken stomach bursting if he took another bite or had even one more drop of coffee or juice.

He turned to Wassim and said, "You don't mind the bishop praying to Christ?" He was aware that Elizabeth was listening.

Wassim had finished eating as well and had pushed the plate away from himself. "Let him pray to Christ," he said. "What is the difference? He can pray to Great Baboon if he wants."

As if she were his official interpreter, Fatima jumped in. "We are guests here. I tell my grandchildren that when the bishop says 'Christ,' for us he is saying 'Allah.'"

"But I gather your husband no longer believes in Allah."

Johnny wasn't sure why he was pressing the issue. He regretted prying almost immediately, but especially when the dark cloud that seemed perpetually to hang over Wassim expanded to overshadow Fatima's face as well.

"My husband has seen many things," she said, her voice taking on a harder and more defensive tone. "Has lost many things," she added, unable to stop herself from glancing at their grandchildren. "Allah, the Most Merciful, the Most Compassionate—but sometimes it is hard to understand why He allows certain things to happen."

"I think we can agree on that," Johnny said, eager to pacify Fatima and move on to another topic.

Throughout, Elizabeth hadn't said a word, but had listened to everything.

Miles came to ask if Johnny would be willing to help with the clean-up. Johnny got the impression that his help wasn't strictly needed as much as Miles wanted to set the right tone from the outset, that everyone should contribute. It was while he was doing dishes that he realized why, at least in part, he'd pressed Fatima and Wassim on their belief in God.

He scraped food off the plates and into a large pail lined with a garbage bag, while a woman named Theresa cleaned the dishes he handed her with soap and water. Her husband Steven, whom Johnny recognized as the other man who'd tried to carry him in the nave, dried with a towel.

They spoke as they worked; unlike Wassim, they didn't blame him for bringing the infected (Steven said he'd do anything for Theresa, and certainly wouldn't do any less than Johnny if she were lost outside somewhere). It didn't take very long in the conversation for Johnny to realize that Theresa at least had no idea the zombies were demon-possessed human beings.

The bishop and his inner circle, including Steven, did know, he was sure of that; and so he'd assumed everyone else had been told. Wassim called them *hiwanat*, animals; that wouldn't be accurate if he knew the truth, and it would be hard to believe in demons but not in God. Theresa spoke as if it were a plague, and expressed her hope, more than once in a relatively short conversation, that someone somewhere was working on a cure. The night before, Michael didn't want Johnny to go downstairs until his bite had been bandaged—or, to say it another way, masked.

Not wanting to cause a panic he could understand. But why keep the truth from the rest of the people? It was inconceivable that Michael, the bishop, or anyone else who was outside during the night did what they did without knowing the true nature of the zombies. They warded them off with crosses and pushed them back with hymns. So why keep that knowledge a secret?

When he was done cleaning, Johnny left the kitchen, hoping to find the bishop. He didn't have to search for long. At the eastern end of the basement, several rows of chairs had been pushed together, with a central chair set apart for the bishop. Izzy sat in the front row with the youngest children.

"That's a very good question," the bishop was saying. "Perhaps you're right, or maybe Jesus felt that the young man had more work to do in this life—take care of his widowed mother, for example. Life for a Christian isn't about doing what we want or what makes us happy. It's about serving God by serving others, serving the people who need us."

There were a few more questions from the children, while Johnny and some other adults stood at the back and against the walls, watching and listening. Johnny felt that he wanted to ask a few questions of his own, but he kept his mouth shut and soon the children were dismissed for the moment, and told to go play.

The bishop seemed intent on returning to the church upstairs, but Johnny intercepted him.

"I need to speak with you."

The bishop stopped, blinked as if noticing Johnny for the first time. "Mr. Salibi," he said. "What would you like to say?"

"My wife was captured by them," he said, placing special emphasis on the final word. "Can you do something to help her?"

The bishop's small black eyes, set deep within his face and underneath an overgrowth of eyebrows, scanned Johnny's face quickly. He seemed to reach the proper conclusion about how much Johnny knew, and nodded slightly before responding, as if in acknowledgment of their shared knowledge.

"That is not an easy question to answer," he said finally. "However, I would like to discuss it with you at a later time."

"And I would like to discuss it with you now," Johnny said, his tone still more aggressive than he intended it. He realized this wasn't the best approach to take with a man like the bishop, but seemed unable to help himself. "Can you help her, yes or no?"

The bishop looked around, perhaps fearing that others would overhear their conversation, especially since Johnny's voice had risen in intensity. "As I said, that is a question I would like to discuss with you at a later time." The bishop began to turn away, but stopped himself. "Mr. Salibi, I am the head of this community. You are very welcome here. However, there are certain protocols to follow."

"Yes, I'm quite familiar with your protocols," Johnny said. "Don't ask questions and just obey authority."

"No," the bishop said. "That is not the Orthodox way." A thought seemed to seize his mind, causing his features to tighten, his lined brow to furrow with even deeper wrinkles. "This parish would've been better served if the people had asked a few more questions and obeyed authority a little less.

"But in your case, Mr. Salibi," the bishop continued, "I don't think there's much danger of you asking too few questions and obeying too much. I asked you to wait until morning to go looking for your wife. You refused. Michael asked you to wait for him to return with me. You refused. Those were not unreasonable requests, although I understand that your overriding desire was to help your wife. The fact remains that our community is now in the greatest danger it's faced since all of this started because of your refusal to obey even reasonable pleas."

Could he argue? He wanted to. He wanted to defend himself, to stand up to the bishop and show him how he was wrong about Johnny. But the bishop wasn't wrong. When Johnny had his mind set on something, nothing could get in his way. Even now, he desperately wanted an answer about what, if anything, could be done for his wife, even though he'd twice been told to wait to discuss it later.

He asked the next closest question, which at least seemed a natural response to the bishop's comments. "What are you going to do about the zombies outside?" he said. Then, sensing in some way that the question's tone was accusatory and wishing to soften it, he added, "Can

I help?"

"We'll hold Vespers tonight, and Matins in the morning. You are welcome to attend either or both if you wish, or to pray in your own way."

"So you're not going to try and drive them off?" The question was out of his mouth before he could stop it. Because did he really want the bishop to try to drive them off, when Rebekah might be among them still? Before the bishop could answer, Johnny said quickly, "Will the services and prayers be enough to keep them away?"

Bishop Joseph held up his palms to the ceiling. "If it's God's will that they be enough," he said, his voice even softer than before.

Feeling paradoxically calmer and more reassured than he would've expected himself to be, Johnny watched the bishop walk away and disappear into the stairwell.

Chapter 5

I F *it's God's will.* It should sound like a cop-out, a way to escape responsibility, a technique to dodge answering a question directly, but it didn't. Johnny had always found it a mark of real as opposed to affected holiness, because it revealed at once a profound understanding of the way the world worked and a deep humility. The understanding was that nothing happened unless God allowed it; the humility was the acceptance of that realization, the willingness to subject one's own will to God's will. Of course, it like all things could be faked, and Johnny had known many people who threw the expression "God-willing" into every sentence without seeming to really believe it or commit to its implications; it seemed more like punctuation or throat-clearing than a conscious expression. But sometimes "if it's God's will" came out of the mouths of those who deliberated and acted, and were ready to accept the implications of their statement. If their work came to fruition, praise and glory to God; and if it came to nothing, praise and glory to God.

Even to Johnny though, who knew this, the expression did not come naturally; rather, if he was honest with himself, it didn't come at all. His own will was much more important to him than any other consideration; God's will was well and good so long as it didn't contradict his own desires. Self-will, he thought, was an aspect of human nature from the very beginning (what else had caused humanity's fall in the Garden?), but it had only grown more pronounced with the progress of civilization. In the past, for most people, life dictated enough terms that a certain humility had to be learned: one couldn't have strawberries in the winter, because there weren't any growing; or work throughout the night, because it was too dark; or eat themselves to morbid obesity, because there wasn't enough food. But now most people in the developed world weren't subject to seasons or the spinning of the earth: they could have any kind of fruit or vegetable whenever they wanted, and could light up a home or office with enough electric light that they could turn night into daytime, and they had readier access to more food than was good for them. Most people, most of the time, wanted what they wanted when they wanted it, and now more than ever they felt a sense of frustration or even outrage when they couldn't have it.

Well, not now more than ever, Johnny thought. Now less than ever before, perhaps. The church had some gas-powered generators into which they'd plugged the refrigerator, freezer, stove, and some other appliances, so they could have bacon and eggs and toast, even coffee. But how long before they could no longer power the generators? Miles had given him a tour of their set-up, and there was enough gas in the tanks Johnny saw to last them another few weeks, maybe a month.

It was cold-cut sandwiches and cream of broccoli soup for lunch that day. Johnny helped in the kitchen, slicing the last of their fresh vegetables (the zombie threat, always present but now so imminent, seemed to shift Miles from his scarcity and frugality mentality to a use-it-or-lose-it mode). There were others with him in the kitchen, but Johnny hardly noticed them; he'd spent the morning talking and listening (mostly just listening during Miles's tour of the basement and kitchen), and being introduced to everyone. After over a week of near solitude, he found the experience draining. Later he would learn that many of the survivors had gotten very good at sensing when someone needed to be left alone with their own thoughts, and that's what the kitchen crew did for him—left him alone—after Miles was done with him.

If it's God's will. Was it God's will that the world collapse? Was it God's will that countless lives be lost, human beings ripped apart by other human beings? Demons possessing people to an extent never before seen in the history of the world? Demons possessing Rebekah?

Maybe God didn't will it in the sense that He desired it to happen; but nothing that had happened was against His will, or it wouldn't have happened. *Couldn't* have happened. God was complicit in every-thing.

Was it thoughts like those that made Wassim lose his faith? Johnny wondered. It would be an easy thing to do, to arrest God and put Him on trial (*in absentia*, Johnny supposed). *God in the dock* was the way C.S. Lewis had put it. It would be an open and shut case: God was in charge, and the world was a complete disaster. And yet, Johnny knew, God had already been arrested and put on trial. The verdict had been handed down—guilty—and the punishment was torture and execution.

If he were Muslim or Jewish or anything else, it would be easy to hate God for allowing the zombie apocalypse, perhaps hate Him so much that Johnny could convince himself that He didn't exist (surely it was better to deny God's existence than admit it but hate Him). How could he stop himself from thinking dark thoughts about a God who stayed safely in heaven while the world burned and His creation suffered? How could he justify a God who did nothing to interfere?

But Johnny was a Christian. God had become man and suffered. God could've easily stopped the humiliation and pain of the Crucifixion (to say nothing of the humiliation of the Incarnation, the act of becoming human in the first place); He could've spoken a word and wiped the world clean, spoken another and started over with a new and better creation. What would that have cost Him?

God made a different choice, though. He chose to work in and with and through the fallen creation that had rebelled against Him. Directly, in the world and not outside of it; patiently, through thousands of years and countless generations; painstakingly, with co-workers who were stubborn of heart and slow of mind. He chose to work with the broken, jagged pieces of the world that were left to Him, rather than melt everything down and start over. He chose to do so even knowing that down that path lay suffering, and not just suffering for others, but that His own work of recreation couldn't be completed unless He Himself took on corrupt creation and imparted His own incorruptibility to it. Unless He Himself suffered in the world as well.

And suffering is exactly what Jesus promised to those who followed Him. He said, "Pick up your cross and follow Me." Every Christian's life was a struggle down the dusty streets of Jerusalem to Golgotha; every Christian death was a martyr's death. All would be raised to new, everlasting life in Christ; and to everlasting joy for those who love Him. But the resurrection to a new life, a life where God Himself would wipe away every tear, and where there would be no death or pain or sorrow or crying, for those things will have passed away—that life came later. First there was the long, painful walk that ended in death.

Almost mechanically, he'd been grabbing tomatoes from the big colander to his right and slicing them thinly. Someone else took the slices from his cutting board and placed them on plates; he hardly noticed. But now, as he tried to split down the middle a piece that he'd cut too thickly, the knife bit into the bottom of his index finger and he cursed out loud. Then he couldn't help but smile a little. He'd cut himself while musing on the nature of suffering; he felt that it was perhaps God waving hello.

Someone brought him a band-aid; he sprinkled pepper on his finger and wrapped it. For the first time in a while, he seemed to become aware of his surroundings again. He listened for sounds of howling from outside, but still he couldn't hear any. *They're being very quiet,* he thought; *or they've finally left, decided we're not worth the trouble.*

Needing to know, he walked out (Steven had taken over to slice the few remaining tomatoes) and dragged a chair over to the window facing north, just left of the kitchen. He climbed onto the chair.

The zombies stood on the other side of the street, as if the group was fixed in that spot. But the individual zombies themselves moved in place, swaying a little, and sometimes bumping into one another. *There's so many of them.* Johnny estimated their number at thirty, maybe even forty. Enough for each zombie to have one of the survivors in the church.

In the bright daylight, he watched them, in part scanning their faces for his wife's, but also getting his first good, clear look at them. If he didn't know any better, it would be easy to mistake them for plague-ridden animals, to use Wassim's word. Many of them, men and women, were missing great chunks of hair from their heads; it looked like someone (perhaps they themselves) had yanked it off in large clumps. Some had cuts and lesions on their faces and necks and, as he saw on those from whom most of the clothes had been torn off, all over their bodies too. Blood had poured from their cuts and coagulated on their skin. Their whole figure from top to bottom was polka-dotted with dried blood and black bruises and mud and grime and other kinds of dirt. A few looked gaunt and emaciated, their cheekbones and ribcages sticking out under their skin. One zombie, whose toothless mouth was open the whole time Johnny watched her, had drool dribbling on her chest, but she did nothing to wipe it away. Another's nose was running, but he let the snot fall on his mustache and mouth without movement or even awareness.

It would be funny if it wasn't so sad and pathetic, he thought. But not just pathetic, horrific too. There was something about their stance, something about their silence, that frightened him. They were waiting for something, as the zombies the night before had been waiting for the invisible field to set them free. More than anything, they reminded him of hungry attack dogs who were held back from devouring their prey by a leash. A leash that they could sense was about to snap.

And, perhaps worse thought of all, it wasn't their fault. Someone else was keeping them from wiping their noses and mouths; someone else was using and abusing their bodies; someone else filling them with a mad fury while holding them back (perhaps waiting for the right time to attack—nightfall?—or perhaps for no other reason than their master's perverse pleasure). And yet these weren't reanimated corpses; they were living creatures who needed to eat—the first word that came to his mind was *feed*—or they'd starve to death.

How much were they aware of what was happening to them? Johnny wondered. Then, thinking of his wife, he pushed the question away.

He might have stayed there forever, watching the macabre and grotesque scene, but after a while he heard the door behind him come open and he turned to look. The bishop emerged, followed by Michael.

The subdeacon glanced up at him as he moved past (slower than he'd seen him move before, Johnny thought), but didn't acknowledge him with more than a slight nod.

Johnny stepped down from the chair and returned it. He found Izzy and brought her to their table, but switched seats so that now he sat next to Elizabeth. His intention was to put himself between Izzy and Elizabeth, but too late he realized it must have seemed that he meant to place himself beside the young, attractive woman.

With that thought in mind, he said, "You're one of the bishop's inner circle." He desperately wanted her to understand that his interest in her was purely opportunistic and professional, not personal...a sure sign that his interest in her was personal. The guilt at having such a feeling, especially at such a time, gave a hard edge to his words.

If she sensed animosity in his tone, she didn't let on. "Hi, I'm Liz Stone," she said, sticking out her hand. "I don't think we've been properly introduced."

The three young brothers were carrying over the dishes and setting the table with the help of their grandmother.

Elizabeth's hand hung in the air. He took it. "Johnny Salibi."

"I know," she said. "And I've already met that little one. Izzy and I have a lot in common. Even our names—my parents called me Lizzy when I was young."

Izzy, who'd been watching them, was kicking her feet under the table like a dog wagging its tail.

"Stop fidgeting," Johnny said to her.

When he looked again at Liz, she said in a soft and kind tone, "You have a very beautiful daughter."

"She gets it from her mother." He'd made the joke a hundred times since Izzy was born, but this time it had a forcefulness and weight he hadn't exactly intended.

Everyone began to stand. After the bishop asked God to bless their food, Johnny helped Izzy make her sandwich. She wanted just one piece of toast with cold cuts and nothing else; he felt like arguing with her, forcing her to take another piece of toast or top it with a slice of tomato, or at least to squirt mayo or mustard on her bread. But he felt that he'd just chastised her unfairly, and let her eat the sandwich she wanted.

"You're very good with her," Liz said later.

He'd spent most of the lunch trying to ignore her, although in fact he often had to ask Wassim or Fatima to repeat themselves, because he'd been eavesdropping on Liz's conversation with the three boys. She mostly asked about the books they were reading and what they liked about them, whether they were looking forward to today's lessons, who had the most marbles now—inconsequential questions about the inconsequential lives of three boys whose great misfortune it was to have to pass their formative years in this dying, burned up world. Yet Johnny listened to every question she asked, and every word they gave in response.

By slow degrees a silence descended on the basement, as conversations were cut off and the other background noise of people shifting in their seats, picking up and putting down glasses of juice, passing around plates and bowls of food, sometimes accidentally banging against another bowl or pitcher—all of that noise was muted as people picked up on the sounds coming from outside.

Presently the howl of the zombies filled the hall. Shadows danced into the room, like dark gremlins. Johnny looked up; framed in the windows was a forest of blood-stained legs and grotesque, deformed, angry faces looking through the glass and yelling.

Someone screamed out in terror. A child began to cry. The bishop called out in a loud voice, "Don't be afraid!"

But he seemed unprepared or unwilling to do anything else. Johnny turned his head quickly to look at Liz, who stared up at the windows wide-eyed and mouth slightly open, in a stunned silence that confirmed his suspicions: they never expected them to attack in broad daylight. They had no plan for this.

Izzy gripped his arm, and buried her face in his shoulder.

Johnny's thoughts raced. They couldn't just do nothing, as the bishop seemed prepared to do. Perhaps he thought they were safe: even if the zombies broke the glass, it wasn't as if they could come squeezing through the small windows. And the entry to the basement itself seemed secure enough. It had been a blessing in disguise: at some point, someone had broken the set of glass double-doors that led outside. They'd been boarded up and, since they weren't serviceable, Miles had started storing extra furniture in the alcove leading to the doors.

Still, Johnny thought, how long before the zombies tried to knock down the church's front doors again? And when that happened—unless the bishop expected the children and elderly people like Wassim and Fatima to fight—they were so far outnumbered by the zombies that they wouldn't survive the hour.

"Don't be afraid!" the bishop called out again.

Yet Johnny could detect fear even in his voice; the zombies weren't supposed to attack until nighttime, Johnny imagined him thinking. And why did it matter? Because, he supposed, Bishop Joseph believed or just hoped that the Vespers service would provide a shield for the church.

Johnny looked up at the windows, locked eyes with a zombie who was staring right at him. He stood, scooping Izzy up and hugging her tightly with his left arm. "Holy God." He sang out each syllable, softly. Why not? Hadn't it worked the night before? "Holy Mighty"—each syllable a little louder now. Why not? If they were going to die today, he wanted these to be the last words on his lips. "Holy Immortal." He was a bit startled to realize someone else was singing too: Liz had joined him. "Have mercy on us."

Together they sang the words again, stronger and less hesitant this time. "Holy God," and more voices joined theirs. The zombies had been driven into an even more intense frenzy, and seemed to want to drown out the hymn with their howls and yells. A few began kicking at the windows with their bloodied, shoeless feet. "Holy Mighty." Johnny forced himself to ignore the zombies and focus on every syllable. "Holy Immortal." The zombies howled and kicked. "Have mercy on us."

Again they sang the words, and again, and again, and Johnny was transported, so lost in the song that he couldn't have said how long they stood there singing.

Eventually the other voices died away. Johnny seemed to return to himself. He looked around. Some people were standing, though most were seated. Some were crying silently, others were staring down at the table in front of them. Some were holding each other. Everyone was quiet; everything was quiet. The zombies were gone.

He turned to look at Liz, but her face was set as if in stone and her eyes were locked onto something at the front of the hall. He followed her gaze to the bishop, who was staring at Johnny. The look on Bishop Joseph's face was not grateful or scared or even just relieved; it was a look of disappointment, frustration, and even anger.

Chapter 6

THE bishop broke the silence. "Come," he said, his voice so calm and rational that it was easy to think that everything that had just happened was nothing more than a mass hallucination. "Let us complete our meal in peace. We can meet and discuss after lunch." Then he sat down and began to eat again.

The everyday noise whose absence caused the hall to be so eerily quiet returned slowly, as people sat and pulled their chairs up to their tables, as the low hum of chit-chat picked up again, and as glasses and plates were emptied and refilled.

Johnny sat Izzy back in her chair and kissed her on the forehead. "You're okay, right, honey?" She nodded. He picked up her plate and half-eaten sandwich from the floor, placed the sandwich on his plate (he couldn't eat now if his life depended on it, he felt) and made her a new one.

When Johnny sat down, Wassim gave him a slight nod and said, "It's a nice song," and seemed to feel that covered or conveyed everything.

The three boys refused to touch their food until their grandmother ordered them to eat. The Medusa's spell that had gripped them seemed to break further with every bite, and soon they were wolfing down the sandwiches and jostling each other, and shoving when one brother swayed too far into another's personal space.

Liz didn't say anything at first. She seemed to be debating something within her self; after a while, one side apparently winning out, she excused herself and stood. Johnny watched her walk over to the bishop, kneel beside him. They exchanged a few words, then she walked back, looking as if her own spell had been broken.

"What was that about?" Johnny said, when she sat down.

She gave him a sharp, quick look. "It was private." Then she turned to the boys again and resumed her conversation with them.

I just saved your life! Johnny wanted to yell at her. *Your life and*

everyone's here. So why are you brushing me off? Why did that grizzled
old man stare at me with his beady eyes like I'd committed a grave sin?

With a shove of his chair away from the table, he stood, then walked
over to the bishop. Michael was sitting beside Bishop Joseph and gave
Johnny a nod and an encouraging smile as he approached. The bishop
himself seemed unaware of Johnny until he knelt beside the old man.

"Did I do something wrong?" he said, whispering. Then, although
he wanted to leave it at that, he couldn't stop himself from adding,
"Because, as I see it, all I did was chase away the zombies."

The bishop turned his head to look into Johnny's eyes. When
he spoke, Johnny was struck once more with the dichotomy of the
strength his voice carried when addressing a crowd, as when he told
them not to be afraid in a loud, authoritative tone, and how weak and
broken it sounded when speaking to Johnny in private. Even his eyes
seemed filmed over with age and tiredness.

"I wish that were true, Mr. Salibi. But I don't think they're quite
chased away."

Johnny didn't wait to hear if the bishop had more to say; he stood
and walked over to the north-facing window, almost mechanically
grabbing an empty chair and dragging it to the wall. He climbed onto
it.

The horde of zombies stood across the street from the church. They
swayed into each other as before, their vacant eyes stared toward the
church as before, their howls momentarily silenced as before.

Johnny felt a wave of despair seize him. He'd assumed (or was
it hoped?) that the hymn had chased them away for good, that the
church was as safe as it had been before he'd arrived, that Izzy could
eat real food and play with other children, that he'd have time to find
and help his wife if that were possible.

But all of their singing had only managed to send the zombies back
to the same place they'd retreated to the night before. How long before
they attacked again? And would hymns or even a full service work to
keep them away next time?

Johnny climbed down from the chair, suddenly aware of the stillness in the room and that almost everyone was looking at him.

"What did you see?" a little boy of six or seven from the table
nearest him said. When Johnny didn't answer immediately, the boy
said, "Did you see them? Are they there?"

Johnny nodded.

As the realization, and perhaps the same thoughts Johnny himself had just had, sank into their minds, the stillness shattered. Yells and howls of their own, some directed at the bishop, pleading for him to help, some at each other as people argued over what they should do ("We need to leave. Now!" a man with a deep, loud voice yelled), but Johnny was shocked that a minority of voices were directed at him.

"You brought the howlers!" a woman yelled. "We were safe before you came!"

Someone sitting beside her, perhaps her husband, said, "Maybe they just want him, maybe they caught the scent of his blood. Let's throw him to them and see if they leave us alone!"

"His wife is out there—" Steven began to say, but someone else yelled over him, "Let him join her, then!" A few more voices rose up in his defense, but now many more called out for him to be thrown out, as if the zombies outside were some dark god who needed a sacrifice to be appeased. *Maybe that's not so far from the truth*, Johnny thought unhappily, looking from one person to the next, who mostly stared back at him with contempt and disdain and hatred.

All of their fear and anger, perhaps since all of this started, seemed to have found a target in Johnny. He couldn't see Izzy, and although he wanted to go back to her, he stood frozen in place. Some of the men and women had already stood so their voices could be heard over the others, but at least they were staying by their tables. He felt that if he started to move, their hesitancy might snap and they would descend on him themselves, tearing him apart as he'd feared the zombies outside might do.

As the cacophony of voices mounted in intensity, one cut through them all. The bishop was walking toward Johnny, so much authority in his voice that by degrees everyone became silent and sat back down, as he asked them to do.

"That's better," the bishop said, when the room had grown silent again. He stood next to Johnny. "If you think that giving Mr. Salibi to those outside will satisfy them, you are mistaken. Believe me when I say that our destruction will never be more certain than at the moment when we turn against one another."

"We're not turning against each other," the woman, the first one to speak out against Johnny, said. "Just on him. He brought the howlers."

Instead of responding to her, the bishop said, "Miles, where are you?" When Miles waved his fleshy hand, he continued, "I'm sorry that our meal has been interrupted. However I believe everyone here has lost their appetite. Will you collect and package the remaining food?"

Miles nodded, stood, and began to point out those he wanted to help him.

"Thank you, Miles. You can leave the cleaning for now." The bishop turned to Johnny's table. Izzy was sitting in Liz's lap. "Elizabeth, will you take the children upstairs to the church? Will you tell them the story of—let's see—how about Ali Baba and the Forty Thieves?"

If Liz was offended at being put in charge of the children, or at being excluded from the meeting, she didn't show it. She began gathering them up to follow her, deputizing the older children to hold hands with the younger ones.

"As the tables are cleared," the bishop continued, "please fold them and take them to the back, then bring enough chairs for everyone over here and we will begin our meeting."

Amid the buzz of activity, chairs were brought for the bishop and for Johnny. They sat in silence, even though Johnny wanted, first, to thank the bishop for probably saving his life and, second, to ask him a thousand questions: why hadn't he told them what the zombies truly were? what did he plan to say in the meeting? when did he think the zombies would attack again? what was his plan for when they did? But Bishop Joseph wasn't looking at him, and Johnny sensed that he'd be ignored even if he did try to speak to the bishop.

Chairs grew around them, more people joining them as their tables were cleaned and put away. Soon everyone was seated and the bishop opened the meeting with a prayer.

Johnny didn't say a word the whole time. After the prayer, the bishop said he saw only two options before them—they could stay in the church, or leave and find someplace else. Those choices framed the conversation, and no one suggested throwing Johnny out to the zombies again, or even mentioned him for the rest of the meeting. For that reason, Johnny felt it best to keep quiet.

He wouldn't have had much to say anyway, and was learning a lot by just sitting back and listening. Almost no one wanted to leave St. George. Many had experienced what the world had turned into before they found the church, or were found by those within the church, and they were well aware how nice they had it there.

Because he'd asked, Johnny knew that the water used to clean the dishes was rain water—but he learned now that it came from two large rain barrels at the back of the church, which he supposed were installed (after his time there) to provide an environmentally-friendly way to water the lawns. Those barrels allowed them to eat with real utensils and on real plates, as opposed to the paper plates and plastic cutlery they used at first, until they ran out. The water allowed them to do laundry, and even to take turns showering.

Then there was the food: meats and breads and vegetables in the freezer to last them weeks, fruits and cheeses in the fridge, along with chocolate, candy and chips and canned goods in the pantry. There was the stove for cooking, and enough space that they could eat while seated in chairs at tables, like civilized people. There were a pair of port-a-potties outside where they could go to the washroom; later he learned that they were left over from the festival that had wrapped up almost a month earlier. He also learned that these were located at the near end of the parking lot, while the far end had been turned into a dump site where they'd been burning their garbage.

The list of things went on. Where else would they find a place large enough to accommodate all of them? Their children had friends here; and they themselves would miss the fellowship if they had to flee and scatter. And they'd miss the prayers and services they offered in the church, too.

Because he'd resolved to keep quiet, as the newest member of this community and perhaps still an outsider, and as someone who'd only recently raised the ire of more than a few in the assembly, he was able to reflect on everything they said. He also couldn't help but notice the order of the things they missed: first, food and comfort; then one another; then the church. So God last. God always last.

At one point, Johnny had wondered why the bishop was letting everyone go on, enumerating all the things they liked about living there, but not really making any decisions. As he saw the looks on their faces, though, he realized that this wasn't a list of *things* they were making, it was a list of blessings. And that was good for them, in both senses of the word: good for them in that they were made to feel better by remembering these things, and good for them in the sense that counting one's blessings is always good for one. Halfway through the meeting, Johnny realized that it had turned into a Eucharistic meeting, a meeting of thanksgiving.

If Johnny had allowed himself to speak, he might have said that all of that was well and good, but things couldn't be the same: first, they couldn't shower or use the port-a-potties with the horde of zombies waiting outside. Second, even if the zombies left, eventually the gas would run out and their generators would die, and they wouldn't be able to keep food cold or frozen, and they wouldn't be able to cook it.

He didn't say that, and no one else did. It would've introduced a dark cloud in the positive atmosphere, and an unnecessary one because all of that was understood. The point right now was that no one wanted to leave, and they were stating all of their reasons why.

When those reasons finally seemed to be winding down, Bishop Joseph said, "I also do not wish to leave this church. In fact, I will not leave it no matter what else happens. I believe we are safe, safer here than anywhere else we can find. I believe that no matter how many times those outside bang on our doors or kick at our windows, as long as we have faith in Almighty God, and we don't succumb to fear, we will be fine. But we must not succumb to fear. I believe that sooner or later, when those outside find they can't touch us, they will leave us be and we will be able to return to the life we have made for ourselves, as good a life as one can expect under the circumstances."

After a short pause, the bishop continued, "For these are strange and trying times, I know. It is easy to forget about Him, to despair, to feel alone and abandoned. But let us never forget God. Let us never forget that He is sovereign, and nothing happens except by His permission. Let us never forget that God has a plan; we don't always know what that plan is or how we fit into it, but we know and affirm and trust this, that God works all things for the good of those who love Him."

Is it God's plan that Rebekah be turned into a zombie? Johnny tried to push the thoughts away, unsuccessfully. *Who loved God more than Rebekah? So is it good for her that she's a monstrous lunatic now, one who claws at her husband's face without awareness, one who growls and howls, one who may be standing outside even now with violent and murderous thoughts on her mind, if anything could be properly said to be on her mind? Is that God working for her good?*

The dark mood seemed to have lifted off of everyone else and settled on Johnny. They were comforted by the happy memories of their *common* experience in this new life, but Johnny didn't share in those memories and he was still an outsider who might never get to experience a shower with rainwater; they were emboldened by the bishop's confidence in God, but Johnny's wife was still outside and Johnny himself might be the first to be sacrificed if the zombies attacked again.

As the meeting broke up, and everyone returned their chairs to the back, Johnny turned to the bishop and said, "Can we have a discussion now? An open one?"

The bishop had stood with effort; his legs seemed rickety, practically shaking with the sudden demand put to them of holding up his weight. "What would you like to discuss?"

Johnny didn't answer at first, because it seemed obvious and it seemed overwhelming. In fact, he wanted to discuss everything, to say everything he suspected and find out everything the bishop knew, to ultimately learn if his wife's condition was permanent or if, like Christ in the Gospels, Bishop Joseph could expel the demon or demons possessing her.

"As a start," he finally settled on, "what are your plans for the zomb—" He stopped himself as the bishop's face clouded over and started again—"for those outside?"

The cloud on the bishop's face didn't clear. "I'm not sure I understand your question, Mr. Salibi." Once again Johnny felt he'd disappointed the old man, as if the conversation and the bishop's level of respect for him may have gone in a different direction if only Johnny had asked a better, or perhaps the correct, question. "I already explained my plans—to stay here, to not succumb to fear, to continue to pray for God's protection."

"That's it? But they could attack us anytime. You must have another plan. Those windows won't hold out forever. The doors will eventually give."

"It is not by sword and spear that the Lord saves."

"Yes, but it is not against flesh and blood that we struggle." Johnny paused, wondering why his tone became so antagonistic when speaking with the bishop, even though he needed his help. "You can call them people," Johnny continued, lowering his voice because someone was approaching, "but I know what they are."

"Bishop Joseph?" Miles said, from a respectful distance. "Can we have a word when you're free?"

The bishop threw an apologetic but final look at Johnny and began to move away. Johnny held him back by gripping his arm.

"I suppose you have reasons for keeping the truth from these people," he said, whispering in the old man's ear. "I don't plan on spoiling things for you. But I need you to speak openly with me." Because he felt as he spoke that he'd once again struck the wrong note, he tried to soften things by saying, "My wife is still out there. I saw her—she's one of them now. Please—if there's anything you or I can do to help her, you have to tell me."

It seemed to work; at first, the bishop's arm had been tense in his hand, but it relaxed as Johnny kept speaking.

Miles had been waiting, but Bishop Joseph seemed to indicate to him by a nod that he'd catch up with him later, and Miles returned to the kitchen.

"Remember," the bishop said, turning back to face Johnny, his voice kind but frail, "that with God, all things are possible."

He patted him on his hands, then moved away. Johnny himself didn't move for a while. Everyone else had been comforted by the bishop's words earlier, but it was these words that brought comfort and relief to Johnny. He hadn't even realized how on edge he'd been until he felt the weight that lifted from his heart when the bishop reminded him that there was at least the possibility of healing Rebekah.

With God all things are possible. From Christ's own lips. And now Johnny had an immediate goal. Something had attacked his wife, defeated her, taken control of her or just of her body. But the bishop could help her, cure her, restore her. And Rebekah and Izzy and he could live together again, maybe even in this church where he should've come in the first place.

And once his own wife were cured, there was a whole world that needed help. The zombie apocalypse had robbed people of loved ones, of fathers and daughters and mothers and uncles and grandchildren and grandparents. But for many of those people, their loved ones could be restored to them, like Christ had restored His friend Lazarus to Mary and Martha.

"Johnny? Hello?"

Johnny snapped out of his daze. The subdeacon had a friendly if slightly concerned expression on his face.

"The bishop asked me to speak with you," he said, when he saw he finally had Johnny's attention. "He said you have some things you'd like to discuss."

Chapter 7

A T the subdeacon's request, Johnny followed him up the stairs and into the church's nave. They sat in the front pew where they could stretch out their legs. Sunlight streamed through the windows. Moving from the basement to the church, Johnny felt as if he'd stepped into another world, or to speak more accurately, that he'd ascended into another world. The saints and angels depicted in icons on the walls of the nave and on the iconostasis at the front of the church stared out with strangely peaceful but enigmatic expressions—even St. John the Baptist, who carried his own head on a platter.

Many icons had been added to the church since Johnny was a child. Still, it was as familiar as a childhood home. In fact, this church was the scene of countless Sunday services and of so many baptisms and weddings and funerals that it was easy to forget about the world as it had become, easy to forget that just a hundred feet or so outside the walls of the church, a horde of bloodthirsty zombies waited for something—darkness to descend, perhaps, or some other sign or signal—before they once again attacked.

They'd sat in silence for too long. "How are you feeling?" Johnny said.

Michael shrugged. "Sore. I'll be okay."

"They did a worse number on you than on me." Whether that was strictly true or not, Johnny didn't know; but neither his nose nor any other bone had been broken in the confrontation outside. He'd had worse days in his youth when he attended karate tournaments religiously, almost every weekend. It never occurred to him at the time how grateful he should be to his father, who gave up every Saturday for about six or seven years to drive Johnny to those events and to watch him compete.

Another long silence followed, and Johnny had the feeling it was once more his to break.

He chose the direct approach. "Those people outside are human beings who've been possessed by demons. Aren't they?"

"We believe so, yes."

"We?"

"I was referring to the bishop and I."

"The others here don't share your belief?"

Michael had been leaning forward, his elbows on his knees, but now he sat back. "I know what you're getting at, Johnny. You want to know—"

"—why you're keeping that information from everyone," Johnny interrupted.

"Because," Michael began, then stopped, seeming to search for a way to put his thoughts into words. It was obvious to Johnny that Michael had expected this question to come up during their conversation, but now that it had, he seemed to struggle to answer it properly. "Because, Johnny—think about it. Some here don't believe in God or demons or anything like that; others feel that God and demons are for the Bible and Sunday mornings, and that those things don't have a place in the real world. They speak of their 'spiritual life' as if they had a couple of different lives like they have different shoes to wear on separate occasions."

"So?"

"So those who have eyes to see have already seen. You figured it out on your own."

"You think they wouldn't believe you if you tried to tell them the truth?" Johnny said, and kept to himself the thought that wasn't testifying to the truth precisely what the bishop and subdeacon were called to do.

"It's not just that," Michael said. "Many of the people here have done horrible things to survive. They view those outside like rabid dogs or some other disease-infected animals, or even monsters. They did those things to survive. There's no judgment here. But can you imagine the weight of guilt once they realize that what they did, they did to fellow human beings?"

In a flash of images in his mind, Johnny saw himself standing in his bedroom and bashing skulls and rib cages with a steel bat, saw himself kicking in the head of the male zombie who'd bit him, saw himself yelling out in anger and boxing his wife's ears. Michael's eyes had filled with a sudden sadness, perhaps as he remembered Johnny's own appearance at the church, bloodied with more than his own blood, and realized what Johnny had done to get there.

"Anyway," Michael said, "the world is horrific enough. Everyone has been touched by it—those of us who've had to do things"—the way Michael spoke the phrase and the casting down of his glance made Johnny realize that perhaps the sudden sadness had nothing to do with him, but with something that Michael himself had done—"and those of us who've seen horrible things done."

"But don't they deserve to know the truth?"

"I think that's a nice ideal, Johnny. But the ones who haven't figured it out by now, or at least strongly suspect it, won't believe us if we tried to tell them. And, like I said, if we tried to force it on them, I believe it would cause more harm than good."

"But if people knew, wouldn't they—"

"—want to help them?" Michael's voice was hesitant. "That would be the worst thing of all." He paused. "I think we're coming to the point. I think this is why Bishop Joseph wanted me to speak with you. We know your wife is still out there; by God's grace, she's still alive. We know you want to help her, to heal her."

"Is that possible?"

"Yes, it is." Johnny couldn't help but notice that so much of what Michael had been saying was couched in uncertain terms, surrounded by hedged bets, but this simple statement didn't have a hint of doubt. "But it's not easy," Michael continued. "It's very dangerous. Whatever demon or demons have possessed her, they won't leave her easily. They'll fight."

"I'll fight back," Johnny said. "In Christ's name. Whatever demon or demons have possessed her, Christ is mightier."

"Of course He is. But are you?"

Johnny didn't respond.

"I know you and Bishop Joseph seem to have gotten off on the wrong foot. But I can tell you, you won't meet anyone with greater faith. The bishop loves the Lord and has dedicated his whole life from childhood to serving Him. Can you say that? He keeps every fast, prays constantly, regularly partakes of the Eucharist. Can you say that?"

"What's your point?"

"Even for a man like that, grappling with these demons took everything in his power. It left him exhausted. Are you ready for a battle like that?"

Michael was so intent on scaring Johnny off that Johnny felt he'd revealed information he hadn't meant to share. "To save my wife," he said, speaking slowly, "I'm ready for any battle, Michael. I'm ready to give up my life if it means I can save hers. And what you're saying is that there is a way. The bishop has tried it and succeeded."

Michael seemed taken aback. He was quiet for a moment, his eyes searching Johnny's face to tease out what he knew. Then his eyes opened wide, at the realization that he himself had inadvertently let the information slip out. "I never said that."

Johnny tilted his head down and lifted his eyebrows, to stare at Michael from underneath them. "You don't have to spare me, or hide the truth for any other reason. I want the truth."

"No, you don't want the truth. You want a way to heal your wife."

"Is that so wrong?"

"It's dangerous, very dangerous. And you seem like the type who'd run off and try it on your own no matter what warnings I gave you."

Johnny wanted to protest and defend himself, but he could certainly understand how he gave Michael that impression over the last day that they'd known each other. "That's fair," he said. "What if I give you my word in the name of the Lord Jesus Christ that I won't try it on my own, unless I have the bishop's blessing to do so?"

Michael nodded. "All right. Yes, of course it's possible. But it isn't easy."

"So he's done it? You've seen him do it?"

"Yes, I've seen him do it."

"You're sure?" *Rebekah is a zombie*, Johnny thought. *But there's a way to bring her back?*

Michael hesitated but seemed to make the decision to forge ahead. "Johnny, I'm sure. You've even met someone here who was once a zombie, as you call them."

"Really? Who?"

Michael sat back. "I'm not going to tell you that."

Johnny wanted to ask why, but stopped himself for fear of upsetting Michael or making him feel that he doubted his words. Instead, he said, "Can you tell me what happened?"

"Why do you want to know?" Michael said. "Can't you just take my word for it?"

"I believe you," Johnny said. "I want to believe you. Help my unbelief, Michael."

Reluctantly, Michael told him the story. It was several weeks ago, on a Sunday morning during the Divine Liturgy. It was only when Michael mentioned Father Gord that Johnny wondered, for the first time since he'd arrived, what had happened to the priest who'd chased him away from this church. Something in Michael's tone, though, deepened the sense of mystery about Father Gord: a strange sadness, a sense of loss or regret, tinged his words.

The bishop had arrived sometime before that Sunday, although Johnny never found out how much before.

"I remember the exact moment it happened," Michael continued. "I was standing by the choir. Father Gord had just called everyone forward to receive Communion, in the fear of God and with faith and love. Those words were hardly out of his mouth when we heard screams from the back of the church. Yells of terror, from the children at first but then from others too. The church was only half full; most of the back pews were empty. A man—a zombie, you'd call him—had wandered into the nave and up one of the aisles before enough people noticed him and began to scream. He was weak, holding himself upright by lumbering from pew to pew; but he was also growling like a feral dog. As he came within an inch of another person, his growling grew in intensity and he tried to reach out for them, to claw them or even bite them. Finally his attempts connected with someone who hadn't seen him coming, an older lady who used to cab to the church every Sunday from her apartment building. This man grabbed her hair from behind and yanked it to the side; she fell over onto the floor, screaming for help. He stomped on her head twice and she was quiet.

"As they yelled in terror and scrambled to get away from this man, the bishop commanded everyone to be quiet. Father Gord was frozen in place, staring down the aisle at the dead old lady and the pool of blood around her head.

"Bishop Joseph strode up to the man, who'd become suddenly quiet at his approach. But now he opened his mouth and blasted the bishop, yelling obscenities about the bishop and his mother, screaming blasphemies about Christ and the Theotokos.

"The bishop took a step forward, and the man fell back a pew. The bishop wore a large golden cross on his chest, the same as he wears now. He lifted it, and the man took another step back. The bishop bent down and checked for a pulse on the old lady.

"I think Bishop Joseph realized what was going on by then. He stood again, and held up the cross. He addressed himself directly to the demons possessing the man, commanding them in the name of Christ to tell him who they were."

When it seemed Michael wasn't going to continue, Johnny said,

"Who were they?"

Michael smiled faintly. "I think that's about as much as I'm comfortable telling you. Except for two more things. One—the bishop cast the demons out of the man. He's downstairs right now, and you wouldn't think him a zombie or former zombie any more than you'd think me one. Very few people know what he did that day, or what he might have done before then."

Johnny nodded. "And two?"

"I know you think Bishop Joseph is naive or lazy or scared—actually, I don't know what you think of him, except that you judge him for not doing more. Don't try to protest, Johnny—you think we should be going outside and chasing them away or trying to cure them, am I right?"

Instead of committing himself to an answer, Johnny shrugged. Of course he wanted to chase away the zombies, of course he wanted to cure them—especially his wife. What else was there to do?

"You have no idea of the effort it takes," Michael said, "or the danger involved. I'm not talking about the physical danger, that's the least of it. The bishop"—here Michael paused, then seemed to force himself to go on—"the bishop is very old now. When he cured that man, he collapsed. Later he said it felt like all the energy and power had drained out of him. It took him days to recover. And when he did, he was like you, Johnny—he saw it as his vocation to cure these so-called zombies.

"We went out together from the church, crosses in hand, the bishop, Father Gord, and I. By that time, the population of possessed persons was starting to rise—it was no longer an isolated case here or there, but cases everywhere. And more being reported all the time."

"So what happened?"

"We had to turn back. When you confront the demons directly, you open yourself up to them. Have you ever tried fasting for an extended period of time?"

Johnny nodded.

"Then you know that's when the temptations are worst. What's that old saying? If you don't believe in demons, try not to sin for a day. And see if all the demons in hell don't rise up against you."

"So all the demons in hell rose up against you?"

"No," Michael said. "But the bishop sensed that something was wrong, and that we were vulnerable to them. He made us come back to the church."

"Because of Father Gord." At the look of surprise that seized Michael's features, Johnny added, "He's the reason I stopped coming to this church, before you came."

"You knew about the embezzlement that long ago?"

The confusion on Johnny's face seemed to clear the surprise from Michael's.

"So if you didn't know about the embezzlement," Michael said, "what was the problem?"

"He was embezzling funds?" Johnny said.

"It was suspected. Bishop Joseph came for an extended visit to see for himself, quietly, what was going on in this parish and with Father Gord. He didn't have any proof, but once we went out together, the bishop sensed that the demons had focused on Father Gord. He sensed that Father had unconfessed sins weighing down his soul.

"He asked us to turn back, then decided to confront Father in his office."

"What happened?"

"Bishop Joseph asked to meet with him in private, so I waited outside. I stood far enough away that I wouldn't overhear their conversation. But soon I could hear Father's side very easily. He was yelling and cursing, saying blasphemous things and accusing the bishop of all kinds of sins.

"I didn't want to disobey the bishop's wishes, but when I heard loud noises of furniture shifting and metal hitting the ground, I opened the door and burst through.

"Bishop Joseph was on the ground, Father Gord on top of him and punching him in the face. I pulled Father off, pushed him away and went to help Bishop Joseph. Father kicked me in the sides, and ignored me when I fell down in pain, resuming his attack on the bishop. He wasn't himself, I knew; whether he'd been taken over by rage or a demon, I don't know, but he wasn't himself. I guess both amount to the same thing."

Michael took a deep breath, then continued. "The bishop's face was bloodied up. I didn't want to take any more chances. I picked up a copy of the Bible, a large gold-covered book, asked Father to forgive me, and swung it at his head as hard as I could. He fell back, and when I held up my cross and asked him in Christ's name to calm down, he yelled at me all kinds of blasphemies, then got up and ran out. I haven't seen him since that day."

Johnny and Michael were quiet for a long time.

Finally, Johnny broke the silence by saying, "I don't get it. He was a priest. In a church, and in an office surrounded by crosses." Before Michael could respond, Johnny said, "How can they attack this church? Why did they attack me even though I held the cross in my hand?"

"It's not magic, Johnny. They fear Christ and His Cross more than anything, but they can get over their fear if sufficiently motivated." Here Michael paused again, as if once more considering within himself whether he should share what was on his mind. "You have spiritual power, Johnny. I heard about the first time you sang the Trisagion— and of course I joined you just now. The bishop fears that you'll use that power to spin the demons into an even greater frenzy and risk all of our lives." Michael shrugged. "He's probably right; they probably are just trying to scare us for now. But I saw what happened: the song transported you into heaven, and they couldn't stand to be near it, so they left.

"I'm not saying you were right; for now we must obey the bishop's wishes. He told me that when Father Gord fled the church, he felt a deep conviction that he had to wait. So that's what he's doing, waiting for a sign from God. And that's what we should do, wait with him. But when that sign comes, we're going to need the kind of power you commanded just now."

Johnny didn't respond. He considered telling Michael that his bishop was so terrified the night before that he'd actually closed the doors of the church when he and Johnny were caught outside, abandoning both of them to the zombies, but he decided to leave it alone.

During Vespers that evening, though, Johnny could barely focus on the service. He couldn't stop thinking about the old lady who'd been killed in the middle of the Divine Liturgy. He kept looking behind him, perhaps half-expecting zombies to disturb these services too, to burst through the doors and attack them. When he wasn't looking behind him, he was looking around, wondering which one was the man who'd been cured of demons—assuming he wasn't among those who'd decided to stay in the basement during service.

Izzy was sitting beside him, listening to the service quietly even though she wasn't used to coming to church. He could see her out of the corner of his eye, looking up at him and probably wondering why he was being so fidgety.

When he'd arrived at the church, and discovered that his wife was missing, the dark thoughts that filled him threatened to choke the life out of him. His greatest fear at the time was that she'd been injured or killed by the zombies. But then he saw her, and it seemed she wasn't dead or even injured, but she'd been turned into one of them herself. The only thought that sustained him then was that maybe the bishop could restore her; but now he was finding out that the bishop himself didn't feel he had the spiritual strength to heal anyone, at least not until he saw this sign he'd been waiting for.

And in the meantime, what was his wife doing? Attacking someone with her bare hands? Tearing apart a little child with her teeth? Eating the flesh of a corpse?

And then there crept up, again, the unhappy thought that followed his defense of his wife. She was possessed by dark forces, so she couldn't be blamed for whatever she did. But how had she come to be possessed in the first place?

Father Gord had perhaps fallen under their influence because of his sins, of arrogance or embezzling money or anger or whatever else he was guilty of. What about Rebekah, though? Her faith was strong; stronger than his own, more times than not. But it wasn't strong enough. Or it was a false faith, seed scattered on rocky ground?

This was the world he lived in now, a world that had gone to hell. The demons had flooded the earth, taken possession of almost all of humanity. That was on the one side; on the other, as far as he knew, there stood a bishop who was waiting (or, to be less kind about it, waiting around) and a small gathering of people in a church.

Despair was a great sin, but as he examined his heart, Johnny didn't feel despair. He felt fear and a deep sense of loss and a longing for the way the world was. But there was no doubt in his mind how things would end. Christ was already victorious. When He had died on the Cross, that moment of utter and complete defeat, He had secured His victory.

The world was dying, but it had to die before it could be raised up again. Christians had always known this day would come. The world, which was so full of corruption, would die but would be raised up incorruptible. And everyone would be raised up too, all to everlasting life, though some to an eternity of joy and light and others to an eternity of sorrow and darkness, depending on the choices they made in this life.

The only questions in Johnny's mind were what role he would play in all of this, if any. And, more importantly, who among those he loved, including himself, would be the sheep Christ welcomed into His kingdom in the next life, and who would be the goats He cast out?

Father, he prayed, *save the souls of your humble servants. Forgive us all of our iniquities and teach us to love You and serve You. Save my wife, Lord, and my little daughter; save my parents, and everyone who has ever said a kind word to me, and forgive anyone who has ever wronged me. Show Your mercy on this hurting and dying world, Lord. Don't hide Your face from us; don't put us away in anger. Don't abandon us, O Savior.*

Teach me to do your will, Father. Use me however You see fit. If I am to wait, grant me patience, Lord; and if I am to act, grant me strength. This I ask in the name of your Son and by the power of Your Holy Spirit. Amen.

Chapter 8

JOHNNY had fallen in with the clean-up crew somehow, but he enjoyed their company and the calm routine of washing dishes. This time Theresa scraped the food bits, Steven cleaned, and he dried. Their conversation was lighter too; they talked mostly of favorite movies and novels and songs, and, at least at first, not at all of what was happening outside. But when Theresa said her favorite movie was *Casablanca*, and Johnny said without thinking that that was Rebekah's favorite movie as well, there was a protracted, awkward silence.

Johnny broke it. "Anyway," he said, and hoped the transition didn't sound forced, "I guess our entertainment these days is cleaning dishes, isn't it?"

"We usually play games after dinner," Theresa said.

"Not that washing dishes isn't therapy," Steven said. "For the first couple of days, we used paper plates and plastic utensils, but we started running out quickly. And Theresa and I found we liked doing dishes."

"Which is funny," Theresa said, "because before—all of this—they piled up in our sink for days on end."

"There was always so much else to do," Steven said.

I guess the whole zombie apocalypse has simplified our lives. The thought came to Johnny, but he refused to voice it. His life had certainly been too complicated and busy before, but nothing about life now was simple. There were less moving pieces, perhaps—survive the zombies outside, find your wife and find a way to cure her were the main ones in his mind—but those pieces were horrific ones, much worse than anything he'd ever had to deal with before. And he still couldn't see the end game—even if they survived these particular zombies, what would happen next?

Only one outcome made sense to him, that this really was the end now, the end of history and the end of fallen humanity. The world had to die before it could be resurrected. . . and this world certainly needed to be resurrected. Even before the zombie apocalypse, it was a world of extreme violence, a world red in tooth and claw. Johnny himself had never experienced anything as horrific as the zombies, but other people had, and perhaps even worse in some ways. If the world had produced a single serial killer, it would be too much; if the world had experienced a single genocide, it would be too horrific. But was there a city in the world that couldn't claim a serial killer? Was there even one century in human history that wasn't marred by genocide? Or, to expand the net as far as possible, was there a single human soul whose life hadn't been mangled by sin? A single human being whose life wasn't pockmarked with betrayals and deep injustices and even casual cruelties, whether that person was committing those sins or having them committed against them?

This was a world being choked to death by sin. And of course it was so, because humanity had delivered it into the hands of the Prince of Devils. But it seemed the time had come for his reign to be broken, even as his back had been broken on the Cross. It seemed the time had come for the world to end, for Christ to reclaim and restore it and reign forever in the Kingdom of the new heavens and the new earth.

Come Lord, Johnny thought, *but in Your mercy and long-suffering, please allow me the time to find and heal my wife first.*

They finished up cleaning in relative silence, Johnny's dark and somber mood perhaps infecting the couple who'd been good enough to let him in on their therapy session, then rejoined the others in the hall.

Enough light was streaming in that some took advantage of it by reading; these had positioned themselves on chairs near the windows. Others were standing around and talking, while a few were napping on some cots that had been set up near the supply room. Among the figures of those napping under blankets and afghans, Johnny noticed the bishop as well as Fatima and Wassim. They didn't seem to be bothered by the noise coming from the western end of the hallway, where the children were playing duck-duck-goose. Izzy was sitting among the others in the circle, but she was facing away from him. Liz was supervising.

In the middle of the hall, a couple of tables had been set up, and Miles stood in front of them, reading out trivia questions in his best approximation of a quiet voice. Each table consulted among themselves, then wrote down their answer on a sheet of paper and passed it up to

Miles. He announced the correct answer and handed the paper back if they were right—so they could keep track of scores, Johnny figured.

He watched them play for a while, from a distance so he wouldn't be asked to join in. At one point, Steven looked back at him, then got up and walked over.

"Want to come on our team? We can use the help."

"That's okay. I think I'm going to go check out that game of duck-duck-goose."

Johnny walked over to where the children were sitting in their circle, and positioned himself along the wall so that Izzy could see him. He waved at her. She hardly took notice of him—the picker was tagging ducks and was almost at her. She sat in a state of excited anxiety, half-looking up at the oncoming boy out of the corner of her eyes, her lips turned up in a wide smile she struggled to contain.

The little boy reached her, touched her head, declared her a duck, and moved on, but her smile didn't fade. The boy seemed intent on never declaring anyone ever a goose, or of making the round of the circle at least twice first, to make sure he picked the right mark, but finally he cried out the magic word and made a run for it. The goose was one of the few teenagers, a young girl who rose quickly but only pretended to chase after the little boy, then pretended to be disappointed when he made it back around and took her spot.

The girl glanced at Liz, and some secret communication seemed to pass between them. She went around the circle, touching the children's heads and declaring them ducks, until she got to Izzy.

"Goose!" the young lady cried.

Izzy shot up and chased after her, her tiny arms swinging at her side like pistons in a machine. Izzy caught up with the teenage girl halfway around and looked absolutely triumphant. She didn't return to her seat, though; she ran over to Johnny and beamed up at him.

"Did you see me?"

He knelt down so he didn't tower over her. "I sure did," he said. "You did good, munchkin. Who taught you how to run that fast?"

He didn't hear her response; a dark thought had invaded his mind. *One day you may need to run that fast, and faster, to escape a zombie who wants to tear you apart. Maybe your own mother.*

He stood suddenly, aware that the smile had dropped from his face but hoping Izzy hadn't noticed. "You should get back to the game, honey."

She nodded and ran to take her place again.

Johnny walked over to Liz. "Thank you," he said, speaking softly so the children wouldn't hear. "That was nice of you."

Liz smiled but didn't look at him. "I have no idea what you're talking about. If you think I've in any way influenced the choosing of geese—" She shrugged, as if the mere allegation left her speechless.

"No, not at all," Johnny said, and finally she glanced at him. "I just meant it's nice of you to organize these games for the kids."

"Ah, I see. And here I thought you were claiming that corruption has invaded even the hallowed game of duck-duck-goose. That kind of cynicism I wouldn't stand for, and would have to throw you in there with the kids as punishment."

As she brushed her hair back over her left ear, he saw the brilliant diamond she wore on her finger. Perhaps for that reason, perhaps for the way she was looking at the children as they played, perhaps because he couldn't think of anything else to say or of a way to leave gracefully, he said, "Are any of them yours? Do you have children?"

He knew the questions were a mistake as soon as he started speaking, but somehow couldn't stop himself.

"No," Liz said. "I mean, yes." She turned to him and roused up a playful smile, but it wasn't as natural as the first one she'd given him. "You asked two questions. None of these children are mine, no. But I did have children. Two boys."

He didn't want to ask what happened to them. "How old?"

"Eight and six. Matthew and Luke."

"Like the Evangelists," Johnny said.

She nodded. "That was my husband's standard joke after Luke was born: if God graced us with two more boys, we could call them Mark and John and have a sure ticket to heaven." She took a deep breath that turned into a sigh. "I like hanging out with the children. It reminds me of my own kids."

"I'm glad we came here," Johnny said. "It's good for Izzy to be around other people. Especially other children."

"She's a great kid. She's very sensitive. She misses her mom, of course, but she's putting on a brave face—I think in large part because she senses how much you're suffering."

Johnny stared at Liz.

"I'm sorry," she said. "It's none of my business. I shouldn't have said anything."

"Izzy spoke to you about her mom?"

"Just that she missed her and wanted to see her. She understands a lot more of what's happening than I would have at her age. She knows her mom is sick."

"And what did you tell her?"

Liz seemed taken aback by the aggression in Johnny's tone. He didn't care.

"I said that we'd do everything we can for her, that for right now she had to be patient and pray for her mom. We prayed together, the first night she was here." Her own voice was still soft. "Was that okay?"

Liz's calm in the face of his own rising temper deflated Johnny's anger. "Yes, I'm glad you did that." After a short pause, he added, "Thank you."

"I better get back to the kids," she said. "They'll want to play something else now. Do you want to help?"

It seemed to Johnny that she asked the question more out of politeness than any real need or even desire for his assistance. "That's okay. I may try to read before it gets too dark."

"Yes!" Liz said, her natural smile springing to her face again. "We have tons of books in the store. Completely disorganized, but I've spent hours in there just digging through the piles."

That sounded like a wonderful way to spend some time, Johnny thought.

"It's dark in there," Liz said, "but there are flashlights just inside the room, on the shelf to the right."

"And it's okay to use them?"

"Sure," Liz said. "We have plenty, and batteries to last a lifetime."

A lifetime that likely won't be too long.

Liz had given him a parting smile and stepped toward the children. She announced that they were going to play a new game.

Johnny walked over to Izzy and picked her up from behind, but didn't say anything until Liz was done explaining the rules of Guess Who. Listening to her, Johnny got the impression that Liz spent some time as a camp counselor in her younger days.

"You want to stay here and play the game?" he said, turning Izzy around to face him.

"Yeah."

"Okay." He kissed her forehead with a loud smack, like he used to do to make her and Rebekah laugh, then put her down again. Izzy didn't laugh. "Be a good girl, yes?"

"Yes," she said, then ran off to see on which side of the hall Liz wanted her to stand.

The bookshop, at the other end of the hall, was an enclosed room without windows. He opened the door and felt around for a flashlight on the shelf. There was a box of them. He pulled one out and clicked it on.

On one shelf, the same one that held the flashlights and some other supplies, were stacked icons and crosses; the rest of the shelves, another six or seven floor-to-ceiling ones, were bursting with books. More boxes took up the space between the shelves, so he often had to step over them as he walked around. These boxes overflowed with books too, and many had spilled their contents right onto the ground. The books were of all sorts—small mass market ones, and tall trade paperbacks, and big hardcovers; books on science and history and math, and books of horror and mystery and science fiction. New books that hardly looked touched and old books with yellowed pages and creased covers.

A small paperback, buried under some others except for its title, caught his eye. He placed the flashlight on the bookshelf behind him, then reached into the box and pulled out the book. *Foundation* by Isaac Asimov. He'd read it in junior high school; and not just the book, but this specific edition. The story was of a man, thousands of years in the future, whose scientific calculations allowed him to predict the imminent fall of civilization, and who decided to collect all human knowledge in a central database so that, ostensibly anyway, the survivors could quickly rebuild the world after the inevitable collapse.

He cracked open the book, held up the pages to the beam of light, and flipped through them. Hari Seldon. Just the name put a smile on his face. It brought back a flood of memories from his youth, when his life was so uncomplicated, when his greatest concerns were how best to ask out Tammy from math class, and whether he'd win a trophy, a medal, or nothing at all in the next karate tournament. When he could spend a whole Sunday afternoon in his room, reading through an entire book or two.

Books like *Foundation*. Good books, but also books with a message that a relatively bright and skilled pre-teen and teenager was only too happy to hear: be as smart and clever as you can be and you'll do all right, and the world will do all right by you. There was no hint in any of those books that the fault lay not in our brains but in our hearts; that the solution to the problems of the world wasn't in the acquisition of more and more knowledge and skills, but in the acquisition of a humble and merciful heart that loves God.

He put the book down and picked up another. It seemed that he'd hit a vein of golden age science fiction paperbacks, the kind of stuff he'd devoured as a kid. One of these books almost fell out of his hands as he held it up to the light, but he caught it by the front cover. On the inside title page, someone had stamped with blue ink "From the library of..." and scribbled their name on the dotted line in messy cursive.

Johnny hadn't met everyone in the church, but he had a feeling he wouldn't find among them the owner of these books. He also didn't imagine this person had donated his paperbacks to the church. Like the flashlight in his hand, like the food he'd just had for dinner, like the generators and gas that powered their refrigerator and stove, the books were stolen goods, taken without payment from empty supermarkets and department stores, from abandoned homes and libraries and maybe second-hand bookstores.

Of course that was fine. Would it have been better to leave the food in the supermarkets to rot? Even if they wanted to buy the generators or the gas that powered them, who were they supposed to pay? Wasn't it better that the books had been salvaged, maybe even saved from destruction by fire, and were among people who might pick them up and read them?

Even so, he couldn't shake the uneasy feeling, the thought that maybe the owner of these books was outside right now, perhaps a zombie, but perhaps not a zombie; or the thought that some other pack of survivors were even now rummaging through his own house and through his books and Rebekah's books, and taking from their home whatever they wanted and what they thought no one would come back to look for. He also couldn't shake the mental image of someone siphoning gas out of abandoned cars, which is how he imagined they'd filled up the tanks in the kitchen, and which, as little as a few weeks ago, would've gotten them arrested.

He returned the book to the box and turned off the flashlight, but kept sitting on the gift shop floor in the dark. They had to do something, he was convinced of that. Not only because the zombie threat was at their door, not only because humanity had lost too much ground to the demons already, but because the despair was so overwhelming that only by struggling could they push it back and hold it at bay. People needed a purpose beyond merely existing. The bishop was waiting for a sign from God, but how long would he wait? And what would happen to them in the meantime, trapped like prisoners in the church, even if the demons and zombies never crossed its threshold?

An hour or so later, the bustling noise from the hall seemed to die down, but Johnny still didn't move until a new set of sounds streamed in.

He left the dark room finally. The sun had gone down and the windows were dark. The hall was dimly lit by candles. Tables were being folded up and carried into the supply room and cots carried out to replace them.

He went to help. Miles was inside the room, directing the stacking of the tables against the wall.

"Oh, there you are," he said, when he saw Johnny. "I've been looking for you."

"How can I help?"

"I've arranged for you to have a cot. Here, I'll show you which one." He was already side-stepping past someone carrying in a stack of chairs. Johnny followed. "There, that one near the kitchen, that's yours, and Izzy can sleep beside you if that works. It's a lot more comfortable than it looks, trust me."

"I don't want to take someone else's cot," Johnny said, following him back into the room.

Miles had gone to the shelf at the back and pulled out a pile of linens. "It's all taken care of, don't worry."

"But I really don't feel—"

"I said everything's worked out. If you make a fuss, I'll think you're second-guessing me and how I run my business. I'll take it as a personal insult and put you on half-rations."

Someone took the linens from Miles.

"I appreciate it, but—"

Miles put a fleshy hand on Johnny's shoulder. "You're still hurt. You're hiding it, but I can tell. So accept this one kindness, get a good night's sleep, and feel better in the morning. Okay?" Before Johnny could answer, Miles continued, "Don't look so conflicted. Does it make you feel better that I'm giving Michael the couch in Father Gord's office? That's the best bed in the house, but he gets it because he needs it more. And because we like him more."

Johnny laughed, but the small sound was almost immediately swallowed up by Miles's hearty, bellowing guffaws in response.

"I had my doubts about you," he said. "But you can still laugh at yourself, so there's hope for you yet. Now go make your bed, there should be linens put out for you by now."

A table was set up a few feet from Johnny's cot, the same table where he'd found the bishop the night before. He supposed Bishop Joseph would sit there again, either alone or with his inner circle, perhaps feeling the need at night to keep watch over this desperate, sad flock he'd been given. Whether he sat alone or with others, though, Johnny figured he could put Izzy to sleep, then approach the bishop and whoever else, and find out what was going on, whether they had a plan or not, and in either case try and convince the bishop to take up that first calling he'd felt, to try again to cast out the demons, even if it meant kidnapping them somehow, bringing them back to the church, and trying to help them one at a time.

The bishop had promised to help Rebekah, and Johnny intended to hold him to his words. Even if, he thought, the promise had been made when the bishop believed Rebekah was running away from the demon-possessed, rather than one of them herself.

As Johnny was making the bed, Miles brought over pajamas for him and Izzy. Johnny wanted to protest that he preferred to sleep in his clothes (dirty as they were, now that he thought of it), but Miles had dropped off the bundle—uncharacteristically saying only that he'd guessed at their sizes and that they could change in the washroom— and moved on, like a whirling tornado, except one that spun and left everything better ordered in its wake.

He found Izzy with Liz; his daughter was sitting on a table and Liz was singing something to her, a hymn or a psalm from the few words he heard. Liz stopped singing when she saw him approach out of the corner of her eye.

He reached out for Izzy and she jumped into his arms. "Say goodnight, honey," he said.

She did and Liz wished her sweet dreams in return. Johnny nodded at her cordially, then headed off to the men's room. An antique-looking but battery-powered lantern was hung just outside the door. He pulled it off its hook, switched it on, then set it down near the sink. The faux-flickering flame provided enough light for them to change by.

The clean and comfortable pajamas didn't help with Johnny's insomnia. He stared up at the ceiling, trying not to move for fear of disturbing Izzy, listening to the low hum of sound, the shuffling of feet as people moved but tried to do it quietly, the whispering voices, the mosquito-like buzz of the gas-powered generators.

"Daddy?"

He'd thought Izzy had been asleep, but from her voice it was obvious that she'd been awake the whole time too. He grunted softly.

"I miss mommy."

"I know, honey," he said, or tried to say—the words seemed to catch in his throat. He swallowed hard.

"Is she coming tomorrow? When the sun comes up?"

"I don't know, honey," he said, and the resolve to speak to the bishop, to do something about the zombies outside and to find and heal his wife, grew as hard as a diamond within him. "I hope so."

"I hope so too," she said.

He pulled her in close to him, hugged her until he felt her breathing slow and knew she'd drifted off into sleep. He was grateful to Liz for keeping her occupied during the day, and even for keeping her active so that now she could get some rest.

He himself drifted into and then right out of sleep for the next few hours. He'd intended to see the bishop, but now that he was lying down, he found he was too tired and too sore to get up again. Instead, he listened to the whispers of those who couldn't sleep either and those, like the bishop and some around him, who seemed to nap a little during the evening but keep a vigil at night; listened even to the humming of the refrigerator and freezer, as if they were having their own conversation in their own private language, perhaps about what a mess their masters had made of the world. All of those sounds formed a comforting background noise against which he half-slept and came awake again, until suddenly a new but familiar sound pierced through the rest and made him sit straight up in bed.

After only the slightest pause to get his bearings, he swung his legs around and stuck them in his shoes, not even taking the time to lace them up before he was off the cot and heading for the staircase.

The long, low howling; the sad, mournful cry. It was a familiar sound, the same sound he'd heard the night before.

He threw open the staircase door, the echo of the wailing still playing in his mind but almost drowned out by the thought that repeated itself in increasing intensity and propelled him up the stairs two at a time: *Rebekah's back*. His wife was outside again.

Chapter 9

IN the pitch darkness of the stairwell he almost tripped but grabbed onto the railing and regained his footing. He burst into the narthex, felt along the wall until he found the door, and fumbled with the latch.

Before he could get it open, he heard footsteps behind him.

"Johnny?"

Michael held a flashlight up at him. By its light, Johnny was able to throw the latch and swing open the door, but Michael was on top of him almost instantly, pushing him away and slamming the door shut again.

"Are you crazy?" Michael had dropped his flashlight. It lay on the ground in between them, shining its glow on the icon of the Virgin and Child. "What do you think you're doing?"

"My wife's outside. Let me out—you can close the door after me."

Michael pushed him away again. "Stop it!" he said. "What's wrong with you? Do you want to be killed?"

The stairwell door leading to the basement came open. By the flashlight's low light he saw the bishop step through, heaving with the effort to go up the stairs faster than he normally would've taken them.

Liz came up behind him, and then a third man, the surly-faced one from the night before, who still looked as angry as ever—or perhaps, Johnny thought, whose face didn't have any other mode of expression.

"What's happening, Mr. Salibi?" the bishop said.

"Help me," Johnny said, looking from the bishop to Liz to the third man. "We can go get her and bring her back here."

"Get who? Your wife?"

"Yes, my wife!" Johnny yelled, not liking the way they had looked at one another or the purposefully calm tone of the bishop's voice, as if he were speaking to a crazy person who needed to be settled down. "You all heard it. She's outside, and we need to help her!"

"Heard what, Mr. Salibi?"

"The wailing! Her wailing, like last night."

The bishop shook his head.

Johnny shot a glance at Liz, who looked mournful and said, "I'm sorry—I didn't hear anything."

"You imagined it," the surly-faced man said.

Before Johnny could respond, Michael said, "Listen to me. I can only sleep for a few hours at a time. I've been up for the last thirty minutes or so, in the nave. If there was something to hear, I would've heard it even better than you. But I didn't hear anything from outside. It's been a quiet night."

"No," Johnny said. "I heard her." Michael grabbed him again to restrain him. "I heard her! Let me go." But he found he couldn't struggle anymore; the energy seemed to have gone out of him. "You're lying because you—you're scared. You don't want me to go outside." He felt a constriction in his chest. It was hard to breathe, but he kept trying to speak, although even he knew his voice was faint and his words barely decipherable. "She's out there, are you—are you listening? She's—out there."

The bishop had walked over and put a hand on Michael's shoulder, who let Johnny go. Johnny slid down the wall, curled up his legs and sat on the cold floor, his vision blurring with tears or dizziness.

He had to get outside, had to, right now, Rebekah was outside, had to help her, had to go.

But he couldn't move. He felt that not even to save his life would he be able at that moment to summon the energy to command his legs to lift him from the ground.

Something soft but firm was placed gently on his head, then he heard, as if from a great distance, words spoken with calm and confidence, and knew that the bishop was praying over him.

Later Johnny was aware that his breathing had returned to normal. He wiped at his eyes with the clean sleeves of his pajamas. The bishop's face was kind, the wrinkles pulled back in an understanding smile.

"I believe you had a nightmare, Mr. Salibi. I'm afraid none of us heard the sound you described."

Johnny nodded.

"Are you able to stand?"

Michael and Liz helped him up. The stairwell door came open again and the surly-faced man walked through, holding a glass of water. He offered it to Johnny, who emptied it in one gulp.

"Thank you," Johnny said, returning the glass to the man. "Thank you," he said, facing Bishop Joseph. "But my wife *is* out there. Maybe

I didn't hear her tonight, but she is still out there."

"Of course we know that," the bishop said. "We haven't forgotten."

"But you won't do anything about it. I don't blame you, I know you're scared." He glanced at Michael. "I don't blame you for anything, I really don't. I know it was fear that made you abandon us out there. Don't look so surprised—I saw the doors were closed. But it's okay— and I'm not asking you to go out with me. All I'm asking, all I need to know is—if I find Rebekah and bring her back here, can you help her?"

"You're mistaken, Mr. Salibi." The bishop's eyes were still looking at him kindly, but in his voice was again that tone of disappointment and weariness. "We fear God; we don't fear His enemies. We didn't abandon you or our subdeacon. We closed the front doors and went out the side doors."

"Not just to protect the church," the surly-faced man said. "But to get to Michael from behind them, to get to him quickly and without trouble, and sneak him right back in."

It became embarrassingly obvious to Johnny how right they were and how wrong he'd been to think poorly of them, to not realize and remember that they were out there with him, in spite of the closed front doors.

"Listen, bud," the surly-faced man continued. "I know you just lost your wife, but come on. How about some self-awareness here? We wouldn't have had to engage them at all if you didn't go rushing right into them."

Johnny had been staring sheepishly at the ground, but now his gaze snapped up.

"My wife isn't lost," he said, at the same time as the bishop said, "That's enough, Isaac," and stepped between them almost imperceptibly.

"Mr. Salibi, will you pray with me?" Bishop Joseph said.

Johnny almost declined, almost claimed that he was tired and wanted to go back downstairs and get some rest. But he stopped himself from saying anything and simply nodded.

While Liz and Isaac exchanged a few words with the bishop before returning to the basement, Michael and Johnny went to sit at the front of the church. When Bishop Joseph joined them, he led them in a short prayer. Johnny felt moved to say something himself, and he spoke the words of Psalm 50 in a small, still voice. Then, encouraged by the way the bishop and the subdeacon nodded in silence, he continued with Psalm 120. In his early teenage years, Johnny had memorized the entire Psalter, to see how hard it was to do after reading that bishops in the ancient church were required to know all the psalms by heart.

The three of them sat and stood and prayed and talked through the rest of the night. It was morning before they stopped, the rays of the dawning sun creeping through the high windows and breaking the spell that seemed to have transported them into a different world.

Johnny felt confident in a way he hadn't for a long time. He felt strengthened, and renewed, and most of all he felt even more certain of what he had to do.

The bishop seemed to realize this as well; he asked Michael to go down to the basement and ask Liz, Isaac, and Steven to join them in the church.

While he was gone, Bishop Joseph said, "I won't send you out alone."

"I'm not unrealistic," Johnny said. "I know finding Rebekah won't be easy, and bringing her back here safely will be even harder. But I have to try, and I believe with God's help that I can succeed." The bishop nodded for him to go on. "There's no need for anyone else to endanger themselves. Especially Liz—I would feel more comfortable if she stayed behind."

The look on the bishop's face was curious, but Michael and the others, including Liz, came into the nave before Johnny could explain. They sat down in the pew just behind them.

"Those outside have not left," the bishop began, after both he and Johnny had turned around to face the small group. "They await the moment when the protection over this church falters. For that reason, I believe a small group that goes outside now will not be in any more danger than usual."

"To get more supplies?" Isaac said.

"To look for my wife," Johnny responded, although the question had been directed at the bishop. "You don't have to come, though. I can do it alone."

"To get more supplies," the bishop said, "and to look for Mr. Salibi's wife."

"Do you need more supplies?" Johnny said.

This time his own question was directed at the bishop, and this time Isaac replied. "No, he just doesn't want you to go out there alone and get yourself killed—or worse."

Bishop Joseph placed his hand on Johnny's knee to arrest his response. "We are always in need of more supplies," the bishop replied calmly. "And we need to get them sooner than later, before they're destroyed."

Liz shot a constraining glance at Isaac, but it didn't work. "We've gone through all the homes within sight of the church," he said. "We've raided every store in Riverview Mall, and checked every car for gas between here and there. Our own cars are almost out of gas. Where else should we go?"

"We can go to my house," Johnny said.

"I don't think—"

"It's not far. And I've stockpiled all kinds of things in my basement, when all of this started. Lots of food—canned vegetables and fruit and tuna and all kinds of other stuff. Bags and bags of chips and cookies."

"Water?" Liz said.

"Plenty. Stacks of bottled water."

"We ran out," she said. "We've been boiling the rain water—but it doesn't taste all that good. And it would be better not to use up more gas than we have to," she added, almost sheepishly.

"Stacks and stacks of bottled water," Johnny said again, as if he were describing a mythical land flowing with milk and honey. "And honey!" he added. "Izzy can't get enough of the stuff, so I've got whole boxes of honey. Soft drinks too."

"I still don't think it's a good idea," Isaac said.

"And first aid kits! Bandages and painkillers and antiseptics. And toilet paper, bundles of it. And hand sanitizer, huge bottles of refills."

The bishop and Michael exchanged glances.

Johnny felt an almost overpowering desire to convince them. Because he wanted to see his house, yes, but also because, now that he thought of it, the house was the first place to look for Rebekah. Maybe, if she'd been pushed away from the church, she'd drifted back to their house out of habit or muscle memory or whatever.

"It wouldn't be stealing at least," Johnny said. "It's all my stuff, and I give it to you freely." He didn't add that technically most of it belonged to the bank, because he'd charged everything to his credit card but the world had collapsed before the statement came due.

"How do you know it's all still there?" Michael said.

"It's in my basement cold room. I keep wine in there too, so the door is locked just in case." Because he saw the skeptical look on Isaac's face, he said to the bishop, "Maybe my whole house is burned down, maybe it's overrun by zomb—by those outside." He meant to add more, to end on an optimistic note, but the words died in his throat. What he'd said was true—there may be nothing left of his house; of his books; of the framed photos of his family; of the little picture book Rebekah had made when Izzy turned a year old; of the hand-written letters he'd sent to Rebekah the year they were dating long-distance, all of which she'd kept because she found it so quaint, especially since she always replied by email—nothing left but ashes.

The bishop seemed to be turning things over in his mind. Finally he nodded, looked at Johnny and said, "All right." Then he faced the others. "Take an hour to have breakfast and get ready."

They got up to leave. Johnny grabbed Michael's arm.

"Do you have my bat?" he whispered.

"That's not a good idea," Michael said in a normal tone. He started to move away again.

Still Johnny held him back. "I won't use it," he said. "Just as a last resort."

"Sorry, no," Michael said.

Johnny followed him down the stairs, Michael using a flashlight to show their way. "I know what they are now," he said. "I won't use it if I don't have to. But what if something happens? We need a way to protect ourselves if worse comes to worse."

"Worse will come to worse if you take anything but a cross."

He opened the door and walked through. The tables and chairs were already set up for breakfast.

"Michael—" he said, calling out after him.

The subdeacon kept moving, shaking his head slightly without looking back.

After changing into his jeans and t-shirt, Johnny went to the kitchen to see if he could be of assistance. The food was already laid out. There seemed fewer bowls of eggs (hard-boiled this time) and no bacon, but seemingly endless stacks of toast and plenty of jars of jam.

Steven and Theresa stopped talking when he walked in, and looked up at him.

"I'm sorry, I didn't mean to—"

"It's fine," Steven said.

He put his hand on his wife's arm for a second, gave her a look, then began to place the bowls and plates on the counter. Johnny helped.

Theresa watched them quietly for a moment, then walked out of the kitchen without a word. Also without exchanging words, Steven and Johnny finished up. When Johnny left, Theresa was standing just outside the door and stopped him.

"Promise me you won't do anything stupid," she said.

"I'm sorry?"

"I know your wife is out there. I pray you find her and that she's safe."

Johnny met her gaze and held it, almost defiantly.

"But my husband... promise me you won't put him or anyone else in danger. Okay?" She didn't give Johnny a chance to respond. "Going on these expeditions is his way of proving that he isn't scared. But he's terrified. We all are."

Steven stepped out of the kitchen too, and stared at his wife unhappily. He grabbed her arm, a more aggressive version of the gentle, caressing, calming touch he'd given her a few minutes before.

"Enjoy your breakfast," he said to Johnny, moving her away.

Everyone was already seated at Johnny's table. He gave Izzy a kiss on her forehead as he sat down, then apologized that he hadn't been there when she woke up.

After the bishop asked God to bless the food, and while everyone else was passing the plates around, Johnny leaned over to whisper in Liz's ear.

"I'd like you to stay here," he said. When he saw her eyebrows go up, he added, "To take care of Izzy. In case something happens to me."

She didn't respond, but accepted the plate of toast from Fatima and helped herself to some pieces, then passed it on to him as if Johnny hadn't spoken.

"Eggs?" Wassim said to him, holding up the bowl in which only two were left.

"Sure," Johnny said, taking the bowl and removing an egg. For the first time, it seemed to him that Wassim looked on him with approval. "I'll share with Izzy."

He offered the last egg to Liz, who smiled politely but shook her head.

"It's okay," he told her. "I don't mind."

"She won't eat eggs on Wednesdays," Fatima said quietly.

"Silly this fasting," Wassim said, speaking to Johnny as if to a confidant as he took the bowl back and helped himself to the last egg. "Silly, but soon all of us will be fasting." He cracked the egg against the side of his plate and began to shell it. "But maybe we don't live that long, I don't know."

Fatima hit him on the arm then threw a sidelong glance at her grandchildren, who were too busy playing a game of pinching each other in turn (the point of the game was to not scream out in pain, it seemed to Johnny) to really notice.

"Liz—" he whispered, leaning over again.

"Stop it," she said, with so much insistence that he left her alone for the rest of breakfast.

When they were done, the boys cleared the table at Fatima's urging. Johnny picked up Izzy, perhaps a little too protectively, and looked around for someone he could trust to watch Izzy.

"I'm going to go away for a little while, okay, munchkin?" he said, scanning the room. "I've got a job to do, but I'll be back soon."

"Are you going to pick up mommy?"

"I don't—" He stopped, started over. "I'm going to go see her. I'll bring her here to see you when she's not sick, okay?"

"I want to see her now."

"I know, honey. When she's feeling better. Okay?"

Izzy nodded reluctantly.

Before he could find anyone else, Liz found him. She had with her the teenager from the duck-duck-goose game, the one who had tagged Izzy. "This is Katie," Liz said to Johnny. "She and Izzy are friends. Right, Izzy?"

His daughter nodded and squirmed to get out of his arms. He put her down.

Liz returned her attention to him. "Katie's agreed to keep an eye on Izzy for a little while."

"Thank you, Katie," he said.

"No worries," she said, holding out her hand for Izzy.

Liz turned away and left before he could thank her. He went to the kitchen to help clean, but there were already people at the sink, working and engrossed in their own conversations. Finally he spotted Steven, walking out of the gift shop with a book and several flashlights in his hand.

He waved at Johnny and walked over.

"In case we need to hole up somewhere for a while," Steven said, holding up the book.

Johnny forced a smile to his face. Steven handed him one of the flashlights.

"Listen, Steven," he began.

"Don't you start with me. And don't listen to my wife, she's a worrywart."

"I'm just saying—"

Steven tapped his book against Johnny's chest. "I'm going," he said. "And whatever happens out there, I will have your back."

"I don't doubt it," he said, a grateful smile springing naturally to his face this time.

"That's settled, then. I'll meet you upstairs?"

"Yeah, I'll meet you there."

Johnny waited in the nave, along with the bishop and Michael. Steven was the last to come upstairs, and though he didn't let on, Johnny could tell he'd been fighting again with his wife.

"Just one last question," Johnny said. "Are we sure it wouldn't be better to go out at night? To have the cover of darkness?"

He could tell the idea was unpopular even before he asked his second question. But it was Isaac who answered for the group.

"The cover of darkness wouldn't help you as much as you think," he said. "And might hurt us a lot. Fear is our biggest enemy out there."

"There's nothing to fear," Johnny blurted out. He wanted to say more—he had this feeling, this sudden fountain of conviction rising within him. *Keep Christ in your heart*, he wanted to say, *and there won't be room for any of them! And don't fear those who destroy your body but can do no more to you; fear Him who has power over both your body and your soul.* Yet he still felt like an outsider in this group, and an outsider who was imposing on everyone to leave the safety of the church sooner than they may have strictly needed to.

Expectant glances were turned toward him.

"God will protect us," he said, a little lamely.

"Indeed," the bishop said. "Let us pray."

They bowed their heads and Bishop Joseph led them in a prayer that asked Christ to accompany them on their journey and to keep them from all harm. When he was finished, Michael gave them each a cross, and Isaac handed out empty backpacks.

The group moved toward the exit doors south of the altar. Although each door had latches to keep it closed and locked, chains had been wrapped around the two vertical handles as an extra precaution. Michael took out a key from a pocket deep within his tunic and clicked open the padlock, then removed the long, serpentine chains.

"There's a blue sedan, a Chevy, about thirty or forty paces outside these doors," Isaac said. "That's what we're heading for. I'll unlock it as soon as we're close. Get inside as quickly as you can. I'll jump in the driver's seat—"

"I should drive," Johnny interrupted. "I know the way."

Isaac shrugged but didn't pass over the keys. "Fine, Johnny in the driver's seat. Liz, you go beside him and Steven and I will get in the back. I'll run out first, then Liz, then Steven, then Johnny holding up the rear. Johnny, I'll give you the keys when we're inside the car. Everyone clear?"

They all said they were.

Isaac looked at Michael, whose hand was hovering above the latch. Johnny gripped the wooden cross tightly in his right hand.

Isaac nodded.

Michael responded with a nod of his own, then flipped the latch and threw open the door.

Chapter 10

SUNLIGHT streamed through the open door and into the passageway where they stood. No one moved.

Michael scanned the area outside, his hand clutching the handle, ready to slam the door shut. After a moment, he took a step forward, his hand never leaving the door, and looked around some more.

He turned his head. "Go," he said to Isaac.

Isaac ran past him, then Liz, then Steven.

As soon as he stepped outside, Johnny became aware of the warm sunlight on his face and the slight, fresh breeze. He kept his feet moving and his gaze fixed as much as possible on Steven's back, but he couldn't help but take a deep lungful of the crisp morning air. He heard birds chirping in the distance. He felt like an imprisoned man who'd been let out for fresh air and sunshine after years of confinement.

The parking lot was empty, with only cars and trees in sight. The cars were parked at all sorts of angles, looking not only abandoned but as if they'd been simply discarded. Some still had their doors open, and Johnny saw Isaac pushing those closed as he ran by them. Johnny realized how smart that was, since a zombie could be in any one of the cars and could step out of an open door and attack them from behind.

The trees were tall and leafy; they created a natural fence on the eastern and southern side of the lot.

The group moved quickly but quietly, heading toward the southeast corner of the lot, and finally he saw the blue sedan—hidden in the shadows cast by the overhanging leaves, behind a pick-up truck and an SUV.

Johnny heard the locks release, and saw Isaac get into the back seat on the passenger's side, quickly followed by Steven on the driver's side. Speeding up past the SUV, Johnny raced around the front of the Chevy, opened the door, and jumped in.

He placed his cross in the pocket to the front of the gear stick, then pulled the seatbelt over him subconsciously and clicked it in place.

"The keys, please," he said, reaching back for them.

The next few minutes would replay in his mind countless times. First he heard Liz yell his name in panic and fear; he turned his head and focused on her because he thought something was wrong with Liz herself, and in doing so withdrew his hand without meaning to. The keys dropped to the ground and he heard them clink as they bounced against something hard, while at the same time he became aware that his door had come open.

Liz stared past him and yelled at him to close the door.

Even before he could straighten himself out, though, Johnny felt a pair of strong hands descend on him, grasp him by the shirt, start to pull him out. If Johnny hadn't been wearing the seatbelt, the zombie might have succeeded.

The hands were digging into his skin with their overgrown nails. Johnny grabbed the zombie's arms and tried to pull them off. But the zombie, a tall, gangly young man who couldn't be much older than eighteen, was incredibly strong, He was silent the whole time Johnny tried to twist his wrists and pry off his fingers, even when Johnny used his elbows to smash into the zombie's arms to try and break his grip.

Liz was holding up her cross at the zombie, but that seemed to have no more effect on him than Johnny's own attempts to free himself.

Isaac had stood, was now on top of him, was leaning over him—but didn't seem intent on helping Johnny with the zombie. Instead, Isaac reached out for the steering wheel, then gripped it with his left hand. Johnny had no idea what he was doing until he saw the keys flash in Isaac's right hand.

Out of the corner of his eye, he saw the passenger side window darken. Before he could warn Liz, he heard the sound of glass shattering. Liz started to scream, then her voice was choked and cut off as dirty, bloody hands wrapped themselves around her neck.

The car's engine roared to life.

"Help her!" Johnny yelled at Isaac, as Isaac yelled at him, "Drive!"

Johnny found the brake pedal with his foot, let go of the zombie's arms to grab the gear stick, shifted the car, and floored the acceleration pedal. The Chevy lunged forward, the door slamming shut on the tall, gangly zombie so hard that he finally let go.

"Don't slow down!" Isaac was behind Liz, trying to pry off the hands from her neck; the zombie was holding on and being dragged along.

Johnny sped up, came within an inch of hitting a parked car, then another as he swerved in the opposite direction. Finally, unable to stand Liz's panicked taps against the dashboard, or Isaac's ineffectual cries to go faster, he positioned the car straight toward an oversized pick-up truck.

"Sit back!" he said to Isaac. "Put your seatbelt on!"

"What are you doing?" Steven yelled from behind him. "Are you crazy?"

"Do it!" Johnny yelled. Liz's taps were getting fainter.

When he saw that Isaac had sat back, Johnny gunned the car forward, gaining acceleration, then shifted his foot and slammed on the brakes as he cranked the wheel. The car spun around, and its side slammed into the pickup truck.

Sore as he was, the sudden jerking against the seatbelt made Johnny cry out in pain. Liz alternated between coughing and taking deep gasps of breath.

"Are you okay?" he said. "Should we go back to the church?"

She shook her head.

Johnny glanced at the rearview and said, "Are you guys okay?"

In the mirror, he saw four or five more zombies racing toward them. They were only a few steps away now. He pressed on the pedal, took the car through the rest of the parking lot, and out onto Down Street.

"Oh my God," Steven said.

The entire horde of zombies that had stood outside the church seemed to be aware of them. Crying out—strange and angry cries of anticipation and victory, like a pack of hyenas about to feed—they started to run toward the small, dilapidated car.

"Keep going or go back?" Johnny yelled, his foot hovering over the pedals.

"We should go back," Steven said.

"Drive!" Isaac barked. "Get us out of here!"

Johnny hesitated, took a moment to study his rearview and to scan the faces of the zombies. Of course, he wasn't sure what he would do if he saw his wife among them. The ideal would be to find her alone (in their home?), so that they could try to take her without violence and bring her to the bishop.

He felt a hand slap the back of his seat. "What are you waiting for?" Isaac yelled again, in a voice that made it clear he'd had enough. "Come on!"

Johnny pressed his foot on the gas pedal and the car went speeding down the street. The wind howled through the open window. The passenger side-view mirror, which was hanging on by a cable, issued its own protests as it banged and clanked against the metal of the car.

"I'll go the long way," he said, turning left on Main Street.

What he'd only glimpsed two nights before, as he had made his escape to the church in darkness, became starkly obvious in daylight as he drove through the streets, slowing down a little now that he'd put more distance between themselves and the pursuing zombies.

Bodies were strewn everywhere, cast down like fallen leaves in Autumn: bloodied, mangled, decaying bodies on lawns, and folded over fences dividing backyards, and even in the middle of the roads. Bodies, too, that seemed to belong to people who had decided to give up on life, and sat down on their front porches or against the side of their homes to die of exposure and dehydration; bodies, perhaps belonging to the possessed, that seemed to have been cut down by bullets as they attacked or tried to escape; charred bodies that had been collected together and burned, but where the fire had gone out before completing the job.

He'd prepared himself for the sights. Still, he felt something bitter rising up in his throat and had to swallow it back.

Johnny turned another corner, then slammed on the brakes. A child stood in the way, a little girl of maybe eight or nine, wearing a tattered blue-white dress. She had long brown hair, frizzy and uncombed.

"Is she—?" Johnny started to say, speaking mostly to himself.

The child didn't move.

"Keep going," Isaac said. "Don't stop."

Johnny kept his foot on the brakes. "Maybe we can help her. She's just a kid."

"Keep going."

Reluctantly, Johnny inched the car forward, turning slightly to avoid her.

She tracked him with her eyes but didn't move otherwise. Her gaze was a strange mixture of wary and feral, as if a sense of caution was only barely suppressing the desire to leap at them.

He reached up and turned the rearview mirror so he could keep watching her.

Liz put her hand on his arm. "I know what you're thinking," she said. "But listen to Isaac—keep going."

"She's just a kid," he repeated, his gaze still fixed on her image in the mirror.

"We can't save everyone," Isaac said.

Johnny pressed hard on the brakes. The car jerked to a stop.

"Seriously," Isaac said, "you're putting all of our lives at risk. Keep going. We'll get the supplies at your house and come back."

Johnny picked up the cross with one hand and opened the door with the other.

"This is a mistake," Liz said.

Ignoring her, he stepped out of the car. The child watched him.

He held up the cross and stepped toward her. "What's your name?" he said, when he was a few steps away.

She had winced at the sight of the cross but hadn't moved. "We have many names."

Her voice, so unnatural and flat, sent a cold quiver through him. "Why are you tormenting this creature of God?"

"Who are you," the child said in that ugly and flat voice, "to question us?"

"I am no one," Johnny said. "But I belong to the One True God and in His Name I command you to depart from this little child."

"No!" she screamed, the flatness gone from her voice, replaced by a fiery anger. "No, no, no!"

He felt power surging through him and raised his voice. "In the Name of Jesus Christ, the Son of the Living God, He Who Is, He Who Was, and He Who Is Coming, I command you to leave this His precious child alone and to bother her no longer."

As he spoke, though, the little girl began to convulse. She fell onto the ground and made horrible retching sounds. Nothing came from her open mouth, but her body still shook.

Johnny stopped speaking, but the violent reaction continued. The little girl looked like she might explode from the intensity of the convulsions.

"Stop!" he yelled, terror seizing him and constricting his throat so that his voice had lost its sense of authority. "Leave her alone!"

The little girl gave one last major shake, as if a strong electric current was shot through her body, then collapsed on the ground.

He rushed forward to help her, fell to his knees to pick up her head. Foam had formed around her lips and two trickles of blood below her nostrils.

She was dead. The head he picked up gently was malleable as a doll's, the body lifeless and unmoving. He pressed his fingers against the side of her neck, but there was no pulse. Her eyes were still open and staring.

Someone touched his shoulder. "We need to keep going," Liz said.

"What happened?" he said, still cradling the little girl.

"Come on," she said. "There's nothing more you can do for her."

He allowed himself to be pulled away, but his gaze remained fixed on the child until they reached the car.

Steven and Isaac were standing outside, crosses in hand. Their faces betrayed sympathy, pity—and something else. It was neither anger nor judgment, but Johnny couldn't pinpoint exactly what it was.

"I'm sorry," he said.

"We should keep moving," Isaac said, opening the door and getting back into the car. Steven did the same.

"Come on," Liz said, opening Johnny's door and helping him in.

Someone had turned off the engine. He started it up again.

"I don't know what happened," he said.

"You tried to help her," Liz said, then seemed to realize something and her voice changed a little, became a little more sincere. "You gave her peace."

He didn't respond, and didn't say anything for a long time.

There were more zombies to avoid on the roads, and more dead bodies all around. He drove past them all in a daze. Finally the sound of a dog barking snapped him out of it; the dog, a large Doberman, came running out of one of the houses and chased them.

The dog looked strong, healthy, and well-fed, and Johnny shuddered to think how that came to be.

"We're a few blocks away," he said to break the silence in the car. Then, to no one in particular, he said, "It's strange that all of these bodies are outside, isn't it?" He caught Isaac's glance in the rearview. "Isn't it?"

Isaac shrugged, then went back to staring out his window as he responded, "Not really. They were either smoked out of their houses, or chased out by a spouse who'd turned, or dragged out of their cars by the possessed or by survivors who had run out of gas in their own cars, or were trying to escape, or were given up and tossed aside dead by whatever demons possessed them. You want me to keep going?"

"No," Johnny said.

They drove the rest of the way in silence, the wind blowing through the cracked-open window and causing Liz's auburn hair to fly around, so that she often had to comb it back and down with her fingers. Red marks were still visible on her neck. She caught him looking, and Johnny smiled at her in a way that he hoped would be sympathetic. He was impressed that she hadn't uttered a single word of complaint—not about the little girl he'd killed accidentally, whom she'd warned him to leave alone; not about the zombie who had choked her, whom he'd killed on purpose; not about the broken window and the wind blowing in her face. She smiled back, and he returned his gaze to the road.

It felt nice to drive again, and except for the dead bodies and the abandoned cars and homes, he could almost pretend that the world hadn't fallen apart. When they turned onto his street corner and he caught sight of the brown-shingled roof of his home, though, he gripped the wheel tighter and had to swallow back a lump that jumped into his throat. At least the street was empty of walking zombies, he thought.

He drove past the homes of his neighbors, past the dead bodies that he tried not to look at—either out of respect or from fear of recognizing anyone, he wasn't sure. Or maybe he just didn't want to see his own wife's body, given up and tossed aside dead by whatever demon or demons had possessed her.

With a deep breath he hoped no one noticed him take, he pulled into his driveway.

Chapter 11

HE pulls into his driveway.

As he steps out of the car, the storm door comes open. Rebekah has heard him pull up and has come out to help with the groceries, bags of which fill the back and passenger seats, and boxes of which fill the trunk. Her features are pulled in tightly, lines of worry creasing her forehead; he imagines she's spent the whole time he's been away glued to the news on TV or reading about what's happening on the internet. Or watching more YouTube videos.

He smiles at her.

She comes down the stairs. "Everything okay?"

"Fine," he says. "No problem."

He releases the latch on the rear door and lifts it up; she opens the back driver's side door. "This is a lot of stuff," she says.

"Most of it is non-perishable," he says, then grunts as he pulls out one of the wide boxes.

She has put plastic bags all along her arms and seems to be carrying her own weight in groceries up the stairs and into the house.

"So it wasn't bad?" she calls back to him.

It was bad. He's been out longer than expected because he had to go to three different grocery stores and a Walmart to get everything he wanted. The shelves are looking more and more bare and they aren't being replenished; the floors are dirty with splattered eggs and wilted produce, but they aren't being cleaned. The manager at the last store was working the only checkout line himself; he told Johnny that all of his employees called in sick that day. People are scared and starting to panic; one man at that grocery store actually pushed an older woman out of the way to get the last carton of milk, and it was only when Johnny asked him what the problem was that the man, after sizing Johnny up, smirked and walked away. Johnny gave her the milk, which she ripped out of his hands ungratefully, perhaps fearing he was just teasing her and might pluck it away when she reached for it. The man stood by his own car when Johnny left the store, and tracked him with his eyes, but didn't do anything else.

"It's fine," he says, placing the box full of canned fruit and vegetables on the kitchen counter.

The TV is on in the living room; currently, a loud man in an excitable voice is yelling to everyone that they need to get to the car dealership *now!* for a never-again-to-be-repeated inventory sale.

"I'll just bring everything in, then put these in the cold room downstairs, okay?"

Rebekah is loading groceries into the fridge. He can tell from the hunch in her shoulders and her non-response that she doesn't believe him that everything's fine, and that she's weighing her next words carefully. There's something she wants to tell him.

He heads for the door before she has a chance, brings in more boxes of canned food and bottled water, setting them by the door this time. When he comes back with more groceries, he sees that Rebekah has moved the boxes into the kitchen so they can sort through them. Finally he brings in the wooden bat which he bought at the Walmart and places it in the front closet, in the corner.

"Don't worry," Rebekah says from the kitchen. "I already saw the bat in the car."

He carries over some of the bags. "It's just for protection," he says. "In case we need it, that's all."

She closes the fridge door. "Things are bad, John," she says; it's never a good sign when she calls him that. "People are dying—people are killing each other. This disease is everywhere across the whole planet. Things are bad."

He steps forward and wraps his arms around her; he feels her sink into him, bury her head in his shoulders. The tension in her body seems to finally slip out and he has to hold her tighter for fear of dropping her.

"I know, honey." He pulls back to kiss her forehead, but she forces him into a tight embrace again.

He's scared too, terrified even. As little as two weeks ago, news reports of people acting in strange and often violent ways were rare and unique, frightening stories from the theater of the bizarre. Even during the next week, when the reports became disturbingly frequent and widespread across the globe, Johnny dismissed them as a selection or reporting bias, the way news of certain scandals (financial ones or sexual ones involving politicians or priests, for example) seemed to come in waves too. In the last few days, though, it became impossible for him or, he supposed, for anyone to dismiss what was happening. At the school where Rebekah taught, two boys beat each other so badly that Rebekah said she couldn't tell one bloody mess from the other by the time she and the principal were able to pull them apart, still yelling and attacking anyone who came near them. The next day, a man jumped out of the high-rise where Johnny worked. According to the lady he spoke with outside when the building was evacuated, the man, a middle-aged father of three, began yelling obscenities and cursing God; then, when his coworkers approached him, the man ran straight for the windows and crashed through them without hesitation, plummeting seventeen stories to the ground. As Johnny drove home that afternoon, the radio announcer warned him to stay off the highway heading east, because a young mother had apparently stopped her car in the middle of traffic, gotten out and taken her crying baby out of his car seat, and launched him off the overpass. Police were on the scene but no one was leaving any time soon; the young mother had been beaten to death by those who witnessed what she had done.

By the Wednesday of that week, their mayor was joining her counterparts in cities across the world in urging people to stay calm, to carry on with their lives as normal, and to let the police handle the copy-cat crimes of those who disturb peace and order at the slightest provocation.

This is Saturday morning, and the reports have only gotten more violent and more frequent since the mayor's plea.

But he doesn't want to betray his fear in his voice or in any other way; Rebekah is already scared, Izzy has been quieter than normal, and Johnny demands of himself that he put them at ease as best he can.

"It's going to be okay," he says, finally. "We have enough food and water to hole up here for weeks if need be."

She pulls back and looks at him wide-eyed.

He's said the wrong thing and he tries to back-pedal smoothly. "I'm not saying that's going to happen, Rebekah. Just that we can. That we'll be okay even if we have to stay in this house for a little while." He's the one to pull her back into a tight embrace this time.

He holds her quietly for a while. "Where's Izzy?"

"Downstairs, playing."

He nods, has the urge to go down there and give his little girl a big kiss. He pulls away from Rebekah and gives her an encouraging smile. She smiles back. But her eyes, always so expressive, betray all of the fear and doubt she's feeling, and in them he sees a hint of the question that seems about to force itself out of her lips.

"What's wrong?" he says. He doesn't want her to ask him to leave their home again, but he much more doesn't want her to look so sad and lost.

"Some people came by from the church."

"Which church?"

"St. George."

He takes a step back and crosses his arms.

"They're gathering there," she says. "They're going to pray together until all of this is over. They have food and water and supplies and—"

"We can pray here by ourselves," he says. "And we have food and water and supplies."

"Johnny—" she says, but he cuts her off again.

"Let's just ride this out until the authorities regain control, okay? Whatever's going on, we're safer here than in some church with a bunch of other people, don't you see that? If this is a disease, the last thing we want to do is crowd together. It's best we quarantine ourselves until they get the cure out."

"And what if they don't get the cure out?"

"Then we're all dead and it won't matter anyway."

She doesn't react to his outburst except to force her own voice to be calmer. "I just think it might be better for us if we go to the church and be with other people. Maybe there's a risk, but there's a risk to being here alone too. There have been home invasions. Lots of them."

Although he hates it when she talks to him like that, it always works; the contrast in their voices makes him acutely aware of how loud he'd raised his tone. "I know," he says softly, but in her eyes he can tell that she won't give up, that she believes in leaving their home as strongly as he believes in staying. "I can protect us."

"We're safer with others, in the church," she says. "If this is about Father Gord—"

"It's not about him," he says, but his voice betrays the truth. More calmly, he continues, "I don't care about him. I just think it's stupid to gather in large crowds when there's a plague or epidemic or whatever this is."

She nods her head slowly.

He uncrosses his arms and places his hands on her shoulders. "I didn't mean stupid," he says. "You're not stupid, that's not what I was saying. You have good reasons for wanting to go, I know that. But I don't want to leave our home right now. I think we're safer here, I really believe that. I know you're scared, but there's nothing to worry about. I will protect us if anything happens. Can you trust me on this, please? If by the end of the weekend things aren't better, we can talk about it again—to go to the church or to go somewhere else, okay?"

"Promise?" she says.

"Cross my heart."

He doesn't know it yet, but the mayor will hold another press conference early the next morning. In that one, she won't ask people to continue going to work and visiting shopping malls and going out for dinners as she had only a few days before; on that Sunday morning, she'll beg people in a weary voice on the brink of breaking down to stay at home unless it was absolutely necessary to leave, to keep their emergency radios on for further news, to be patient with the city as they tried to contain the spread of this new and serious disease.

He doesn't know it yet, but that night the TV signal will go dead; then the power will cut out, taking the internet with it. Their cell phones won't be able to find a signal and, a few hours later, no one will be broadcasting on the emergency radio frequency.

He doesn't know it yet, but his decision to stay will keep his family locked in the house for the next nine days. Although the front windows are set high above the ground, he will board them up before going to bed on Sunday, after he catches one of his neighbors standing in the street and peering into their house and straight at Johnny with a hungry look in his otherwise vacant eyes. They will spend that night listening to howls and cries, and it will seem to them that their whole neighborhood has become infected. The next morning, convinced he heard someone trying to come in through the patio door at the back of the house, he'll board up and reinforce that too.

He doesn't know it yet, but as day follows night and night follows day and no one is broadcasting on the emergency radio and the howls from the zombies outside don't abate, he will take advantage of the rare moments when Izzy is asleep to talk to Rebekah about what they will do if their home is attacked. He will concede that if there are other survivors, the church is their best bet of finding them; but Rebekah will not agree with the details of Johnny's plan. Rebekah wants to stay together the whole time, but Johnny insists that he should draw away the zombies so that his wife and his daughter can escape first. She is again uncertain, and he will again ask her to trust him.

He doesn't know it yet, but after those nine days of forced confinement, the zombies will discover his house like bloodhounds catching the scent of formerly hidden prey. They will break through the plywood and glass on the patio door and flood into his house.

He doesn't know it yet, but that night will not go according to his plan. He will lose sight of Rebekah and Izzy, and they will not be at the church waiting for him. He will fear the worst.

He doesn't know it yet, but the next time he sees his wife after that, she will have turned into a zombie herself, and she will try to kill him.

Chapter 12

THEY opened the car doors and stepped out, crosses in hand. Johnny looked around; everything seemed quiet and clear.

His garage door had been broken. Was it zombies looking for survivors, he wondered, or survivors looking for a car? Either way, they would've been disappointed. The SUV he and Rebekah had bought the year they found out they were pregnant with Izzy—the car he'd almost gone crazy to fill up on his way home from the Walmart, forcing himself to wait patiently in the long line-up of frustrated and honking drivers that extended to the end of the gas station and into the streets—had been stolen from his driveway the very next day, the day the mayor went on television asking people not to leave their homes. At the time, he'd wished he'd parked it in the garage; but now, looking at the broken wood of the sectional door, he realized that it probably wouldn't have made a difference.

"We should get you cleaned up," Isaac said.

Johnny looked at Liz as she dropped her hand from her face. The blood had run down to her neck but seemed to have clotted. A piece of glass stuck in her cheek reflected in the sunlight. Bruise marks lined her neck and throat.

"There's tweezers and bandages in the bathroom," Johnny said. "I'll grab them; you guys wait here."

"What do you mean?" Isaac said.

"Let me go in first and make sure the house is empty."

"That doesn't make any sense."

"We go in together," Steven said.

Johnny didn't want that. If Rebekah were inside, he didn't need things escalating. And if his house were still overrun by zombies, despite the quiet and peaceful appearance of things from the outside, he didn't need the bottle-neck at the front door of three other people trying to escape.

"It's better this way," he said, turning around and focusing his gaze on Isaac. "You'll have more light out here anyway. You can take care of Liz while Steven and I start moving stuff into the car."

He stared at him until Isaac finally shrugged.

"Come on," Isaac said to Liz. "Sit down in the seat and let's have a look at you."

Johnny grabbed the railing and climbed the stairs to his front door, the same stairs he'd climbed a thousand times before. The storm door's top hinge had been broken off and the mesh screen stuck out dangerously. The metal frame leaned across the wooden door as if trying to protect it. The attempt had failed, though; the lock on the inner door had been broken and it had come closed only by its own weight. Johnny pushed it open.

Holding the cross in front of him, and trying to move slowly and quietly, Johnny stepped into his house. Thin streams of light squeezed through the boarded-up front windows and into the living room, which looked empty. His gaze jumped to the clock on the wall above the TV; it had stopped, as if it knew the world had ended and its services were no longer needed. The insane urge to change its batteries tried to seize him.

As he walked toward the bedrooms he peeked into the kitchen; it was empty too. Disappointment mixed with relief inside of him.

A strong whiff of decay invaded his nostrils as he stepped into the hallway and out of the breeze the broken windows let into the living room and kitchen. Bodies were piled outside the master bedroom; broken, mangled, bloodied bodies tossed on top of one another like a pile of dirty, discarded clothes. Except the dirty clothes still had people in them.

He forced himself to keep walking, despite the sight and the stench. The light streaming through the boarded-up window of Izzy's bedroom was faint. Johnny's heart thudded as he pushed open the door. He gave his eyes some time to adjust as he peered inside. For a moment, he thought he saw someone or something lying on Izzy's bed. Catching the yell for help in his throat and suppressing it, he forced himself to keep looking and soon the shadow resolved itself into Izzy's stuffed lion.

He closed the door for reasons he couldn't have explained to himself, and turned toward the master bedroom again.

In the hallway, Rebekah had hung a series of picture frames. These caught his eye suddenly. In the first, younger versions of themselves stared back at him. They sat on a grassy hill, eating a picnic lunch they had packed, their bikes out of focus and almost out of frame behind them. The picture was at an odd angle; Johnny had done his best holding the camera at arm's length and taking a self-portrait without being able to see what he was shooting. Rebekah looked particularly stunning, her hair tied up, a thin film of sweat giving her a healthy glow, and a happy, content smile on her face. The second picture was of their wedding day; he looked a bit dazed, she looked delightful as always. In the third, Johnny leaned by the hospital bed where a tired and sweaty and unglamorous but gorgeous Rebekah lay, a tiny alien-looking creature on her chest; Johnny and Rebekah beamed at the nurse who took their picture, his own goofy smile so wide that it looked like it might leap off his face.

Rebekah felt the series highlighted the story of their lives together. Johnny told her it was weird and corny, but now he found he couldn't tear his gaze from them, his eyes darting from one picture to the next. For a few moments, the horrors around him disappeared; nothing existed in his world but the photos and the memories they evoked.

The sound of footsteps snapped his attention back to the present. He turned slowly and reluctantly, resentful of the intrusion and wondering why they had come inside when he'd asked them to wait for him. The question died on his lips.

"My God," he said in a thin voice, taking a step back.

The man who stood at the other end of the hall smiled, revealing a mouth from which most of the teeth had been broken or knocked out. His build was large, the oversized muscles of his shoulders jutting out of the collar of his V-necked short-sleeved shirt. His arms were monstrous, each one twice the size of Johnny's.

Johnny held up the cross in his hand. "In the name of Jes—"

The zombie was on top of him, having traveled the distance separating them with astonishing speed, almost as if in a single step. With a dismissive slap, he knocked the cross out of Johnny's hand, then tried to grab Johnny by the shirt.

Johnny fell back, tripped, landed on top of the dead bodies outside the master bedroom.

The bald head and toothless grin popped into his view.

"In the name—"

He was able to get even less out this time; the zombie plunged his large arms down and gripped Johnny's neck.

His legs were pinned under the large and heavy frame, but Johnny had enough give to drive his knees into the man's crotch. No reaction. Johnny kneed him again, and again, making contact each time, but the zombie kept squeezing Johnny's neck as if nothing had happened.

Even as his vision began to blur and he could feel his larynx about to give way and collapse, Johnny forced himself to focus. *In the name of Jesus Christ, the Son of the living God,* he thought, *I command you, dark and evil spirit, to depart from this man, to leave this house, to. . . .*

The words trailed off in his mind. He couldn't remember what he wanted to say. He felt very tired; it had gotten very dark. He tried to cough but couldn't.

From far away, he heard a loud bang, then another, then a third.

Something heavy fell on top of him. He heard something else—his name. Someone was calling it. Rebekah? Her voice was muffled, but she sounded upset, hurt, even panicked.

His eyes snapped open.

The large zombie was on top of him, dead. Johnny turned his body to try and slide out from underneath him.

"Johnny!" Liz cried again.

Her small hands were gripping the large man's shoulders, trying to pull him away from Johnny. He helped, using his arms and his legs, and together they were able to flip the zombie over. His large bowling-ball head bumped hard against the wall, causing one of the pictures to fall down and crash against the ground.

Liz stared into Johnny's face. "Thank God you're okay."

Johnny reached back, picked up the frame—it was the third one, the day Izzy was born—shook off the glass, and pried out the picture with trembling fingers, his vision still swimming.

"Come on," Liz said, reaching down to put her arm underneath him.

"Wait," he said, shaking her off and looking around. "My cross."

"There's no time," she said. "Do you have anything we can use to put in front of the door?"

The sound of grunting finally impinged itself into his consciousness. He got up with Liz's help, then followed her down the hallway. He saw her cross poking out of the back of her jeans, and the black plastic handle of a gun that had been shoved in beside it.

In the entrance, Steven sat on the tiled floor, his back to the door, his legs stretched out against the closet. Isaac stood over him, shoulder pressing against the swaying door. Both had strained looks on their faces.

"It's all in the basement," Johnny yelled out, then ran down the stairs, the thought not occurring to him that more zombies could be down there until his foot hit the vinyl floor. Heart thudding, he peered into the darkness, his hand on the railing in case he needed to race back upstairs.

His eyes took a moment to adjust; the basement looked empty.

The tall metal shelves where he kept his tools stood in a neat row just outside the cold room. He grabbed some pieces of wood from the pile he'd leaned against the shelves, then the hammer and a box of nails, and ran back upstairs.

"Hurry," Isaac said, speaking through clenched teeth. The door was bulging, giving way a little before Steven and Isaac and Liz could push it closed again. Johnny didn't hear anything from the other side.

He dropped the wood on the ground to free his hands, then ripped open the package of nails and stuck a bunch of them in his mouth. Liz had come out of the entrance, picked up a board, and now handed it to him.

Stepping over Steven's outstretched legs, Johnny hammered one end of the board into the door. It bulged out again, even more than last time. He hammered in two more nails.

"Take it!" he yelled, handing the hammer to Isaac, then using all of his strength to try and force the door closed. Isaac kept his hip and knee against the door, held the board up with one hand and pulled a nail out of Johnny's mouth with the other. Steven grunted loudly, his body coming off the ground.

As soon as the door closed again, Isaac hammered the other end of the board into the door frame.

"In the wall, too," Johnny said.

Isaac pulled out another nail, struck once, but it was wasted: the nail went right through, hitting nothing but drywall.

"Try again!"

Isaac pulled out the remaining nails from his mouth, struck again with no more luck, and then a third time before he hit a stud.

"Liz, more nails!"

She handed a couple to Isaac, who hammered them in.

Steven finally relaxed and sat, or deflated, back down. The board seemed to be holding.

"Let's go," Johnny said, helping Steven to his feet.

"We should put in another board," Isaac said, his gaze fixed on the door.

Johnny watched it too and couldn't help but feel the same; the zombies on the other side had started howling now to accompany their banging on the door. But it didn't make sense—they'd be boarding up the front door and the zombies would be streaming in behind them through the back patio door. He'd hoped the zombies had abandoned his neighborhood, but they clearly hadn't. And now that he and the others had attracted their attention, it wouldn't be safe outside. They needed time to think and regroup.

"We can go out the back," Liz said, as if she'd read his mind, but poorly. She started in that direction. "There's a door there."

"No, to the basement," Johnny said. "The door locks. Come on."

Liz shook her head and seemed about to argue, but as she looked down the hallway her mouth came open. She stood speechless, the blood draining from her face, which confirmed Johnny's suspicions.

"Let's go," he said, running forward, almost tackling her to the ground in his attempt to push her toward the basement door. As he passed the hallway, though, he couldn't stop himself from turning his head to look at what she'd seen. Just outside his house, a gaunt, even emaciated zombie stared back at him. An elderly gentleman, naked except for white briefs, which he had soiled. Wispy white hair flowed off of his head and chest, and his ribs stuck out from under his skin. On his face was a slight, patient, knowing smile. A victorious smile, Johnny felt. Then, with a shock that almost stopped Johnny dead in his tracks, the mental image of the dirty old man resolved into a familiar pattern. He recognized that man—or his mind was playing tricks on him.

Johnny blinked hard to clear away the association, forced himself to keep running, his hands on Liz's back and pushing her forward.

She ran down the stairs and Johnny stepped out of the way so that Isaac and Steven could go too. When they were through, he slammed the door shut and threw the deadbolt.

The others hadn't gone down but were crowding the staircase and watching him. Isaac had pulled out a flashlight; he held it so the light shined on Johnny.

"The people who used to live here before we bought the house installed the deadbolt," he said, in response to their questioning gazes. "They used to rent out the basement."

For several moments they listened quietly for sounds from beyond the door, but didn't hear any.

"We should reinforce it," Isaac said, his light beam playing on the door's surface.

"I've got more pieces of wood in the storeroom."

Even if he didn't believe there was a point to boarding up the door—which he did—the exercise was good for them in and of itself. By the time they put several boards across the door and frame, and wedged in a two-by-four in the slot so the door couldn't be pushed back, the tension that had seized the group seemed to have ebbed away in part. Whether it was because they all felt safer, now that the door was boarded up, or because some time had passed and still no sound could be heard from the other side, or whether it was just the distraction of working together on a specific goal, Johnny couldn't say.

Then again, Johnny thought, maybe the zombies weren't trying to knock down the door because they'd finally realized they didn't have to waste that kind of effort. How long could he and the others hide out in his basement? In his mind's eye, he saw the victorious, patient smile of the eerily familiar old man in his soiled underwear. How long could they hold out?

Johnny recognized the thoughts as dark, defeatist, and counter-productive. He chased them out of his mind as he followed the others down the stairs.

The basement was composed of two parts, an open area and en-closed rooms. The middle, open area was bordered off by four speakers on stands; at the back was a brown leather couch with two matching chairs standing guard and set at an angle on either side, and a large-screen TV facing the furniture. A dark curtain pulled across the single, tiny window set high on the wall blocked out whatever light it might otherwise let in. The first enclosed room was a bathroom, the second a bedroom that Johnny had converted into Izzy's play room, which held her toys and a Tickle Trunk full of princess dresses and other Halloween costumes. The third was the supply room; beyond that was the cold room, which could lock (another consequence of renting out the basement, Johnny had always figured). He kept the key hidden where the previous owners had hid it, just above the door, in the false drop-ceiling of the supply room.

Johnny pulled the curtain from the window to let in a bit of light.

Isaac and Steven sat down on the couch; Liz and Johnny on the individual chairs.

"Can I get someone something to drink?" Johnny said, as if this were nothing more than four friends hanging out together at his home.

Everyone shook their heads.

"What's our plan?" Isaac said.

The others seemed to look to Johnny for an answer. "I have no idea," he said. "Maybe we take a moment to regroup? See what we can arm ourselves with from down here?"

"Why?" Isaac said, seeming to be directing his words at Johnny but fixing Liz with a stern look. "You didn't kill enough people today?"

She seemed to know what he meant; she pulled out the gun from behind her back and handed it over to him.

He checked the chamber.

"I used them all," Liz said. "I'm sorry."

"All right," Johnny said. "What do you suggest?"

Isaac didn't answer; he seemed to alternate between shaking his head and shrugging.

"Where did the gun come from?" Johnny said, turning to face Liz.

She looked at Isaac. "It's his. He was a cop before—before all of this happened. He was my husband's partner."

"What happened up there?"

"We were waiting outside, like you asked," Liz said. "Isaac was looking at the cut on my face. Steven saw—"

"—people approaching," Steven said. "Four or five, maybe. They came out of your backyard."

"They were almost on us when Steven yelled to get inside the house."

"We barely got the door shut behind us," Isaac said.

"The guys held it closed; I went looking for something to wedge into the door. I saw you and that very large man choking you to death. I didn't know what to do; I ran back to the front door and took Isaac's gun from under his shirt. I didn't mean to use all the bullets."

"You saved my life."

Isaac turned on him with a ferocious look. "You caused her to kill another human being. You get that, right?"

"You're the one carrying around a gun," Steven said from beside him, quietly.

Isaac sat back. "That gun was a last resort," he said. "I felt better having it on me."

"Did the bishop know?"

Isaac didn't respond, which was answer enough.

"We can point fingers and blame one another once we're out of the woods," Johnny said. "For now, I think Isaac asked the right question. What's our plan?"

The question hung in the air for a long time.

When the silence was finally broken, it wasn't by any of them. It was shattered by a loud, sharp bang coming from the top of the stairs, so sudden and so loud that they all jumped in their chairs. The second and third hard thumps against the door were no less unnerving for being less unexpected.

"I guess they got tired of waiting," Johnny said.

Chapter 13

HE walked over to the staircase and looked up. For the moment at least, it seemed the reinforced door wasn't buckling under the assault.

A part of Johnny wanted to spring into action, to arm himself and the others with whatever they could find in his basement—hammers? two-by-fours? crowbars?—in case the boards snapped and the door finally gave in and zombies streamed through. But he stood immobile at the bottom of the stairs, staring up.

"You okay?"

He'd been so focused on the rhythmic drum-beats on the door that he hadn't noticed Liz coming up to stand beside him. His intention was to lie, to tell her that he was fine, that he was just trying to decide on their best course of action. Instead, he heard himself say in a matter-of-fact tone, "I'm scared."

He regretted the words as soon as he said them; and yet Liz's reaction wasn't what he would've expected. The furrows in her forehead cleared and her shoulders relaxed and dropped—he could almost see the tension leaving her body.

"I'm scared too."

"What a wimp," he said, shaking his head.

She smiled distractedly in acknowledgment of his joke. When she spoke again, it seemed to him that she was sharing something that had been on her mind for a long time. "So it isn't un-Christian of us?"

"To be scared?"

She nodded.

"No, I don't think so."

"It doesn't show a lack of faith in God?"

He shrugged. "Maybe scared is the wrong word. I don't get the sense from you that you're scared in the sense of terrified past endurance, or that you're full of anxiety, worried about what we're going to eat or drink."

"It's not like that, it's more like—"

"—you're full of sadness?"

Looking up at the ceiling, she breathed in deeply and seemed to be turning thoughts over in her mind. After a second or two, she met his gaze again and said, "That's a good way to put it, I guess—full of sadness."

"'Sorrowful unto death' is how Christ put it."

Her pause to process his words was momentary. "In Gethsemane," she said.

"Yeah. Christ knew that He would defeat death by His death; He knew that the whole world would be saved. He knew that He was born to die on the Cross. But He was still—"

"—sorrowful unto death."

"Because—" he began, a deeply held but previously unarticulated truth seeming to rise fully-formed from his subconscious, "—because before all that good stuff was all the bad stuff. Before the victory over death, He had to suffer the defeat of death, and before the glory of the Resurrection, He had to undergo the shame of the Crucifixion." He shrugged again. "He didn't hide from His feelings; and He certainly didn't try to hide them from His Father. He knew the Father has power over all, and He prayed that He wouldn't have to undergo this suffering if there were any other way creation could be saved and restored. But, as always, He said, 'Not My will, but Your will be done.'"

Liz had been nodding along with him. "For me, it's this sense of darkness closing in, and a feeling of helplessness because you can't do anything to stop it."

"You can just endure it, I guess. The best you can."

She looked up at the ceiling again, seemed to be trying to organize or crystallize her thoughts. In that stretch of silence, he heard a loud thud that momentarily surprised him; he'd almost forgotten where they were or what was happening around them. Across the room, Isaac and Steven were engaged in their own conversation in hushed tones. He leaned back against the wall.

"This world is coming to an end," she said. "And I guess it's good that it does; it's a world of violence and decay, full of corruption and horrors. I know the world has to pass away so that God can raise it up again, raise it up in incorruptibility, restore it to the way it was supposed to be. I know that, I just wish..."

Her voice trailed off, and though he felt he knew what she was about to say, he held his tongue and waited.

"...I just wish that I wasn't here to witness it. I wish I hadn't seen the things I've seen. And I wonder, and this is maybe the worst part, how much more will I have to see before it's all over?"

"Me too," he said. "Sometimes—in my worst, darkest, most selfish moments—I want to walk up to God and punch Him in the face. For all of this. For creating this world, even, when He knew it could all go so bad and cause so much suffering and pain to come into existence."

She had raised an eyebrow and was half-smiling at him.

"But then I remember," he said, "that humanity got to punch God in the face, and to do much worse to Him. And I think: He knew that was a possibility too, when He made the world. He knew that if His beautiful and good world went bad, and He wanted to restore it rather than destroy it and try again, or not try again—He knew that He would have to restore it by entering into it and absorbing all of its corruption in Himself. And He did it anyway; He thought it was worth the price, even the price of the Cross. I don't know if that helps you," he continued, "but it's always helped me put my own suffering in perspective. Not that it minimizes any of it at all, but it allows me to see God suffering right along with me because of the corruption of this world.

"It's hard for me to think, in those dark moments, that it would've been better that I'd never been born, or even that the world had never been made—obviously God doesn't think so, despite the cost to Himself." He flashed one of his impish smiles. "And I'm humble enough to admit that maybe God knows a little more than me."

"That's quite humble—and very generous of you."

He waved off the mock compliment with feigned modesty. Then, in a more serious tone, he said, "The thought does give me a sense of hope, though. I suffer like He suffered, and I will die like He died; and I hope that I will rise in glory as He rose in glory, me and all the people I love."

"St. Paul," she said with a slight smile, as if they were playing a guessing game.

"You don't have to answer this if it's too personal," he said suddenly, bringing up his knee so his foot leaned against the wall.

She nodded for him to go on.

"You mentioned kids. Are they—?"

It was the wrong question to ask, or at least the wrong time to ask it. The small smile fell from her face, her eyebrows pulled in tight on her forehead, and her gaze dropped rapidly to the ground.

"You don't have to answer," he said quickly, stepping off of the wall.

Perhaps she thought he was moving away; she placed her hand on his arm to hold him there. "It's okay. It's not a secret."

"But if it's difficult to talk about—"

"It's normal to be curious. We've all been asking each other about our families, about our lives, about what happened. I had two boys, Matthew and Luke—that's right, I told you that; you made the joke about the Evangelists. Matthew was three and Luke was only one."

Johnny waited quietly.

"They were at daycare. I'd gone back to work a few months before— I'm a graphic designer—and put them in the same place Matthew used to go before Luke was born. It was a good daycare and we were lucky they took us. They kept attendance small, no more than eight kids. They had a beautiful little space on the first floor of a building downtown, only a few minutes from my work. I knew the girls who ran the place; I'd spoken with them a hundred times."

He'd intended to be patient and allow her to tell the story at her own pace, but he couldn't stop himself from asking, "What happened?"

"I got a call at work—from Isaac. He said something had happened at the daycare. He sent a patrol car to get me. When we arrived, there was police tape blocking the entrance and all these people were around... office workers and parents, and everyone was yelling at everyone else, demanding to know what was going on." She seemed to snap out of her reverie, and met Johnny's gaze for the first time since she began telling him about her children. "The kids were used to getting a snack at ten o'clock, usually a cookie and some juice or milk. The girl who made their snacks that day—Sarah—put rat poison in their milk. She'd been working at the daycare for four years. She loved children and couldn't wait to have her own, she once told me. But that morning, she decided to lace all the children's milk with poison. Julie—the other lady who worked there—came into the kitchen, saw what Sarah was doing, and tried to stop her. Sarah bashed her head into the countertop until Julie stopped moving. Her screams of pain and panic sent the children into a frenzy and made the people in the office above come to investigate. Sarah barred the doors quietly and without rushing, according to the people who could see through the window at the front. Then, just as calmly, she drew the curtain. The people outside banged on the door; finally someone made the decision to break the glass with a nearby chair. When they got in, Sarah was holding a large and bloody chef's knife in her hand; children were dead or dying from the cuts she gave them, while others were hiding under desks or in the closets and crying. It took three large men to subdue Sarah and get the knife out of her hands."

"Matthew and Luke?"

"They were dead by the time the police arrived. Isaac told me that it looked like Matthew had tried to get in between Sarah and Luke. I don't know if that's true or if he said it just to make me feel better."

"I'm sure it's true."

"We called my folks. We couldn't reach Bill's parents."

"Your husband?"

She nodded. "My parents said they were leaving right away. It only takes five hours to get here. Isaac stayed with me, despite all the calls he was getting and frantic text messages from his supervisor. Finally he decided that the city wasn't safe anymore, and that we'd leave as soon as my folks arrived. They never did, and we never heard from them again."

"But you stayed in the city."

"It was my fault; I refused to leave my house, or even to get out of bed. By the time Isaac convinced me that more was going on than we imagined, it was too dangerous to leave. We agreed to hide out in my church until things settled down. There were only a few of us there—at St. Vincent's, I'm Catholic—and when we were overrun, we escaped up the street to St. George. Only Isaac and I made it."

"I'm so sorry," he said, feeling lame about such a trite response but not being able to think of anything else to say.

"Everyone you saw at the church has a story like that, or even worse." She hesitated for a moment, then said, "You do too."

Isaac stood suddenly and walked over to them.

"Is your husband still with us?" Johnny said.

She looked over at Isaac as he joined them, shook her head. "He died while I was pregnant with Luke. I had a craving for Rocky Road ice-cream—we had other kinds but I wanted that one—so I sent him to the gas station just before midnight. He walked in on a robbery, tried to stop it, and was killed."

"I'm sorry to interrupt," Isaac said, "but someone needs to go talk to Steven, or I'll murder him myself."

"What's going on?" Johnny said.

"He's freaking out and refusing to listen to reason."

Johnny went over to Steven, who was sitting on the couch with his head slouched, staring straight at the floor but not seeming to see it or anything else.

"You okay?" Johnny said, sitting beside him.

Steven didn't look up or turn his head. "No, no, no," he said in a distant voice.

"What's wrong?"

"Everything's wrong. I'm never going to see Theresa again. We're going to die in here."

"That's not true," Johnny said. The others were standing beside them and watching. "We'll find a way."

"No, no, no, no, no, no." Steven shook his head, each turn punctuated by an additional *no*. "There's hundreds of them upstairs. They could break through any time now. They're just toying with us; just beating their heads and fists against the door to make noises to scare us."

"You can't know that, Steven. And there aren't hundreds of them—hundreds wouldn't fit in my whole house."

"They're there." His voice was quiet but insistent. "Waiting for us. We won't survive the night." He seemed to be listening for something. He shook his head violently.

"Steven—?" Johnny placed his hand on the man's arm, but Steven seemed unaware.

"No, no, no," he said, again.

"Steven, are you listening to me?"

Almost ferociously, Steven's head snapped up and he stared at Johnny. "It's you they want. You're the only one they want." He looked up at the others. "They want him, not us."

"Don't be crazy," Isaac said.

Steven stood, started to move past Liz and toward the staircase.

"Where are you going?"

"I'm going to let them in. They just want him, they'll let the rest of us go."

"They're lying to you," Johnny said, as Isaac pounced on Steven to restrain him. They fell to the ground, struggled, then Steven, who was about half of Isaac's size, threw the larger man off of him.

As if nothing had happened, Steven started to climb the stairs.

Johnny ran up to him, took him by the arm. "Listen to me—"

Steven shook him off, kept climbing.

"Get out of the way," Isaac said to Johnny.

Instead, Johnny bear-hugged Steven from behind, wrapping his arms around Steven's, and lifted him up. He tried to walk him back down the stairs, but Steven squirmed and kicked and Johnny fell backward. He might've cracked his skull, except Isaac was there and caught him.

Somehow Steven didn't fall—perhaps he'd grabbed onto the railing, Johnny thought. He'd made it to the top of the stairs, where he stood when Johnny looked up at him, his hand on the two-by-four they'd hammered in behind the door. He tried to rip it out with his bare hands.

As if in encouragement or anticipation, the steady drum-beat from the other side of the door became a frenzied knocking.

"Wait," Liz said, stepping past them and running up the stairs two at a time. She placed her hand on Steven's shoulder. "You're not thinking straight. Come back down with me, we can talk just the two of us." Her hand dropped gently to his own.

He elbowed her in the face, hard, sending her tumbling down.

Johnny ran to catch her as best he could. He wondered where Isaac had disappeared to, but the question was answered in the next moment as the large man came running out of the storeroom, a bundle of strong rope over one shoulder, and went roaring up the stairs.

Quickly Johnny helped Liz to her feet and moved her out of the way. She had blood on her face and tears streaming out of her eyes.

Steven came sliding down the stairs as if he'd been bodily thrown from the very top. Isaac wasted no time in landing on top of him, then flipping him over onto his stomach. Moving just as quickly, he grabbed one of Steven's arms and twisted it behind his back, then did the same with the other.

"Tie them together," he said to Johnny.

Steven struggled against the rope but Isaac's grip on his wrists was firm, and Johnny was able to bind his hands.

"Are you okay?" Isaac said to Liz.

She nodded, but blood still spilled out from her nose and onto the ground.

Johnny walked her over to the bathroom sink and held her hair back. It was too dark to see in the windowless room, but he could hear the steady *plop-plop-plop* of her blood.

When the drops were less frequent, he turned her around to face the open door and the small amount of light filtering through. He reached down to grab some toilet paper and held it to her nose.

"I don't think he broke it," Johnny said. "That's good news, right?"

She didn't respond; instead, she plunged into his chest and he felt her heave and heard her sob. He wrapped his arms around her. "I know," he said.

As he held her quietly, he could also hear Steven's voice filtering in from outside, but couldn't make out the words. It seemed Steven was speaking non-stop; or, to be more accurate, murmuring non-stop.

"Johnny," Isaac called out after a few moments. "You better come see this."

Liz let him go.

Steven was still belly-down on the floor, his face turned to one side, his eyes tracking them, his mouth working away but his words unintelligible.

Isaac's knee was still pressed into Steven's back.

"What's he saying?"

"Threats, mostly," Isaac said. "He's going to kill us, apparently."

Now that he was standing beside him, Johnny could finally make it out for himself—"You will suffer," Steven was murmuring, "all suffer, suffer and die. Your lives are ending, they will end in torment for you. You will suffer and die. We are too many. So many of us and so few of you. We are coming."

The frenzied attack on the door underscored his words.

"You have to help him," Liz said softly, looking at Johnny.

"Me?" Johnny shook his head. "What do you want me to do?"

"You speak with authority," Isaac said.

"I do, do I? You saw what happened to that little girl—you both did."

"We are waiting," Steven murmured. "Do you think the door holds us back?" The loud thumping ceased immediately. "We are giving you a chance! If we have to break down the door, we will break you too. We will kill you; we will rip you apart. But open the door for yourselves and you will be spared, except that one."

"You have to try something," Liz said.

"We are many!" Steven suddenly yelled, and in response the whole basement seemed to fill with the howls and cries of innumerable zombies.

"Turn him over," Johnny said.

Isaac did it.

Johnny leaned down beside him. "Listen to me. In the name of Jesus Christ—"

"Jesus Christ I know," Steven said, a strange, wide smile splitting his face. "But who are you?"

"A servant of Jesus Christ, who commands in His master's name that you leave this man alone."

"I know who you are," Steven said in a drawn-out voice, as if he'd been teasing him all along. "You're Johnny Salibi."

"Is that supposed to scare me?"

"I can tell you about your wife, Johnny Salibi. Don't you want to know where to find her?"

Johnny drew back from him.

"Be careful," Liz said softly. "We know they lie."

Johnny considered his words before answering. He was desperate to have news of his wife—every hour that she was out there, the chances of finding her (or at least finding her alive and well and whole) plummeted. But Liz was right, he couldn't trust anything this creature said.

"All I want from you," he said, getting close again, "is that you leave this man alone. Leave him now, in the name of the—"

"You're right," Steven said, the voice hard and sharp again, the grotesque smile dropping from his face. "You're right not to ask about her, Johnny Salibi. You won't like the news. She's dead! We drowned her."

Johnny was breathing hard, his body tense, every fiber of his being pulsing with the desire to grab Steven's head and smash it into the ground, a small part of his mind holding him back and reminding him that this wasn't Steven speaking, and that the demon possessing him would love nothing more than for Johnny to attack his body.

Out of the corner of his eye, Johnny saw Isaac watching him carefully. Ready to pounce on him and restrain him, Johnny figured.

"I can tell you where to find her body if you want," Steven said.

"He's lying." Liz kneeled down beside Johnny and placed her hand on his shoulder. "Everything he said—all of it could be just lies. You know that, right?"

Johnny stood, shaking off her hand without meaning to, afraid his resolve couldn't survive the sight of Steven's slight, sly smile and provoking eyes much longer.

He paced the basement for a while, to the background noise of Steven laughing and Isaac telling him to be quiet, of the howls of zombies that had started up again with the renewed drum-beating on the door.

Rebekah's dead, he thought, more than once. *They drowned her. She's gone—Rebekah, full of life—now dead. They killed her, brought her maybe to the river in sight of St. George and forced her to place her head under its surface until the water filled her lungs.*

Finally, unable to *bear* his own thoughts or the angry sounds from the basement and from the top of the stairs, he turned to face the other two. "We have to get out of here."

"What about Steven?" Liz said.

Johnny didn't know; perhaps he didn't care. At that moment, nothing mattered but getting out and away.

"We leave him here," he said. "We go back to the church."

"We can't do that," Liz said.

"She's right," Isaac said. "We can't just leave him tied up like this. He'll starve to death."

"We can lock him in the cold room, with the food."

"And what if he comes back to himself? What if this demon finally leaves him, and he realizes we locked him up in a small room by himself?"

"I don't know!" Johnny yelled. Then, more calmly: "I don't know. We can come back for him—later. Come back with more people, maybe."

"He'll be dead by then," Isaac said.

"Like my wife?"

"Don't take that tone with me." Isaac rose to his feet. "I'm talking about Steven. I wasn't implying anything else."

"Everyone needs to calm down," Liz said. She stepped in between them. "Johnny—"

"—stop saying my name. I don't know what to do, okay?"

"Then pray," she said.

"What?"

"Lead us in prayer. Isaac and I."

He didn't want to pray, he wanted to act, to get away from Steven and from the zombies outside, to return to the church so he could think straight again. *Where two or three are gathered in My Name, I am with them.* The words came to Johnny unbidden, and arrested his rising feeling of panic. He felt his breathing return to normal.

"I believe in one God," he said, "the Father Almighty, Maker of heaven and earth, and of all things visible and invisible."

As he recited the Creed, he was so focused on the words that it was only at the periphery of his awareness that Johnny knew Liz and

Isaac were saying it with him, that Steven went on yelling and crying—sounding like the barking of a rabid dog, noise without content—and that the thuds and thumps against the door continued.

"And in the Holy Spirit," they said, "the Lord and Giver of Life, Who proceeds from the Father, Who together with the Father and the Son is worshiped and glorified, Who spoke by the prophets."

He began to return to awareness of his surroundings. The banging on the door had ceased, the howlers were silent once more, and Steven wasn't yelling either. He lay on the ground where they'd tied him up, eyes closed, his face still as that of a corpse.

They completed their prayer by saying, "I look for the resurrection of the dead, and the life of the age to come. Amen."

"Is he—?" Liz said.

Isaac walked over and kneeled beside him, placed his fingers on Steven's neck. Johnny stood over them and prayed that God would spare him. *It's my fault he left the church, Lord; he didn't have to. Grant him more days—not just for him and his wife Theresa and for us, but as a loyal servant to help with the holy struggle until You appear in glory. Save Steven and save us all, O Lord, so that we may give thanks to Your holy name and triumph in Your praise.*

Isaac stood and approached Johnny.

"Well?" Johnny said, his eyes still on Steven. He couldn't be sure, but he thought he saw his upper body moving slightly.

"His pulse is shallow," Isaac said, placing a grateful or congratulatory hand on Johnny's shoulder, "but he's not dead yet."

Chapter 14

ISAAC picked up Steven and carried him to the couch, where he and Liz propped him up with some of the pillows Rebekah felt had gone out of style and were no longer worthy of family room status. Johnny used to tell guests that their basement was a graveyard for demoted pillows.

"Can we get him some water?" Liz said.

"Of course." Johnny went to the cold room, unlocked it with the key hidden in the drop ceiling, and brought back a case of bottled water.

"How is he?" Johnny said as he ripped off the plastic, pulled out a bottle, and handed it to Liz.

She unscrewed the cap and held the bottle to Steven's lips, her face furrowed with worry. "He's alive," she said without looking at Johnny.

Eyes still shut, Steven drank water until he coughed. Two streams spilled over his chin and down his neck. Liz tried to wipe them with her sleeve, but Steven pushed her arm away in a distracted, almost unconscious manner. He'd opened his eyes but they seemed not to be focused on anything or anyone in particular.

"Are you okay?" Isaac said in a wary tone, perhaps ready to defend himself if Steven wasn't himself after all.

"Yeah," Steven said, shimmying up the cushions to reposition himself. Suddenly he cried out as if a shock had been sent through him, and he raised his shoulder to his neck.

Without a word, Johnny left for the cold room to get some aspirin. When he returned, Steven's hands had been untied; he was holding the bottle of water. Liz sat on the couch beside him, and Isaac still hovered over both of them warily.

"Some things are a blank," Steven said to Isaac, in response to a question that Johnny had missed.

Johnny uncapped the bottle and handed Steven a pill.

After a moment of hesitation, Steven took it and tossed it into his mouth, then took a swig of water, holding Johnny's gaze the whole time.

"Other things are very clear," Steven said after he'd swallowed, speaking slowly and with what Johnny felt was a sense of import.

Johnny glanced at Liz, whose look of concern hadn't faded from her face, then to Isaac.

"It doesn't matter," Liz said. "Is your head starting to feel better?"

Steven nodded, his face softening as his gaze met hers.

"Did I do something wrong?" Johnny said. He resisted the urge to add, *Sometime between healing you of demonic possession and getting you water and painkillers, I mean.*

Steven turned his head slowly to look up at Johnny. His eyes, buried in their deep sockets, almost disappeared as he narrowed them. "I heard you," he said, still speaking in that slow, accusatory manner that made every word sound like a stab through the air.

"Heard me say what?"

Steven half-laughed, a derisive expulsion of air from his mouth completely devoid of humor.

"Steven—" Liz began, but he stood up suddenly.

"I heard you. You were going to leave me." About a foot shorter than Johnny, Steven stood right in front of him and stared up at his face. "You were going to abandon me."

Under the weight of the accusation, Johnny's resolve to be patient and understanding with Steven broke down and his words were as quick as Steven's were slow, though they matched his in intensity and contempt. "You want to hash this out, Steven?" he said, so ferociously that Steven took a step back and almost fell into the couch. "All right. You were going to sell me out, do you remember that? Like an idiot you believed them when they said you'd be safe if you turned me over, and you were going to do it." Isaac grabbed Johnny around the chest with one arm to restrain him and pull him back; Liz had stood and positioned herself between him and Steven, but Johnny barely noticed. Holding his ground, he continued without pausing, "You said you'd have my back no matter what, remember? But at the first sign of trouble, all your courage left you and you gave yourself over to the demons. What kind of coward lets that happen?"

Steven had been practically leaning back to get away from the ferocity in Johnny's voice, but at the last question he straightened up again. "Why don't you ask your wife?"

"That's enough!" Liz said, as Isaac finally managed to pull Johnny away. She forced Steven to sit down on the couch again, then motioned for Isaac and Johnny to do the same.

"You can let me go," Johnny said to Isaac. "I'm not going to do anything."

"Well that didn't take long, did it?" Liz continued, when they'd sat down in the chairs beside the couch.

Johnny didn't trust himself to speak. Externally he was calm; his breathing was normal and his hands were resting gently on his knees. But inside—he burned with hatred and resentment toward Steven, the coward who had succumbed to the demons, the weakling who had put all of their lives in danger, the ingrate whom he had cured, the—

Johnny came to awareness of himself with a start; his eyes went wide, but only Liz was looking at him and noticed. *Get away from me, Satan*, he thought. *I know this man was not healed by my power, but by the power of the Mighty One of God.*

Immediately an avalanche of thoughts tried to crash into his mind, but he refused to indulge any of them.

"Steven," he said, and waited until Steven turned to look at him. "Forgive me, please. I had no right to judge you."

Obviously taken aback, it took Steven a moment to reply. "I'm sorry about what I said too."

The tension seemed to leave the room, betraying its previous presence by its sudden absence.

"I didn't want to abandon you," Johnny said. "I just—" He stopped and started again. "I was upset and scared. I felt this panicked desire to get away. I didn't know what else to do."

Steven nodded. "I would've probably done the same as you, I guess."

"So what do we do now?" Isaac said. "We can't stay here." He seemed to have been throwing furtive glances at Steven the whole time, and Johnny thought he knew what was going through Isaac's mind: Steven had been captured by the demons once already, what was to stop it from happening again? Or to any one of them?

"It's quiet outside, isn't it?" Johnny said.

The mad howling had stopped, as had the beatings on the door. Johnny stood and walked over to the window, looking up. Over the top of the window well, he saw only the scratched and dented side of the Chevy. Even so, he sensed that they were there, waiting quietly.

"Anything?" Isaac said from his seat.

Johnny shook his head. "Maybe they're trying to lull us into a sense of confidence. I don't imagine they've gone far."

"They haven't," Steven said. "They want you."

Isaac jumped to his feet like a tense spring suddenly being released. Johnny was by his side in an instant, and put his own restraining hand on the big man's arm.

Steven's eyebrows had drawn together; he seemed to take a moment to review what he had said and why it could have produced such a reaction. "I'm not saying we should hand him over," he said, "just that they want him."

"Why me?" Johnny said, as Isaac sat back down.

"I don't know. But they hate you."

"It makes sense," Isaac said, in that matter-of-fact tone that implied he was saying something they should all already know. "I told you— you have power from God. They hate you because they fear you."

Johnny hardly heard him, though; a question had occurred to him, a question that he both wanted and didn't want to ask, each with an equal level of desperation. He went back to his own chair and sat down, his gaze fixed on the ground.

"It doesn't matter," Liz said, misinterpreting Johnny's mood. "Let's talk about something else."

In large part because he didn't want her to think he'd been worried about his own safety, he said without looking up, "Is it also true what you said about my wife?"

"About being weak? No, I... I was just—"

"Not about that. About her being...." Johnny couldn't bring himself to say the word. Not caring what the others might think, he pulled out the picture of them from his back pocket. For a moment, looking at her face, he thought he could hear the echo of her giggle.

After a long pause, Liz said, perhaps in answer to a questioning look from Steven, "When you were under the influence of the demons, you told Johnny that his wife was dead, that she'd been drowned. You offered to take him to her body."

"I don't remember that," Steven said. "I'm so sorry."

Johnny put the picture back in his pocket and took a deep breath before looking up at Steven. "So you don't know if it's true or not?"

"No. I'm sorry."

From upstairs, Johnny heard a sound—a creaking, as if someone who'd tried to stand still for too long had shifted their weight. Now that he was attuned to it, he heard it again and again, repeated across the floor above him.

The others didn't seem to notice the sounds.

"Isaac's right," Johnny said. "We can't stay here. They're being quiet for now, but I think they're still in the house. I think they're waiting for the right time to raise their voices again, and maybe the right time to break down the door."

Perhaps without meaning to, Steven and Liz looked over their shoulders at the staircase, as if to confirm that the zombies had not yet burst through.

"My guess is they're waiting for darkness to fall," Johnny continued, half-speaking to himself.

"What's your plan?" Isaac said.

Johnny stood, walked back to the window out of nervous energy more than any particular purpose. They were here because of him, he thought, because he believed (or wanted to believe) that his wife might have come to the home they'd shared. They could've stayed in the safety of the church. Or relative safety, he corrected himself; for was the church even that safe? An army of zombies stood at the ready in front of it. But ready for what?

Then again, he went on thinking, what were the demons doing at all? Why were they still persecuting humanity? They knew Christ was victorious over them; they knew that sooner or later He would appear in glory and they would be cast into Hell for eternity.

There was the answer, he felt. They knew they would be cast into Hell for eternity, and they wanted to drag as many as possible down with them. *For the devil has come to you, in great wrath, because he knows that he has but a short time.*

A rebellious spirit within him was awakened or reawakened; a deep desire to oppose the devil in the power of the Holy Spirit, to save as many human beings as would be saved before Christ's return. But was it possible? When the Son of Man comes, will He find even one faithful person remaining?

If you give yourself to them, they will let the others go.

The words surprised him for their suddenness and for being discordant with his other thoughts. Did they come from his own mind, he wondered, or were they whispered into there by something external to it? He had no way of knowing.

The others had been waiting patiently, perhaps in hope that Isaac was right and Johnny did have a plan. He turned to face them, and looked at Steven.

"Do you think they were telling the truth, when they said that they'd let you all go if I stayed behind?"

"Who cares?" Liz said, as Steven looked back at Johnny blankly. "That's not an option."

"It is," Johnny said simply. "It is an option."

"How about we hear some other ideas?" Isaac said, standing up to match Johnny. "Ones that don't involve anyone sacrificing themselves?"

"I can think of only two others," Johnny said. "We stay here and wait for them, to break down the door or...." He let the words trail away; he'd wanted to say *or take over one of us again, and maybe murder us in our sleep*, but thought better of it. "Or," he started over, "we take up arms with whatever I have down here, open the door ourselves, and try to survive against whatever and whoever's out there. Killing lots more people in the process, and almost certainly getting ourselves killed too."

Liz stood as well, and then so did Steven. "You can't be serious," she said. "We can't believe anything they say."

"I know that. But it may be your best bet to get out alive."

"*Our* best bet? What about you?"

He wanted to respond, but ended up just shrugging. How could he explain it to her, or to any of them? He didn't want to die, and he didn't want to face a bunch of zombies or demons by himself. But much more than that, he didn't want to be responsible for Liz's or Steven's or Isaac's death. He hardly felt he could think straight until he knew they were back in the church, as safe as they had been before he'd dragged them out, at least. He wished he'd come alone—or never come at all.

"No, there has to be a better way," Isaac said, crossing his arms over his chest. "Can't we try praying or something?"

Give yourself up, and they will be safe. It's the only way.

"I'll be praying the whole time," Johnny said, "believe me. And if we had no choice but to stay here, I'd say our best option is to hold a full vigil, praying every hour of every day until Christ comes. But I need to get you back to the church—and I'm not sure how well we can keep our minds focused on God while running for our lives from a horde of zombies."

"Don't call them that," Liz said.

"Sorry," Johnny said. "I'm just saying—it's too risky."

Liz took a few steps toward him and looked into his eyes, searching them for something. "Why do you want to do this?"

"I don't," he said wearily. "But it's worth it if it gets you back safely."

"What about Izzy?" she said.

Steven sat back down suddenly, buried his head in his hands and massaged his forehead. "I wish we'd never come out here."

His voice was barely audible, but Johnny heard it, and in hearing his own thought expressed back to him aloud, he suddenly disagreed vehemently. "We couldn't stay in the church forever," he said. "Just like we can't stay here." He took a deep breath, then sighed it out. "The world is dying, yes. But we're still alive. And while we're alive, we have to work. We have to be good stewards of this dying world until the end. God spared us—for what reason, except to serve Him a little longer? For what reason, except that the world and those in it still need us, or people like us?

"I wish you'd never come too," he continued, speaking more slowly and less excitedly now. "This is my conviction, and I know not everyone shares it. I know the bishop doesn't. I shouldn't have involved you. I'm just trying to make this situation better as best I can."

"He's right," Isaac said.

Liz's wide eyes turned on him in disbelief.

"Maybe it's best. God will protect him."

Johnny could hardly believe that he'd won Isaac over either. But now that someone else was on board with his plan, he had to fight back the temptation to distance himself from it, to tell them that maybe it wasn't such a good idea after all.

Give yourself up, and they will live. Give yourself up, and those outside will take you to your wife.

"No." Liz looked back at Johnny. "You don't have to do this alone. You don't have to do everything alone, okay?"

"Liz—" He felt himself about to grab her by the shoulders, but resisted the urge. "I need to get you back safely to the church." *I can't lose someone else*, he wanted to say, but again he stopped himself. "I have to find my wife. I have to do everything I can to find her. Maybe the demons are lying and they'll just kill me the first chance they get. But I don't think that's their plan; if it were, they would've broken down the door by now and overwhelmed all of us. Do you understand? Maybe I can use whatever they're planning to do with me to find out if my wife is still alive. I have to try."

He paused for breath.

Time's up, he thought, and again didn't know if it came from his own mind. Later, he couldn't be certain if he'd had the thought just before or just after the basement erupted with noise: the loud and angry howling like the cries of vicious and hungry dogs, that seemed to come from all around; the heavy and repetitive stomping against the floor that shook the ceiling from one end of the basement to the other; the insistent, relentless banging on the reinforced door, the groaning and creaking of which was only partially drowned out by the other sounds.

They've decided to burst through. They've had enough.

Even as the others exchanged panicked looks with him and each other, the room darkened with shadows. Through the window, a forest of legs—naked ones and ones covered in jeans and pants, but almost all caked in blood and mud—tried to block out the sunlight.

"That's enough!" Johnny yelled. "I'll stay here with you!"

Immediately, the entire army of zombies stopped. From the ones in the house stomping on the floor to the ones banging on the door to the ones howling from outside—as if they were controlled by a single mind, all of the noise they were making ceased at once.

"Load up your backpacks with water," Johnny said, rushing to the cold room to bring another case, stacking on top of it all of his first aid kits.

When he came back, Liz was standing waiting for him. He thought he'd have to argue with her, despite the fact that there was no time to argue, but she only pressed the cross she'd been holding into his hands. "I'll do what you say, but you have to take this."

"Okay," he said.

Before he could move past her, she brought up her hand to his chest. Her fingers slipped past his collar, closed around the brown rope around his neck, and pulled out the crucifix so it rested on top of his shirt.

He smiled at her. Then he whispered, "Please take care of Izzy for me until I can join you again."

She seemed to want to say something. Instead, she swallowed hard and said, "I will."

Isaac and Steven had loaded the four backpacks. Johnny put the new case down and tore open the plastic wrapping, then went back to the storeroom while they loaded those bottles as well.

He returned with a crowbar and a sledgehammer.

"I think they'll let you go," he said, dropping the tools on the couch. "But take those just in case. If they turn on us, we'll have to defend ourselves."

Isaac slung a backpack over each shoulder. Steven zipped up the other two and handed one to Liz. Half a case of water remained. Impulsively, Johnny picked it up with one hand. "You're going to let them go," he said, whispering but aware the others could hear him. "And you're going to let me toss this into the back of the car first."

Isaac had picked up the crowbar and was halfway up the staircase. Johnny grabbed the regular hammer by the stairs and followed him. Working together in silence, he and Isaac removed the boards that had held the door closed. Over the sounds of the squealing nails as they were pulled from the door and the frame, and over the sounds of the creaking of the boards as the wood bent, Johnny thought he could hear breathing—loud and coarse exhalations from a dozen or more noses and mouths—just on the other side of the door.

When the last board was out and tossed to the bottom of the basement, Isaac handed the crowbar to Steven and took the sledgehammer from him. He knocked away the two-by-four. Johnny handed his hammer to Liz, and picked up the case of water again.

He took a deep breath and prayed, *Lord Jesus Christ, Son of God, have mercy on me, a sinner.*

Johnny looked back at Isaac, who stood behind him, gripping the sledgehammer in both hands, holding it over his shoulder at the ready.

Chapter 15

JOHNNY pulled back the deadbolt. Then, squeezing his cross even tighter, he pulled back the door as well.

Almost immediately, a wave of foul air rushed into the stairway like a fast-moving fog. The mixture of the pungent smell of urine and the farm-like stench of manure convinced Johnny that more than one of the zombies had soiled themselves, perhaps recently; the smell was so overpowering that Johnny subconsciously began to hold his breath. As the door came fully open, a sea of monstrous faces stared back at him and the zombies began to howl in laughter, like hyenas, their mangled and dirty faces splitting in half with too-wide smiles. Johnny couldn't believe how many of them there were. He stood frozen on the top step, but it didn't matter; the zombies filled the landing and the hallway as far as Johnny could see. There wasn't room for him to move forward even if he wanted to.

Instinctively he searched among them for his wife. As much as he wanted to find her, a part of him hoped he wouldn't—not among this group whose features were twisted with devilish pleasure. The faces that looked back at him belonged to men and women and boys and girls, but only barely; dirty faces with bald heads or just bald patches where hair had been pulled out; heads and necks polka-dotted with cuts and bruises and crisscrossed by rivulets of dried blood. Bad enough were those staring vacantly with their mouths hanging open; even worse were those staring right back at Johnny, their mouths exploding with guttural, ugly, angry laughter.

Even so, despite the horror of twisted humanity that constituted their faces, and their naked and half-naked bodies torn and bruised and bloodied, their eyes were their most bone-chilling feature, from the unnaturally wide, bloodshot ones to those yellowed or filmed over, to eyes that were gouged out, leaving bloody sockets in their absence.

"Let us pass!" Johnny yelled. He held up the cross to make sure they could all see it. A few zombies paused, but the majority went on laughing. None of them moved away even an inch. "I will stay! But you must let us pass. Otherwise, we will fight to our deaths."

He had the strong sense that whoever was in charge—or, to speak plainly, whichever demon or demons were dominant in this area—didn't want him to simply die. It seemed to him that they had a different plan for him. The thought chilled him in part—especially as he faced a wall of distorted, dirty, smelly humanity and wondered if he'd be numbered among them before the sun set that day—but it also bolstered his sense of confidence that they wouldn't want to push him or the others into fighting for their lives.

The zombies began to move away from the landing, up the small staircase and down the hallway, marching like refugees from a bloody civil war. Isaac pushed past Johnny, swinging the sledgehammer down to hang by his side. A long double-row of escorts walked them past even more zombies; Johnny's kitchen and living room and hallway leading to the bedrooms were packed. Maybe a hundred or more zombies filled every available square foot of floor, giving way only to create the narrow passageway that led them to the front door, which stood open. Outside, zombies in similar numbers surrounded their car and filled the driveway, spilling out into the street. If he'd thought to make a run for it—and Johnny hadn't, not until he saw the overwhelming crowd of zombies that made the idea so untenable.

His group had kept quiet up to that point. As they descended the stairs to the driveway, he heard Liz whisper something to herself. It sounded like, "There's so many of them." His own thoughts echoed hers: even if this wasn't the whole city's population of zombies, called to assemble at his house for some reason, was it reasonable to hope that any other survivors were left? At best, it seemed, only those who remained in the church had survived; at worst, maybe even they had succumbed. In addition to searching for his wife among the sea of twisted faces, Johnny found that he was also scanning for other familiar faces.

He spotted one almost immediately as the zombies cleared away from their car like insects scattering from a wrecked anthill. This was a doubly-familiar figure; he stood motionless by the driver-side door, fixing Johnny with a cold stare. Now that he was getting a good look at this half-naked old man with once-white underwear, Johnny could no longer doubt his first flash of recognition.

"You will leave this place," he said in his raspy voice, turning his attention on Isaac. Johnny looked at the others, but none of them seemed to recognize the old man—because they'd never met Father Gord, he thought, or because the present sight was so ghastly and incongruous with the healthy-looking, well-groomed priest that they couldn't bring themselves to connect the two.

Isaac strode up to him, but the old man didn't budge at all. Although Isaac towered over him in every way—Father Gord was now thin and wasted away, his ribs poking out from the wrinkled, paper-like film of skin that covered his body—there was a dark quality to his eyes that made even Isaac stop short of shoving him out of the way, as had perhaps been his intention.

After a short pause—during which Father Gord held Isaac's gaze in a defiant stare, his narrowed, black-pupiled eyes filled with hatred and disdain—he smiled, humorlessly but victoriously and contemptuously, and stepped to the side so that Isaac could open the door.

The others had been waiting with Johnny. Isaac barked back to them, "Come on, get in." Johnny saw him struggle to adjust the seat to accommodate his larger frame, especially with the bags which were still strapped to his back.

With tentative steps, and eyes that seemed to catch every motion of the nearby zombies, Steven walked around to the other side of the car. He was tense as a harp string, and hypersensitive to every sound as he slowly opened the door, but then got in quickly and slammed it shut.

Johnny opened the back door and tossed in the case of water. Liz was still standing near the staircase. Leaving the door open, Johnny walked back to her. "Go on," he said.

Isaac fired up the engine. He rolled down the window and called out her name in a monosyllabic bark.

Liz ignored him and looked into Johnny's eyes, searching for something, confusion and disbelief written all over her face. *Please don't do this*, Johnny thought. *Just go.*

Isaac barked her name again, more insistently this time.

She broke her gaze with Johnny almost forcefully, then stormed to the back of the car and got in. Through the open window, he heard her say to Isaac, "We're not really leaving him here, are we?"

Isaac's own voice was cold and matter-of-fact. "It's for the best," he said. "Trust me." He rolled the car backward down the driveway, slowly because the zombies cleared away from the car at only a leisurely pace. "We'll be back for him," Isaac added; then he looked out the open window and called out to Johnny, "We'll be back for you!"

He watched them roll out onto the street, pause to shift gears, then drive away.

"You're alone now," the old man said delightedly, as the rest of the zombies closed in around him.

Worse than alone, Johnny thought. *I'm surrounded by all of you.*

"Your friends were only too happy to leave you."

"I told them to go," he said, though now that they'd gone, he really wished that they hadn't.

Even outdoors, the stench of all those zombies was overpowering; the heavy breathing from their stuffed noses and toothless mouths was irritating; and the old man—he didn't want to think of him as Father Gord—with his cheerful yet violent tone was terrifying.

They shouldn't have left him alone, Johnny thought; at least they could have died together. He pushed the thought away as ignoble. *Lord Christ, give me strength.*

"They'll come back for you," the old man was saying. "We hope so; with Bishop Joseph too. But"—here his too-wide smile grew even wider—"who will they get when they do?"

Johnny tried to ignore the sinister smile and teasing tone. "You may not get your wish," he said. "The bishop isn't stupid enough to leave the church. Certainly not to come rescue me." The old man seemed about to respond, but Johnny took a step toward him so that only a few short ones separated them and said, "Where's my wife? Do you know?"

An image appeared in his mind instantly, as vivid as anything he'd ever seen with his eyes. In the vision, he and his wife attacked one another, although neither seemed to be themselves. They descended on each other with wordless cackles and unimaginable violence and gusto. He tore out her hair and she clawed out his eyes; he bit her hands and she bit into his cheek; he bashed her head into the concrete curb of some street.

The zombies, including the old man, had erupted into their chilling howls of derision-filled laughter.

You think you're scaring me by showing me this nightmare vision. Johnny kept the thought to himself, trying not to betray the joy and relief he felt. *Your plan is to take possession of me, then make me kill my wife? Fools! If that's your plan, that means Rebekah's not already dead; it means she's alive, and not drowned like you said.*

The old man's eyes narrowed further.

Another vision played in Johnny's mind. This time he led a group of zombies into the church and to the altar. The bishop stood in front of the sanctuary, with Isaac and Liz on either side. Four zombies attacked Isaac, brought him to the ground and dashed his head against the marble floor so that his blood flowed out like a tiny river down the steps. Two other zombies had rushed up to the bishop, beat him with their hands until he fell, then kicked his face and body until he was a curled-up, shaking, bloody mess. Her face twisted with horror, Liz stood in front of the royal doors, arms spread to protect the altar behind her, all the while screaming at Johnny to leave this place, entreating him in Christ's name to depart. He saw himself walk up the bloodied steps slowly, gently place his hands on the sides of her face, then snap her neck in a single, quick twist of his arms. He tossed her body down the stairs as the rest of the zombies began to kick and bash themselves against the iconostasis to topple it over, while he himself moved toward the wooden altar.

None of that is going to happen, Johnny thought, but he'd be lying to himself if he tried to pretend the vision hadn't shaken him. Even more than the first one with his wife, perhaps because this one wasn't diluted by the relief he felt that Rebekah was still alive, or perhaps because he couldn't gloat with this vision that they'd revealed to him more information than they'd intended.

"Nothing to say?" the old man asked.

Rattled as he was, Johnny spat out his own question without having to think. "Where's my wife?" *That's all I care about right now*, he told himself.

The old man stepped toward him; more zombies had closed in on his sides and from behind him as well. He felt their breath on his neck. The air was so foul he found it hard to breathe himself.

"Didn't I tell you?" the old man said. "We're going to reunite you. You want that, right?"

Johnny had the strong desire never to respond to him in the affirmative, for any reason.

"I know what you're thinking, Johnny Salibi. You're thinking you can resist us, that your God will protect you no matter what we say to tempt you away from Him. Right?"

Johnny didn't respond; he felt light-headed.

"You don't have to answer me." The old man's voice seemed to be coming from far away. "I know it's true. But I don't want to tempt you, Johnny. I want to make a deal with you, like we made with your wife."

The mention of Rebekah brought Johnny out of his daze; he shook his head and took a deep breath, despite the stench.

"Here's the deal." The old man had stepped closer, was now whispering. "Sooner or later, you will succumb to us. Everyone does. But if you give yourself over to us now, we won't make you kill Elizabeth Stone. We'll spare you that experience. Doesn't that sound fair?"

He's lying, Johnny thought, trying to look over the old man's bony, white-haired shoulder and not into his narrow eyes that seemed entirely composed of ink-black pupils.

"Ha! Not interested? I thought as much. You are a man of your age, Johnny Salibi; a man of instant gratification. That is why we've brought your wife here."

The old man stepped to stand beside Johnny, gripped his arm with surprising strength. Down the driveway and into the street, the eerily silent zombies parted, creating a macabre corridor at the end of which stood Rebekah. Her clothes were torn and dirty with mud and sweat and blood, her hair matted down over her face, her eyes staring but vacant.

The sight gave him renewed strength. He turned quickly and pushed away the old man, who tried to hold onto him. Johnny broke the grip with a quick flick of his arm so he wouldn't go down with the old man as he tripped and fell.

He held up the cross and ran down the corridor toward his wife, not surprised yet that none of the zombies tried to stop him. He held the cross high, began to say, "In the name of—" when a jabbing pain in his mind made him scream and fall to his knees.

The old man's voice played over another vision. In this one, several zombies grabbed Rebekah, two of them pulling in opposite directions until her arms ripped off; another yanking out clumps of hair as her body fell to the ground. Throughout, Rebekah somehow managed to survive, crying desperately and mournfully, a cry of deep pain but of even deeper betrayal.

The vision was so vivid that Johnny actually yelled out for them to stop; for a moment, it looked like it was happening before his very eyes, that Rebekah's bloodied torso was on the pavement of the street, tendons and bones sticking out, her blood everywhere. But he saw her standing there still, motionless and eyes vacant; and he remembered the old man's words that had played over the vision: *This is the new deal, Johnny Salibi; the here-and-now deal. Give yourself over to us and we'll spare you this experience. Isn't that the love no man has greater than, to give up your life for hers?*

Johnny stood, the headache fading a little. He stared at his wife. *I love you*, he thought. He wanted to rush forward and hug her, catch her up in his arms like Superman and fly her away from this mad and ugly world.

As if they read his mind, two zombies stepped forward and grabbed Rebekah by her arms.

Give yourself to us right now, the old man's voice spoke in his mind again, *or watch her die right now. The choice is yours.*

Johnny looked down at the cross in his hand. He wouldn't watch Rebekah die; he'd fight them to his own death, the cross lifted high until he could no longer hold it up, the name of Jesus on his lips until he could no longer speak.

Christ our God, receive our spirits in Your Heavenly Kingdom.

He swallowed hard, prepared to launch himself at the zombies holding Rebekah, when he heard the screech of tires and the honking of a horn.

It looked like another strange vision playing out. The blue sedan came racing toward him from the street down which it had disappeared, Liz behind the wheel, Isaac's large black frame half-sticking out of the front passenger window, a modern knight on a steel horse with a sledgehammer for a lance. He swung and knocked out every zombie between him and Johnny. Liz hardly slowed as they came up to him, but Isaac tossed aside the sledgehammer and wrapped his arms around Johnny, picking him up as Liz raced on.

"No, wait!" Johnny said, screaming into the wind over the roof of the car. He looked back as Liz turned the car left, but saw only a mob of howling, angry, pursuing zombies. None of them his wife.

Halfway down Main street, Liz stopped the car suddenly. Isaac dropped Johnny as the back door came open.

"Get in!" Isaac yelled.

"You don't understand," Johnny tried to say, but Isaac spoke over him, "Get in now!"

The mob of zombies had turned onto the street and was running with remarkable speed toward them, their howls desperate and loud.

Watching them approach in the rearview, Liz yelled, "Johnny, come on!"

He jumped into the back. Liz took off so fast that Johnny had to pull in his legs before the door was slammed shut by the force of the car's rapid acceleration.

She looked up at him in the rearview and smiled widely in relief; he felt a euphoric sense emanating from all of them, their reward for a successful execution of such a risky and daring rescue operation.

"We turned around as soon as we got to the end of the street," Steven said.

Isaac looked around the headrest at him, a triumphant twinkle in his eyes. "I told you we'd come back for you," he said. "I just didn't say when. I had no intention of abandoning you to them for very long."

"Thank you all," Johnny said, trying to sound sincere. "Thank you so much. Really."

Even in his own ears, the words sounded artificial and forced, the gratitude he should have felt overwhelmed by the sadness of having lost his wife for yet another time. And also by the despairing thought that even if he did find Rebekah again, what could he do differently? How could he win against the demons, except by fighting them until he died?

His mood, such a stark contrast to their own, infected the others. In the rectangular frame of the rearview, he saw Liz's smile drop off by degrees.

They drove in silence until they came into view of the church.

Chapter 16

A s they turned on Down, Johnny heard Isaac curse and Liz gasp
out loud. Their way forward was completely blocked; a wall of
zombies stood near the church, two or three people deep and stretching
onto the sidewalks on either side of the road.

"You'll have to drive through them," Isaac said, as Liz slammed on
the brakes. "Lord forgive us, there's been too much killing today, but
there isn't any other way."

Steven leaned forward, stared out the front window. "No way, we'll
never make it. There's too many of them."

Johnny leaned forward too. "We're not going to drive through them,"
he said. "Isaac's right. Too many people have died today because of
us."

Isaac turned his head. "But not you," he said. "You're alive."

I was ready to die, Johnny thought. *You think you saved me, but
you saved me for more struggling, for more days to live in a world gone
mad.*

Through the broken window, he heard the zombies howl like dogs,
trying to tempt his group forward or scare them away, or maybe just
drive them mad.

With a quick jerk of his arm, he opened the door. Steven yelled at
him in panicked tones, but Johnny ignored him and stepped outside.

"What are you doing?" Isaac said.

Ignoring him too, Johnny held up the cross and cried out loud, "My
name is Johnny Salibi, a servant of Jesus Christ, the Lord." At the
name of Jesus, the zombies howled even louder. Johnny looked up
at the three crosses on the three domes of the church and continued,
"Leave this holy place, for holy things are for the holy! Do you think
we fear you?"

"Johnny, get back in the car!" Isaac barked.

"We do not fear you! We pity you! We ridicule you! We spit on you!"

The howling had become frenzied, the front line of zombies trembling with rage or desire to shut Johnny up, but holding their place for the moment.

Isaac tried to grab his arm, but Johnny took a step away. At the edge of his attention, he thought he heard Liz tell Isaac to leave him alone in a tone that implied she knew what he was doing.

"Soon—you know this!—soon the Lord will come in glory and you will be judged for what you've done. And you will be judged by men!"

Those were the magic words. As loud as they'd been howling before, at that sentence their yells became deafening. They broke their formation and stampeded forward, their faces contorted by rage, blood and spit flying out of their open, screaming mouths.

Johnny jumped back into the car. Liz didn't have to wait for him to tell her what to do. By breaking ranks, the zombies had created an opening on the left side. Liz veered to avoid some of the faster zombies that had reached the car and were trying to block its progress. In the meantime, Steven had given his hammer to Isaac, who swatted away the zombies trying to grab him through the open window. Although *swatted*, Johnny felt, might be the wrong word as sometimes it included smashing them in the shoulder or slamming down on fingers that had gripped the door frame.

The car went over a bump. For a moment, Johnny thought it was a fallen zombie, but almost immediately he realized Liz had gone over a curb, was now driving on the patch of grass on the outside edge of the parking lot. She went over the curb on the other end and down to the paved lot, then accelerated ever faster as she drove past the parked and abandoned cars. She brought their car to a sudden, jerking stop in front of the doors from which they'd emerged only that morning, though to Johnny it felt like a lifetime ago.

"Where's the stuff?" Johnny said.

Liz popped the trunk, as both Isaac and Steven opened their doors. Liz ran around the front of the car and to the church doors, where she barely had enough time to knock before one of them came open and Michael stood beaming at her.

Johnny held up the cross and watched the approaching line of zombies, who had slowed down and were now moving toward them almost reluctantly.

Isaac and Steven ran past him, loaded down with the backpacks and the case of water.

Liz called out to him; then Michael; then Isaac and Steven too, in increasingly baffled tones.

Johnny kept watching the tortured approach of the zombies, who seemed unwilling to keep moving forward, but unable to stop. *What is it you fear?* he wondered, not for the first time. *The church? The cross? The altar?*

Strong arms closed around him from the side, and picked him up effortlessly. Johnny almost screamed out in his surprise, but gained control of himself as he realized it was Isaac, racing back to the church with him. The large metal door slammed shut behind them.

"Thank God," Michael said, speaking almost to himself as he threw the latch. He turned around and continued, "Thank God you're okay." He took the cross from Johnny, who only reluctantly gave it up. Michael didn't seem to notice. "We've been praying for you. Bishop Joseph and I, the whole time you were gone."

"Thank you," Johnny said.

The bishop was sitting in the front pew with Liz and Steven. The backpacks and case of water had been placed on the floor at the bottom of the marble stairs, the pathetic spoils of their mission laid out before them.

As the rest of the group approached, the bishop greeted Isaac and expressed his own gratitude to God for his safe return. Johnny had the strong desire to escape, and as the bishop turned his small black eyes to meet Johnny's, he cleared his throat to cut off anything the old man might say.

"Thank you for praying for us," he said quickly. "If it's all right with you, I'd like to go see my daughter. Is that okay?"

If the bishop felt disappointment or surprise, it flashed on his face for only a moment, so brief that Johnny wasn't even sure it had been there. "Of course," he said.

Resisting the urge to look at anyone else, especially Liz, he walked down the aisle quickly and out into the narthex. By habit he had turned at the doors to cross himself, and saw Liz looking back at him over her shoulder. He turned around again and went down the stairs, holding the railing because of the dark.

Izzy found him before he found her; he'd hardly opened the door and stepped into the basement when he heard a young voice call out, "Daddy!" and saw her running toward him.

He kneeled down to embrace her as she launched herself into his chest, then squeezed her tightly and picked her up.

"I missed you, munchkin," he said, kissing her forehead.

"I missed you!" she said, as if he'd stolen the words from her mouth and she was trying to reclaim them. "Did you see mommy?"

"I saw her, yes," he said, before he could think of a lie. "She's still sick." Unabashed disappointment registered on Izzy's small face. "She misses you too, honey," he said, then almost reached into his back pocket to pull out the picture of exhausted, sweaty, gorgeous Rebekah and a one-day old creature who might be a tiny girl or a tiny alien. But would it make Izzy happy to see the picture, he wondered, or would it just upset her even more?

"Come on," he said, "we have some catching up to do."

They found a quiet corner and Johnny and his daughter sat on the ground, cross-legged and facing one another. Johnny asked Izzy to tell him all about her day. Playing with the plastic toes of her shoes, she told him in minute detail about the games she'd played, the lunch they'd had, how she had helped Fatima with cleaning up their table, and then colored some books with her. That seemed to make her remember something, and she was up and away like a dart, racing toward Fatima, who sat at a table near the back reading to her three boys. He saw Fatima smile, nod, and hand over a book to Izzy, which she brought back to Johnny.

"That's some very nice coloring," Johnny said. This particular book was *Tales from the Bible*, appropriated from the bookstore or the Sunday school room, Johnny figured. Izzy had colored in Adam and Eve plucking the fruit (from a purple tree with purple leaves, according to Izzy); had colored in Old Man Noah and the elephants and giraffes and lions sticking their heads out of his purple boat on the purple waters; had colored in Baby Moses floating in a basket on the purple Nile, but had left the young shepherd holding a sling-shot tragically empty.

"You didn't color in David, honey."

"I didn't have time."

"Well I want to see what color you're going to pick for his eyes. I'm going to guess purple."

"Purple is my favorite color," she said.

"I had a feeling it was."

She nodded.

"Last week red was your favorite color, do you remember that?"

She shook her head, her eyebrows drawn together in the skeptical look that was a carbon-copy of her mother's.

He laughed. "Let's go to the table and finish coloring, okay?"

They worked together for the rest of the afternoon, Johnny serving as his daughter's artistic director, suggesting colors to fill in the different outlines. Izzy's mind worked in such a way that whatever shape was largest needed to be in purple, but she gave free rein to Johnny's direction on the other, smaller outlines. She held the crayon with practically her whole hand and colored in the pages with a deep and joyful concentration.

He tried not to think about the others upstairs, but kept catching himself glancing in the direction of the stairwell door. It didn't come open by the time they needed to start setting up the basement for dinner.

Glancing in that direction subconsciously as he came out of the storeroom loaded down with another folded table, he caught Liz looking around the basement.

She smiled as their gazes met and intercepted him. She helped him pull out the table's legs and set it upright.

"You okay?" she said.

He had started to move back to the storeroom to get another table, but she followed. "I'm fine," he said without looking at her.

"What's going on with you?" She grabbed his arm to stop him.

Johnny almost unleashed on her, almost asked her what kind of question that was given everything that had happened that day, let alone that month. But the confusion and concern in her tone was matched by the look on her face, which arrested the words and made him take a deep breath to calm himself before answering.

In that calm state, he intended to say something untrue but pacifying, something understandable that would satisfy Liz's curiosity and put an end to the conversation, something like, "I really am fine. It's just been a stressful day." Instead, he heard himself say, "We left Rebekah behind."

Liz's hand dropped away from his arm. "What?"

"They brought her there. She was standing on the other side of the street when you drove up to rescue me."

Liz's eyes were wide and searching, the speed of their movement perhaps mirroring the thoughts racing through her mind. "I'm so sorry," she said. "I didn't know. We could've tried to pick her up. We—"

"It's okay," he said, trying to interrupt the torrent of words.

"I thought she was—" She cut herself off.

"She's not," Johnny said, firmly.

"We can go back!" Liz said, brightening up.

Johnny shook his head. What was the point? The demons planned to tear Rebekah apart, to torment him. He would die before he allowed that to happen. Either way, he was now on their radar; his hopes of finding Rebekah, lost and wandering by herself, were now more unrealistic than ever. Somehow he'd attracted their attention, and by doing that, he'd put Rebekah in even greater danger.

"It's okay," Liz was saying. "We can go back tomorrow morning. Or even right now if you think—"

He kept shaking his head.

"Don't worry about us. We'll be fine. It's worth it."

"I wasn't thinking about you," Johnny said. The words sounded harsher than he'd intended them, perhaps because he spoke in a matter-of-fact, flat tone, the way someone might correct an acquaintance for a non-consequential mistake.

"Of course," Liz said, but her balloon of excitement had been deflated.

"I'm sorry," he said. "I didn't mean—"

"It's not a problem. Really." She looked away from him. "I'm going to see if they need help in the kitchen."

He watched her leave, feeling callous and foolish, and wishing he could take back the entire conversation and start over.

When he was done helping move the tables and chairs out of the storeroom and setting them up, he returned to his own table. The others were already seated.

"Thank you for watching the little one," he said to Fatima.

She looked at Izzy and smiled. "Anytime you want. She's an angel."

Although he sat next to Liz, they didn't exchange more than a few words until halfway through the meal. Until then, it was mostly her asking for the ketchup or mustard or sliced cheese to be passed down, Johnny jumping to meet her needs, followed by a quick thank you from her.

Adding to the awkward atmosphere of the meal was Fatima and Wassim's grandchildren, who stared at Johnny and then at each other, seemingly having a silent contest of wills among themselves. Finally, Osama, the oldest, seemed to screw up his courage and, a half-chewed French fry in one corner of his mouth, he almost spat out, "Is it true you went outside today?"

Osama had the misfortune of sitting closest to Fatima, and suffered the consequences in the form of a quick slap on his upper arm.

"It's okay," Johnny said to her. Then, facing Osama, he said, "Yes. I was outside."

"Is it bad?" Ahmed, the middle child, said.

It's worse than you can imagine, Johnny thought. Fatima was glaring at him, concerned perhaps that he'd terrify her grandchildren; Wassim had put down his burger and was looking at Johnny intently, perhaps just as interested in the answer as the children.

"It's going to be fine," Johnny said, smiling gently and looking Ahmed in the eyes. It was easy to speak the words with conviction; he believed them with all of his heart, so long as he didn't have to commit himself to any particular timeline. "But for right now, we need to stay here."

"For how long?"

"I don't know. None of us know."

"We can't go outside even for a little while?" Mahmoud said.

Fatima was too far away to swat any part of his body, but the glaring look she gave him served the same purpose. Mahmoud put his head down. In Arabic this time, she yelled at them to finish their food.

The boys buried their faces in their plates, looking so despondent that it made Johnny scramble to think of something to cheer them up. But it was Liz who asked, "Why do you want to go outside?"

Johnny's initial reaction was that it was a dumb question, but as the youngest looked up at her with his bottom lip sticking out in a pout, and said, "We just want to play soccer," Johnny realized that he'd filled in his own answers (not wanting to be locked up like prisoners, mostly; wanting to feel sunshine on his face; wanting to return to some sense of normalcy) and hadn't thought of asking the kids for theirs.

Now that he knew their answer, though, he said, "Well, do you have a ball?"

Osama nodded. "But Teta says we can't play in here, we would bother people too much."

Fatima turned her glare on Johnny, as if daring him to contradict her.

"She's right," Johnny said quickly. "You can't have a soccer ball bouncing around in here and hitting people in the head."

The boys half-shrugged in despondent acquiescence.

Johnny looked around the basement as if surveying it, then he and Liz exchanged looks.

"Having said that," Johnny said, "we could declare a soccer tournament. Put some chairs down to make goalposts, maybe other chairs for a stadium. Then anyone who stays to watch and gets hit in the head with a ball couldn't really complain, could they?"

Almost as one, the three boys turned to Fatima and asked her if it was okay. At the same time, however, Wassim said, "I can be the referee for you. I used to coach soccer, before." It was the most animated Johnny had yet seen him.

"You're hired," Johnny said, then turned to Liz. "Do you think that's okay? We should get the bishop's blessing, right?"

"I don't think it'll be a problem." She had thawed toward him, finally—whether through the contagious excitement of the boys, the bemused look on their grandmother's face, or the signs of life their grandfather was finally showing.

He next turned to Izzy. "Do you want to keep score, honey? To count the points?"

"Yeah," she said, nodding excitedly. Then, as an after-thought, she said, "I don't know if I'll make a mistake."

Fatima laughed and said, "I'll help you," which the boys took as tacit approval of the scheme and began to thank her, Johnny, Liz, their grandfather, everyone in sight of their machine-gun fire of gratitude.

"It's not a deal yet," Johnny said, when he could finally get a word in. "Finish your food and I'll ask Bishop Joseph what he thinks."

The bishop found Johnny first. Before they were done eating (two meat patties were left, and Johnny was eyeing one of them), Bishop Joseph approached their table. Johnny was telling the kids a series of riddles.

"I'm sorry to interrupt," the bishop said. "I just wanted to ask if you'd be willing to speak with me, when you're done."

"Of course," Johnny said, wondering why the bishop sounded so hesitant. He started to get up.

"Please, no. Finish your meal. I'll be upstairs. Just come see me when you're ready." He'd glanced at the table, and now reached out to grab the empty bowl where the lettuce had been and the plate that now contained only wrappers of sliced cheese. Liz tried to stop him, but the bishop made a sound like *tut-tut* and carried them off.

Johnny had his third burger, but enough time to eat it was the extent of the patience the boys had for him. Although he tried to help with cleaning up, the boys begged him to go. He hesitated until Liz said, "Go ahead. I'll see if Steven and Theresa need help."

Bishop Joseph sat in the front pew, staring up at the large painting on the wall behind the altar of the Theotokos with the Christ Child.

The phrase "more spacious than the heavens" was printed along the icon.

Holy Mary, Mother of God, pray for us sinners, he thought as he stood at the pew and wondered if he should make a noise to alert the bishop to his presence. The words were from a Catholic prayer he'd learned in elementary school, and which he'd always loved. Mary herself was a great comfort to him, as kind and loving as a grandmother and as enthusiastic and full-of-life as a baby sister. Those were strange feelings for him to have, perhaps, because he and his mother had never gotten along all that well, but Mary for him wasn't a symbol of motherhood—she was a real presence, and not just a presence but a person. It had been a long time since he paid her any attention, though; not since he'd stopped coming to the church; not since things had broken down so badly with his parents that he'd stopped talking to both of them.

A twinge of guilt, now familiar, had struck at his conscience. To force himself to ignore it, Johnny said the first thing that occurred to him, perhaps a bit abruptly: "They're being quiet out there."

The bishop seemed to return to himself and to an awareness of his surroundings. "For now," he said, in the semi-automatic way a person speaks if they've just been awakened. With a slight pulling motion of his head, Bishop Joseph indicated that Johnny should sit beside him.

When Johnny had done so, the bishop said, speaking more clearly, "That's their plan, I think. If they howled all the time, we might get used to it."

"I think you're right. They did the same thing at my house."

"Yes. I wanted to talk to you about what happened at your house."

Johnny was silent for a moment. Had the bishop called him up simply to berate him? As if anything the bishop could say would make Johnny feel worse.

"I'm sorry," he said, in a flat voice. "I endangered everyone's lives, I know that. And I took life, and I forced the others to take life too."

"That's not what I was referring to."

"I crushed a guy with a car," Johnny said, taken aback once more by the bishop's tone, which wasn't condemning as he'd expected it to be, but—probing? The bishop was trying to get Johnny to admit something, but it didn't seem he was looking for a confession. "You understand? We beat people with a sledgehammer."

"You're not calling them zombies anymore."

"They brought my wife out there," Johnny said suddenly, because the image of her standing on the other side of the street, held as if under arrest by two others, sprang into his mind.

The bishop raised his bushy eyebrows, but took his time before responding. "How was she?"

"Alive. She didn't look good. I don't know how much longer she'll survive." He didn't add that he didn't know how much longer any of the rest of them would survive either.

"That's what I wanted to talk to you about, Mr. Salibi."

"Why do you call me that?" Johnny said. "It makes me think of my dad. Call me Johnny."

A curious, yet somehow knowing look flashed through the bishop's eyes. But he seemed to set his curiosity aside and said, "Forgive me, but I'd feel as if I were talking to a child. May I call you John?"

"Sure."

"All right. I think you were right, John; I believe I was wrong."

"About what?"

"About the situation we're in. I've been waiting for a sign, some indication of what I should do next." His voice drifted off a little. "I've been trying to protect and preserve this tiny flock that's been given to me until Christ returns." They'd both been looking straight ahead at the iconostasis, but now Bishop Joseph turned his head to look at Johnny. "When you appeared in our church, hobbling toward me and panicked about your wife, insistent that we all go outside immediately to find her, I thought you were a problem sent to me by God to try my patience. I don't think that was quite what God had in mind."

"What do you mean?"

"You aren't a problem, John. You're the solution."

"No, I'm not."

The bishop's face cracked into a smile, the wrinkles folding over themselves; but it was a sad smile. "I'm very old now, and even more tired. I pray almost all day and all night for this church, for its protection. But every day, it takes more out of me—or maybe I have less to give."

"I don't have anything to give," Johnny said, because he didn't like the direction the conversation was taking and he wanted to put a stop to it.

"That's not true. I heard what happened today—"

"Let me tell you what happened today. They were about to torture my wife in front of me. I didn't want them to have that satisfaction, so I was going to fight them. I was ready to die—no, that's not true. I wanted to die. I wanted it to be over, do you understand? I have a three-year-old daughter, who may have lost her mother for good, but...."

"You're right," the bishop said. "You're the last person I would've chosen for this. You're zealous, but impetuous. You have spiritual strength, but not enough humility. So much power, and so little wisdom to use it."

"Chosen for what exactly?" Johnny said, ignoring for the moment what he perceived as criticisms against his character to focus on the more important, more ominous issue.

"To lead the community, when I'm gone. Don't give me that look. My role was to preserve them for you. But one day you will have to take over and lead them. And do the things you said—take back for Christ as much ground as you can. Heal people, cast out demons from them, increase the flock."

"That was before," Johnny said. "Things have changed. I'm not strong enough to fight them."

"Of course not. But His strength is made perfect in weakness."

"If we go up against them directly, we'll get killed, like you said. We'll be destroyed, or tortured until we beg for death."

The bishop didn't look convinced.

"Besides," Johnny said, "I'm not a leader."

"Yes, I would've thought the same. But now I believe Isaac would follow you anywhere, and I'd never thought I'd say that about anyone in conjunction with Isaac. The subdeacon is devoted to you too." The bishop shrugged. "John, God forgive me if I say this out of hubris, but when I feel this kind of conviction, I am usually not wrong. You'll always have a choice in how to respond, but I think you'll find that this is what you're being called to do.

"But don't worry," he continued, no doubt in response to the very worried look on Johnny's face. "I'm not planning on going away any time soon. So for now I'd just like you to pray with me, if you will."

"So I can learn some humility from you?"

"Because I need strengthening in my own prayers, and because I think it won't do you any harm, and may do you some good." Bishop Joseph paused, his probing glance roving over Johnny's face. "Is there something on your mind, John? Something you'd like us to discuss?"

Johnny couldn't help himself from looking up at the icon of Mary and Jesus. He knew the bishop wanted him to open up, about his parents or some other unresolved issue that Bishop Joseph had detected in him. On the one hand, Johnny felt the urge to talk about what had happened with his folks, to lay it all out for the bishop and see if he felt better for doing so. But on the other, Rebekah had spent years trying to uncover the history with his parents and he'd always regretted the little she could get out of him, because it all sounded so petty when vocalized, and the experience always made him feel lower than whale droppings at the bottom of the ocean, as his own dad used to say.

To avoid having to talk about it, Johnny almost said, *I saw Father Gord today. He's leading them.* But as he reviewed the words in his mind, he realized there was no point in divulging that bit of information, unless it was simply to make himself feel better by sharing the burden with someone else who could understand. But that wasn't enough justification; he'd rather carry the burden on his own, than tell the bishop that his priest was now an emaciated husk of a man in soiled underwear.

Instead, he said, "The demon who brought out my wife?"

There was a pause before the bishop nodded, as if he knew this wasn't really what was on Johnny's mind but was willing to go along with it. Johnny wondered if Bishop Joseph suspected that that there wasn't only one thing, but layers and layers of things, that he was keeping hidden, each for a different reason.

"He said something," Johnny continued.

"What?"

"That I could give myself to them or watch my wife be tortured. He said he was giving me a deal like he'd given my wife a deal."

"He might've been lying," the bishop said. "Or trying to confuse you."

Johnny didn't respond.

"However," the bishop said after a short pause, "I think you're missing an obvious point."

"What's that?"

"There's someone who can tell you what happened to your wife that night."

Johnny almost asked who, but the answer came to him immediately. "She's just a kid," he said, but at the same time he couldn't believe he'd never considered that possibility before.

The bishop seemed to wait for him to make eye contact again. When he did so, Bishop Joseph said, "'Out of the mouth of babes and infants you have perfected praise' our Lord said, when the children in the temple called out to him as Son of David. Children see more, and understand more, than we often give them credit for."

It was true that Izzy had been there, Johnny thought. She might remember enough, and be able to describe enough, for him to know what had happened to his wife that night.

Chapter 17

JOHNNY and the bishop descended the staircase mostly in silence, questions whirring in Johnny's mind. What would Izzy say? What did she remember? How could he talk to her about it without making her relive the trauma of that night?

Those thoughts were brought to an abrupt stop when the bishop opened the door and his beam of light flashed on three young pre-teenagers, the eldest holding a ball expectantly.

"What did he say?" Osama said, looking past the bishop at Johnny.

"What did I say about what?"

"The soccer tournament!" Mahmoud said.

The bishop turned around, directed his flashlight at Johnny's face as if Johnny were about to be interrogated.

"You didn't ask him?" The tone of betrayal in Osama's voice would've been comical to Johnny if it wasn't so condemning.

Johnny shielded his eyes from the light. "I meant to, I'm sorry. Bishop Joseph, would it be all right if we held a soccer tournament in the basement, perhaps tomorrow after breakfast?"

"Ah, a soccer tournament," the bishop said, turning off his flash-light. He kneeled down with some effort to face the children. "Are you good at soccer?"

"I'm the best of us," Osama said, matter-of-factly. "But Mahmoud and Ahmed are good too."

His brothers nodded in agreement.

"So it'll be a good game, then?"

The boys exploded with loud and repeated promises, assurances, and commitments. All the while they gesticulated with so much excitement that it looked like they might spin themselves up and hover right off the ground.

"Okay, I believe you!" Bishop Joseph yelled over their voices. When they quieted down, he said, "It's all right with me. But we have to check with Miles, okay?"

Miles was never a difficult person to find; if his large frame, both height and width, or his bald head didn't give him away, Johnny only had to listen for a moment to identify the direction of the one-man mirthful clamor. This time, however, Johnny couldn't spot him or hear his loud and happy voice directing someone, congratulating someone else, recounting a story, or laughing with his whole, substantive belly.

"I'll go find him right now," Johnny said. Almost all of the tables had been put away. On the few that remained, mostly near the outside walls, people were playing cards or board games. Others had set themselves up on chairs, reading silently or out loud to a small group in quiet tones. It seemed everyone was making use of the last few hours of daylight. At the end of the basement near the bookstore he spotted Liz sitting on the floor, his daughter curled up on her lap, a large book open before them. He tried to catch Izzy's attention to wave at her, but she was too engrossed in the story. She sat listening to Liz's voice and tracing out the pictures with her fingers. Seeing them together, it occurred to him that there lay the solution to his dilemma.

As for Miles, he was nowhere to be seen. Johnny turned toward the kitchen, and saw a small light emanating from the back.

The boys were following him.

"I can manage without an escort, guys."

"We'll just go with you," Ahmed said.

The suspicion with which the boys regarded him made Johnny smile in spite of himself. He missed the days when something like a soccer game was the most important thing in the world, and everything would be all right if adults could just manage to get their priorities straight.

"Go find a quiet corner and do some drills," he said, not unkindly. "Bounce the ball off your knees or something."

The two younger boys watched the eldest, who in turn scrutinized Johnny. "Make sure you tell him we're not going to make a mess or anything," Osama said, finally. "And that it'll be really fun, and he can be referee or whatever he wants."

"I'll do that."

Miles was in the kitchen, half-sitting on a stool, hunched over the long table that ran along the back wall, and scratching with a pen on a pad of paper.

"Is this a bad time?" Johnny said.

The smile dropped from Miles's face when he saw Johnny, a reaction so unexpected that it took Johnny aback and his own polite smile faded away as well. Miles scrambled to get off the stool, approached Johnny with some definite intent in mind, then seemed to lose his nerve and stopped just short of him.

"Yes," he said. "I mean, no, it's a fine time. A fine time for you. Any time, really. Whatever you need." He looked over his shoulder, his hands gesturing nervously at the pad of paper. "I was just taking stock, updating our lists, planning out a meal plan for tomorrow. You know how it is. How are you? Everything okay?"

"Everything's fine," Johnny said, speaking slowly. "Everything okay with you?"

After a slight hesitation, Miles pursed his lips and suddenly slapped Johnny on the shoulders with both hands, a precaution Johnny appreciated because otherwise he might have been launched in one direction or the other. "Great!" Miles said. "Just great, really. I wanted to say— thank you very much for the water. Really. We really appreciate it. Steven brought it down and—well, I just had to say thank you."

Miles's hands were still on Johnny's shoulders, and his big eyes were staring into Johnny's very earnestly. "Uh," Johnny began. "No problem. I know it's not a lot—"

"Nonsense! Please, I won't hear any more of that kind of talk. It's wonderful, don't think otherwise for a single minute. Really wonderful, I can't even begin to tell you." With a final squeeze, Miles let Johnny go. "But you came to see me and I've monopolized the conversation. How can I help you?"

Johnny explained what they were thinking of doing, told him the bishop was supportive if Miles was, then started to explain how it would be good for the morale of the kids and also of everyone else, but Miles cut him off.

"It's done!" Miles said. "Wonderful idea. I agree—fun and exercise for the kids and all that, and a good show for everyone else. I really approve of exercise, you know, though I don't like it myself, as you can see." Miles tapped the sides of his belly and chortled, then went on, "I'll take care of everything. We'll have it all set up after breakfast tomorrow. Oh! Maybe we'll even have a picnic lunch for the people watching, wraps or something like that. I'll have to reorder the menu, but it won't be a problem. Don't give it another thought."

"Wow, great. Thank you." He was so overwhelmed by Miles's helpfulness, and by the inexplicable sense of gratitude or awe that seemed to emanate from him, that he was thrown off enough to speak out loud the thought that had popped into his head. "Let's just hope we don't get attacked before then."

He regretted the words immediately, but Miles only cocked his head to one side and said, "Yes, of course we'll pray that doesn't happen. But you're not worried, are you? Of all the people here...."

Johnny had no idea what Miles was hinting at.

Miles took a step closer, managed to actually lower his voice to a real whisper. "It's okay," he said. "Steven told me."

"Told you what?"

"He swore me to secrecy, don't worry. I'm not to tell anyone—especially his wife—but certainly the secrecy doesn't extend to you!"

"What exactly did he tell you?"

"Come now! He told me what you did for him—the whole thing, everything. It's really amazing, I never would've believed it was possible. But Steven wouldn't lie, he'd have no reason to; and if he wanted to, why tell a lie that makes him look bad? No, I believe him and it fills me with a kind of hope I never thought I'd feel until I saw the Lord Himself riding on the clouds of heaven."

"Miles, calm down." Johnny had never heard anyone before manage to express so much excitement in a soft, contained whisper. "What is it exactly Steven told you I did for him?"

"You healed him. He told me all about it. You cast out demons from him."

"No, that isn't exactly—"

"I get it, humility and all that. And it wasn't your power, of course I know that too; it was the power of God working through you. But there's the point, isn't it? He did work through you. You brought back one of ours, one who'd been captured." Miles waved his arms in a general direction. "Maybe you can do it for the others. Those out there, the ones we lost. Maybe you can help them too. Maybe that's your role in all of this—and what better, what more glorious role could you ever ask for?"

"You're getting carried away," Johnny said, but felt that all of his warnings and hesitation would fall on deaf ears, Miles discounting them as sincere or feigned humility as soon as they were spoken. The thought frustrated him, and pushed him into trying to deflate Miles's enthusiasm. "Did Steven also tell you that I killed someone by smashing their body with my car? That I also killed a little girl by trying to cast out demons from her?"

"No, but—"

"Stop. Don't do that. Don't dismiss the death of two human beings because you're holding out for some sense of hope." He tried to soften a tone that had somehow grown harsher than he'd intended it. "And don't pin those hopes on me, Miles. It's too much pressure. I'll fail you."

Miles spread his arms apologetically. The sad, forced smile betrayed his thoughts as much as his sudden, unnatural silence.

"I'm not trying to hurt you—" Johnny began.

"I know." He spoke at a normal volume now, and even at what might be considered a normal pace for someone else; in his mouth, it sounded like he was measuring out each word before speaking it. "Our hope is in Christ, of course. But God works with and through and in people, doesn't He? It's about synergy; cooperation. That's how He's always worked, from the beginning, and even when He became incarnate, and even to the present day."

They both turned at a noise from behind them; Steven stood outside the open door. "Sorry to interrupt," he said. "Theresa thinks we should wash the linens in the sink; she says they're getting—well, spicy is how she put it."

The transformation Miles underwent was a sight to behold; in one breath, he thanked and gently excused himself from Johnny, as if their conversation had been about nothing more than the supply of drinkable water; in the next, moving past Johnny and out into the basement, he told Steven that they could start the very next morning, but only do one or two a day to make sure they had enough dry linen to go around that night. As they walked away, presumably to discuss the plans with Theresa, Miles simultaneously thanked Steven, congratulated him for his wife's thoughtfulness and care, and expressed his hope and desire for more rain soon to replenish their barrels.

Johnny left the kitchen and heard a familiar, excited, loud voice call out his name. Half-embarrassed, he waved at Izzy, who was waving excitedly at him, then held up a finger to ask her to wait a minute.

The boys were with their grandparents, and they watched him in silent, almost stoic resolve as he approached. He toyed with the idea of pretending that Miles had refused, but their faces were set with such stone-like stillness, perhaps because they'd become accustomed to disappointment lately and had prepared or even resigned themselves for more of it, that he couldn't bring himself to lie to them.

"It's all good, guys," he said. "We'll have a tournament before lunch tomorrow, God willing."

If he'd been embarrassed by his daughter crying out his name, he was much more so by the sudden rush of the boys, whose excitement propelled them into his waist in a group hug that almost brought him to the ground.

When he managed to extricate himself, and assure them that a thousand thank-yous was more than enough, he made his way toward the bookstore.

"Daddy, do you want to hear a story? Liz is a good reader."

"That's good," Johnny said, dropping to his knees to kiss Izzy's forehead. "I'd like to listen to the story later. For right now, can I steal Liz from you for a second?"

"No, Daddy. We're still reading the story."

That's quite the attitude on you, he thought. The judgmental look on the small face—eyebrows pulled tightly together, cheeks lifted— betrayed her considered opinion that only a callous dimwit would interrupt a story before it was finished. *I hope this isn't a preview of your teenage years.* The dark cloud of their present situation cast its shadow on these thoughts too and he couldn't help but add to himself: *if we live that long.*

He gave her another kiss as he picked her up off of Liz's lap, who looked at him with a bemused expression. He set Izzy and the book she still gripped in her tiny hands down on the floor.

"This is important," he said. "We're only going to be a second, and then we'll come back and finish the story together, okay?"

"We'll have to start over from the beginning."

"That's fine. Just wait right here for us."

Liz followed him to an empty spot near the kitchen.

"Is everything okay?"

"Yes, I'm sorry to pull you away like that. But I wanted to catch you tonight. I'd like you to do me a favor."

"Anything."

"I'd like you to talk to Izzy about her mother." Liz waited expectantly. "The bishop pointed out that Izzy was there the night Rebekah was—taken. She may be able to give us some insight into what happened."

"Oh. I see. Listen, Johnny, I don't think—"

"I'd really appreciate it. This won't be easy for her—and I have this terrible fear that I'm going to make it much worse, either by saying the wrong thing or not being able to control my own expressions or emotions. I just can't see myself talking to her about it. She likes you; she trusts you."

The struggle in Liz's mind was apparent on her face: her gaze fixed on the ground and not meeting his own, her eyebrows drawn together, her jaw clenched. She hated to refuse him, he saw, but she didn't feel comfortable acquiescing to his request either.

"Please?" he said.

After another short pause, she nodded. "I don't like it," she said. "But if it's what you want—okay."

He thanked her and watched her walk back to his daughter as a sense of relief swept through him. In that moment, however, he saw as if in a flash of insight that he was being a coward, that he was placing his own daughter in the hands of another person because he was too weak to talk to her himself. He knew, with the kind of honesty reserved for oneself and for God, that his reluctance came from a cowardly fear, and from his own lack of patience, and from his deficiency of the compassion necessary to talk to his daughter about her mother. The man who the bishop thought could lead this community in his absence—the man who Miles thought could stand up to the demons surrounding their church—was a man seemingly unable to speak to his little girl.

My weakness leaves room for Your strength, he thought, and then prayed that God would be with him, would make up the reserve of his patience and compassion, would enable him to find out what he wanted to know from Izzy while allowing her the chance to share her burden and tell him things she might have been holding back for fear of hurting him.

Liz had seated herself beside Izzy on the ground. They were reading the story again. Johnny sat down on the other side of his daughter, and listened to Liz as she read through the rest of the book.

When they were done, Izzy flipped back to the first page and said that they had to start over once more, because Johnny had only heard the ending.

"Are you kidding?" Johnny said. "Do you know how many times I've read that book? I could recite it to you from memory. Let's see—there's a girl who has these magic kisses, and she kisses a frog, which is kind of gross if you ask me, but she seems okay with it; and suddenly the frog turns into a pony!"

Izzy giggled. "He turns into a prince, Daddy."

"Oh—I must have read a different version," he said, taking the book from her and closing it. He picked Izzy up and placed her on his lap facing him.

"Honey, I'd like to talk to you about something, okay?"

She nodded.

"I'll leave you two alone," Liz said, starting to get up.

"You can stay if you want," Johnny said.

She hesitated for only a moment, then nodded and sat back down.

Johnny held Izzy's tiny hands in his own. "Honey, do you remember the night we came here?" She nodded. "You remember when we were in our house, and the—people came inside?"

"The bad men," she said.

"That's right, the bad men came in. You and your mother went into the bathroom. You waited a while, then you slipped out the window." She'd been nodding all along, though a crease had formed in her forehead. "You went up the street, right, honey?"

"Mommy said to close my eyes."

"I know, honey. That's good. Did you have your eyes closed the whole time?"

She suddenly looked down, as if she'd been caught out. She shook her head slowly.

"Izzy, look at me. It's okay. You didn't do anything wrong. You understand what I'm saying?"

"Mommy kept saying, 'Keep your eyes closed.' I tried, Daddy, but they kept opening all by themselves. Everyone was angry."

"You heard a lot of yelling?"

She nodded.

"Did you hear anything specific?"

She hesitated, seemed not to understand the question, then decided to answer it anyway and shook her head.

"Honey, did mommy talk to anyone?"

"Yeah."

He waited. "Who did she talk to, honey?"

"Lots of people."

"What did she say?"

Izzy put up her hand as if pushing someone away. "'Stay away from us!'"

"Anything else?"

"She kept saying it. There were a lot of people. She turned around and around and said it."

"Did they stay away or come closer?"

"Closer. They were trying to take me away from mommy."

"What happened then?"

"I don't remember, Daddy. I was crying."

"It's okay, honey. You're very brave and smart. You're doing a great job. What's the next thing you remember?"

"They weren't angry anymore."

"They stopped yelling?"

She nodded.

"Was mommy talking to someone?"

"He wasn't wearing any clothes."

"What did she say?"

"I don't know, Daddy."

"You don't remember?"

She shook her head. "I didn't understand."

"Did the man say anything back to her?"

She scrunched up her nose at the memory. "His breath was stinky."

"Okay, honey, but what did he say?"

"He said, 'It's a deal.'"

Johnny exchanged looks with Liz, who was staring at Izzy and listening very attentively.

"What happened after that, honey?"

"Mommy made me promise."

"Promise what?"

Izzy looked up at the ceiling as if the words were written on its tiles. "I couldn't be scared. I couldn't cry. I had to close my eyes and not saying anything until I saw you. Oh, and I had to be patient." She sounded out the last word.

He teased out more information from her. Rebekah had set Izzy down on the ground and told her that the men were not going to hurt her or even touch her; that she was going to bring Izzy to Johnny; that Rebekah would have to go to the hospital but that if Izzy was patient, her dad would come and get Rebekah when she was feeling better. That Izzy had to close her eyes and bury her head in her mother's chest and not look up, no matter what. That once she was sure Izzy understood all of that, Rebekah kissed her, then scooped her up in her arms, holding her tightly, then told the bad men that she was ready. Although Izzy couldn't really articulate what happened next, and her energy for this conversation seemed to be running out so that Johnny didn't feel like pushing her any further, he thought he could fill in the gaps himself: whether because Rebekah was stronger than they expected her to be once they possessed her, or because the demons concocted a plan to use her and Izzy as bait to pull the bishop out of the church—most likely a combination of the two, Johnny figured—she was able to hold them to the deal they'd made; she brought Izzy safely to the church and to Johnny.

That night, tucked into the bed Miles once again insisted he take, his daughter lying asleep against his chest, Johnny lay awake. An unnatural stillness pervaded the basement; those outside were so silent one might think they'd lost interest and left (but Johnny didn't dare allow himself to think that). Those inside were just as quiet. In that silence and stillness, Johnny thought and prayed.

Izzy's story had had a profound effect on him. As much as he loved his wife and would've gladly sacrificed his life for hers, he'd also judged her for falling under the influence of the demons. *Judge not*, Christ said; and yet it was so easy, even knowing the kind of person Rebekah was, to try to blunt the stabbing pain of her loss by placing the blame, at least partly, at her feet. *Lest you be judged.* For even in the very act of judgment one judges oneself. *Let he among you who is without sin*, Christ said another time, *cast the first stone.*

At least it never occurred to Johnny to cast stones at God, to put Him in the dock and cross-examine Him about why He'd allowed Johnny's wife to be taken. Or, perhaps less selfishly, to put Him under arrest and make Him account for why He had allowed the demons to destroy countless human lives and almost all of human civilization. Why had God allowed any evil, ever? Why for His own name's sake had He allowed people to be exiled, abandoned by friends and family, mutilated and tortured, and even executed or murdered?

It *had* always occurred to him as odd that some Christians lost their faith when bad things happened to them. Didn't they know that Christ Himself had promised them all sorts of pain and trouble, especially if they chose to follow Him? That Christ Himself had suffered all sorts of pain and trouble?

But not for no reason. Evil ruled the present age, but God had from the beginning been wresting control back, searching almost desperately for fellow workers through whom He could accomplish His aims.

Lord, make me an instrument of Your peace, he said, using the words of Saint Francis.

Maybe Miles was right; maybe Miles was wrong. Johnny had no way of knowing if God really wanted to use him. But he knew that

Rebekah was out there, and that she needed him. And he knew that he would do everything in his power to help her. Even if it meant badgering God incessantly into allowing him to help her, like the man in Christ's parable who in the middle of the night banged on the door of his friend's house until he got what he wanted.

Redeem the times, he thought to himself, *for the days are evil.* And it was St. Paul too who said: *Do not be overcome by evil, but overcome evil with good.*

Overcome evil—that was the call for all Christians. Not just resist or withstand evil, but overcome it. And don't overcome it with more evil, as others might do; overcome it with good, as Christ did.

Lord, teach me Your statutes, he prayed. *Strengthen me and Bishop Joseph and all those who are willing to serve You with fear and love. If it is Your will, accept us as Your fellow workers. Fill us with Your Holy Spirit; help us to help those who have fallen under the influence of the evil ones.*

Stay strong, honey, he thought as simultaneously he prayed to God that somehow Rebekah could hear his words or at least know that he was thinking of her. *I'm coming for you.*

Chapter 18

HIS eyes open slowly to the sound of laughter. Sunlight streams in, the rays curving over and around the edges of the drawn curtain to fill up the room with a golden haze. The sound of chirping, excited birds is overshadowed by that of trilling, happy laughter from the basement. He stretches himself across the bed; his wife isn't there. Smiling subconsciously in response to the laughter, he gets out of bed, walks out of the room, through the hall toward the basement, and down the stairs.

Liz and Izzy are playing on the foam blocks mattress they'd gotten Izzy a few months after she was born.

Is Liz my wife? he wonders distractedly.

She turns to smile at him. "Uh oh," she says, scrunching her nose and shoving it into Izzy's face conspiratorially. "We woke up daddy."

"Uh oh," Izzy repeats.

There was a question on his mind, but he can't remember what it was. "Who's winning?" he says.

"Boys!" Liz says, speaking confidentially to Izzy again as if Johnny can't hear them. "Always thinking about winning. Can you please tell him that there's no winning in a tickle fight?"

Izzy turns and looks up at him with a very serious face. "It's a tickle fight, Daddy," she says, as if explaining the laws of nature to him. "There's no winning, just fun."

"Oh, okay," he says, approaching nonchalantly. His plan is to descend on them both and tickle them into submission, but before he can take another step, he hears a familiar, terrible sound. "What was that?"

"What was what, honey?"

"You didn't hear it?" he says. He walks quickly to the window, cranes his head up, but can't see anything. He hears it again: a wailing sound, a mournful sound. Somehow he feels it's directed at

173

him; somehow there is an important, personal message in that horrible sound. Where has he heard it before?

Liz has stood and come over to place a hand on his back. "Are you okay?" she whispers. "You're scaring Izzy."

"You don't hear it?" he says.

She shakes her head, then makes a cooing sound at the perplexed look on his face. She reaches her arms over his shoulders; he reflexively pulls her into a hug, but pulls away again almost immediately.

"I don't hear anything, honey," she says in response to his searching gaze.

Something's wrong. He can hear it clearly now, a loud, sad, terrible cry for help. Someone is calling for him, someone in a great deal of pain and trouble.

"Honey, what's going on? Talk to me."

He ignores her, races across the basement and up the stairs, and out the front door, almost launching himself off the steps. But he stops short at the sight before him: a mass of bloodied zombies fill his driveway, spilling out onto the street as far as he can see. He turns around quickly, but more zombies are at his back, filling up the entrance to his house. They begin to laugh at him—a humorless, angry, derisive sound—but cutting through it all, he still hears the wailing that has called him out of his home.

The zombies in his driveway part, and in the middle he sees a woman, disheveled hair dangling over a bent head whose gaze is cast to the ground. He knows her. The familiar, terrible wailing is coming from her, though her body seems unmoving.

"Rebekah?" he says.

She looks up; flesh is missing from her face, as if someone has taken a bite out of her cheek. One eye is bruised and swollen shut; the other is bloodshot. She stares at him, sightlessly he feels. She opens her mouth, but he can't hear what she's saying above the sound of the laughing, teasing zombies. Teeth are missing from her bloodied mouth, out of which more blood pours out as she speaks. Her voice is too weak. He hears the wailing sound still; he hears it even as she's trying to say something else to him, as if the mournful cry is coming from her and not from her at the same time. He doesn't understand.

He descends the stairs. The zombies, snarling and laughing, give way before him. He approaches his wife; her mouth is still open and moving, but he hears nothing above the derisive laughter except the sound he wishes he couldn't hear: the wavelike, pathetic wailing, as of a dog dying from its wounds.

"I'm sorry," he says. "I can't hear you over all of this!"

He gets angrier with every word, and by the end he is so furious that he turns on the zombies and yells at them to shut up, screaming until his voice is hoarse.

In the stark stillness that follows his outburst, he hears from behind him a small voice, so faint that it's barely recognizable as his wife's.

"Please help me." The words are soft, sad, and weak; she has whispered them into his ear, or he might never have heard her.

He turns around, but there is no one there. His wife is gone, and so are the zombies; he stands alone in his driveway.

"Rebekah?" he calls out.

From far away he hears the response, the wailing sound that has become the background noise of his universe. It is coming from no direction in particular, or from all directions. It is a pathetic call for help. But not insistent, as if Rebekah knows hers is a plea he can't possibly answer.

JOHNNY'S eyes opened slowly, but the sound of the wailing, the sound that had penetrated his dream, made him sit up quickly. Rebekah was back.

Careful not to disturb Izzy, he slipped out of the cot. In the dim moonlight seeping in through the windows, he saw the bishop sitting at the table near the kitchen, Liz beside him, both in the same posture as the first night he'd met them, as if every night they sat like this for a slow-working artist to complete their portrait.

The sound of Rebekah's wailing urged him toward the staircase. He resisted it, though; the bishop was looking at him with mild curiosity, Liz with a hint of concern. Neither seemed to be aware of the sound he could even now still hear. Was it a figment of his imagination again? Maybe he could convince himself that the bishop's hearing was weakened by age, but what about Liz's? A bubbling feeling of panic tried to propel him upstairs and through the doors, to help his wife as she'd begged him to do with heart-breaking despair in his dream.

Trying to stay calm, he forced himself to walk toward the kitchen instead, the worried lines on Liz's face deepening the longer she studied his own features and the clearer they became as the distance between them collapsed.

"Master, bless," he said.

The bishop asked the Lord to bless him, but waved away Johnny's attempt to kiss his hand. "What's wrong, John?" he said, keeping his voice low to not disturb the others.

"You don't hear that," Johnny said, looking from one to the other, the question sounding more like a statement. "You don't hear it?"

It seemed to him that Liz was not used to speaking first in the bishop's company, or perhaps even speaking at all unless directly addressed. But her concern for him seemed to overwhelm her piety, and she blurted out, "What do you hear?" before looking slightly embarrassed and apologetically at the bishop.

Not seeming to notice, the bishop waited for Johnny to answer.

"My wife. Calling out, like on that first night."

"Do you still hear her?"

Johnny nodded.

He saw the bishop's hands separate and his right hand move quickly in small motions, and knew the bishop was making the sign of the Cross over him. "It's been quiet, John."

Johnny accepted the words without really believing them. In the next moment, though, he couldn't be sure if he still heard the sound, and a moment after that he was sure that he heard nothing at all coming from outside. Feeling his heart rate return to normal, he asked if he could sit with them. As the bishop nodded, Liz got up and offered him her seat.

"I didn't mean to kick you out," he said, as she spoke over him, "No, it's okay—I sit with the bishop when I can't sleep." She shrugged. "I can't sleep a lot. But I'm going to go try again."

He asked her if she was sure, she told him she was, then placed a hand on his shoulder and gave him a supportive squeeze as she left. A pang of guilt flared up inside of him. Rebekah had sacrificed herself to save their daughter—had done what Johnny would rather die before he could humble himself enough to do—perhaps she was even now undergoing enough humiliation and pain to last a lifetime—and he was dreaming about another woman?

"Do you ever sleep?" Johnny said to the bishop as he sat down, faking an easiness he didn't feel.

"As I get older, I find I'm only able to nap for short stretches of time. Besides, I like being down here when it's quiet and everyone's asleep."

"The shepherd watching over his flock by night."

The bishop smiled. "It strengthens me. It reminds me of what I'm doing when I'm upstairs."

"What are you doing?"

"Praying."

"For their safety?"

The bishop hesitated. "Mostly for their salvation. But also that the cup of suffering may pass from their lips if possible." He reached up and adjusted the toque on his head, pulling it away from his ears slightly. Looking straight ahead still, he continued, "It's very easy for a bishop to think of a church as an ark—a little or big boat trying to survive in the storms of a fallen world. That's a good and helpful image most of the time, but like all things it can be misleading if taken too far. And I took it too far; I now realize I was waiting for a dove to swoop into the church, holding an olive leaf in its beak so I could know it was safe to go outside again."

"But now?"

"As we discussed, if this is the end of the present age, it won't be safe to go outside again—not until we see Christ riding the clouds of heaven with power and glory, and hear the great sound of a trumpet."

"And if it isn't the end?"

"We are still the church militant, and we must still live in the present age. We must try to do good."

"I guess Liz or Miles or someone has been talking to you," Johnny said. "You don't have to convince me. I know, and I agree; I just don't think I'm the one who's supposed to lead these people after—" He allowed the sentence to dangle off, and started over. "I'm more of a loner than a leader."

"I must say, I wouldn't trust anyone who actually wanted the job."

"I don't know that I can stand the pressure of being responsible for all these people," Johnny said.

"We are all already responsible for one another." He paused, looked at Johnny with a sudden flash of a smile. "When I was very young, I once heard someone say that at the beginning of Holy Scripture, Cain says to God, 'Am I my brother's keeper?' and the Almighty, perhaps failing to see that it was intended to be rhetorical, spends thousands of years, and the rest of the Bible, answering that question. Isn't that a neat way of looking at Scripture?"

"But—" Johnny began.

"Yes, it's a greater burden, what I'm asking you to—no, what I believe God has called you to do and to be. But I believe He wouldn't lay it on your shoulders without also giving you the strength to bear it." The bishop placed his hand on Johnny's arm. "For now all I'm asking is that you trust me, that you allow us to do things slowly and prayerfully. The road ahead is fraught with danger, for us, for them"—his gaze swept across the basement—"and even for those outside."

"I know," Johnny said, thinking of the little girl in the middle of the road.

"We'll work together," the bishop said. "We'll strengthen one another. You'll help this old man take more risks—calculated risks!—and I'll restrain your. . ." He seemed to search for words and then settled on ". . . impulsiveness."

"It's a deal," Johnny said.

He stayed up with the bishop for the rest of the night without exchanging another word. Every once in a while, he thought of something he wanted to say, but decided against breaking the silence. In those times he was reminded of something Mother Teresa had said about prayer. Someone asked her what she said to God when she prayed. "I don't say anything," Mother Teresa said, "I just listen." "Then what does God say?" she was asked. "He doesn't say anything," she replied, "He just listens."

It seemed to Johnny, whenever he turned his head to look at the bishop, that he and God were listening quietly to one another, and Johnny didn't want to interrupt. Although his mind wandered throughout the night, roving over thoughts strange and prosaic, revisiting memories of aching beauty and of mundane simplicity, remembering events distant and more recent, he punctuated those moments with prayers of his own. One day he hoped to be silent with God, as the bishop seemed to be, as Mother Teresa had said she was, but for now he prayed with words. Or, to speak more plainly, he petitioned with words. He asked God for His continued protection, asked God that the bishop's trust in Johnny wasn't misplaced, that God would help Johnny control his impulsiveness and not put anyone else in harm's way, as he'd done with Steven. As he'd done with Rebekah, too, because he didn't listen to her when she wanted to go to the church in the first place. Most of all he prayed for Rebekah.

She is my cross, he prayed. *I don't know what you have planned for me, Lord, but allow me to do it with her by my side. Heal her, Father, that she may continue to serve You in this life.*

Every time he said that prayer, however, he couldn't help but add another thought, a thought that recognized God's sovereignty, a thought that recognized God's plan must roll out in His own time and by His good pleasure. *But if that is not Your will, Lord*—he had to practically drag the thought from his own mind each time, for despite a lifetime of acknowledging that God is King, a small part of Johnny still rebelled against the idea, a small part insisted that his own will, not God's, must be done. He forced the thought to completion each time: *allow her to die well: painless, blameless, peaceful. And grant her a good defense before Your dread judgment seat. For You work all things for the good of those who love You.*

By the time Johnny became aware of his surroundings again, the sun had risen, natural light was filling the basement, and the sleepers were starting to stir in their cots.

"Come with me upstairs," the bishop said, using the arms of his chair to help him stand up. "Let us complete our morning prayers."

"I'll catch up with you," Johnny said. He went back to his own cot and woke Izzy up with a kiss on her forehead and a light touch on her arm.

She stirred, turning over on her back, and opened her eyes lazily. *They look so much like her mother's*, he thought; *a pair of bright emeralds set in pearls of clear white.*

"How did you sleep, munchkin?" he said.

"I had a bad dream." Her eyes, so wide and expressive usually, seemed to be seeing the visions from the night before even now.

"I'm sorry to hear that, honey." He patted down her hair on her head. "What happened in the dream?"

"I died."

The words made his body turn cold, but immediately he began to protest to her that it was only a nightmare.

She cut him off, with childish exasperation that he hadn't heard the full story. "You and mommy were happy."

He had the sense that she was annoyed he'd tried to insist it was just a nightmare, as if that negated the happy promise that her mom would be reunited with her dad, even if it meant that she herself would be dead.

"That's not going to happen," he said, then lowered his tone when he saw others around them turn to look at him. "Izzy, your mommy and daddy love you very much, and we're not going to let anyone hurt you, okay?"

"Mommy wasn't sick anymore," Izzy said.

"Mommy's going to be fine," Johnny said, though of course he had no way of knowing that was true. He kept going, however, needing to say the words perhaps even more than Izzy needed to hear them: "Mommy's going to be okay and we're all going to be together again. Everything's going to be fine, honey."

Again the words weren't true, not technically, not in the way Izzy could possibly understand them. Even if Rebekah were healed, even if the three of them were reunited—which was his greatest hope—even still the world was ending and things wouldn't be fine ever again, not until Christ came in glory. If Christians had always been the church militant, in the past they could've ignored the war and enjoyed the peace and joy they'd carved out for themselves away from the battlefield. But the war was now not only at their door, the war had crashed through their door and forced them outside. Now there was nothing but battlefield, so that even this little ark of salvation they'd found was surrounded on all sides by dark forces waiting for the right moment to storm through its doors and take it by force. That wasn't the end of the story, though, but how does one explain the mysteries of God's plan of salvation to a little child, even one as bright and precocious as Izzy? How does one speak to a child of mysteries that have perplexed the minds of saints and overwhelmed the imaginations of almost everyone else?

"Promise?" Izzy said.

Liz saved him from having to respond. He saw her approaching, holding a small white dress with a yellow sash across the middle.

"I found this in one of the suitcases," she said to Johnny. "It's a bit wrinkled, but I wondered if Izzy wanted to have it."

He lifted Izzy up so that she stood on the cot. "What do you think, honey? Want to wear that pretty dress today?"

Izzy was feeling shy, as she sometimes did when she hadn't come fully awake yet. But Johnny knew how to interpret the bashful casting down of her head and the slight raising of her eyes to look up at him.

"It's great," Johnny said to Liz. "Can you help her change into it and keep an eye on her for a little while? I need to go upstairs to—"

She waved off his explanation as unnecessary. "I'd love to. Come on, darling." She reached across Johnny to pick her up, her side brushing against his arm accidentally before he pulled it away quickly. Liz didn't seem to notice. "There's lots more dresses in the suitcases," she said. "Maybe we can pick out a few you like?"

"Be good," Johnny called out after them, although he felt the words properly applied to him more than to his daughter or even to Liz. As he folded up the bed sheet, he tried to dismiss the guilt he felt, perhaps caused by the dream he'd had of his happy family, except it wasn't his family. Rebekah was his wife, not Liz.

Yes, but Rebekah's a zombie. The thought popped into his head unbidden; he tried to push it away. *Rebekah's a zombie. Liz isn't.*

The more he fought against that line of thinking, the greater the intensity with which it forced itself on his consciousness. Lost in those thoughts, mechanically he carried the folded linens with the pillows on top to the storeroom.

How do you think this is going to end? he asked himself. *Rebekah is in the hands of the demons. They won't give her up easily. Most likely, she's dead or will be dead soon. Most likely, you'll be dead too, but if you survive, you'll need to carry on with your life. You'll need to think about Izzy.*

Rebekah's alive, he yelled back in his mind, feeling like a man split in two and having an argument, like a madman, with himself. *That's the only thing I care about—she's alive, and she needs my help.*

And even if you're able to cure her, what then? She's been possessed for three nights and two days. Who knows the things she's done—the things she's been made to do? Who knows if she's done irreparable harm to her body?

He folded the cot, picked it up and made his way to the back again, his guilty or broken heart sending flashing images of Rebekah to play in his mind. Rebekah throwing her head back and laughing; scrunching up her nose at something odd or weird he'd said; *arching* her neck so he could kiss it when he swept her hair away gently. But the divided part of him countered with its own images: Rebekah pushing him to the ground; growling at him; trying to kill him.

In the dark staircase, he was startled out of his thoughts by a tall and dark shadow.

"Who's there!" he barked.

"Johnny—it's me, Michael."

"I'm coming," Johnny said, with a bit of annoyance.

Michael laughed and squeezed past him. "Good for you," he said. "But I was going down to tell Miles that the bishop would like to have matins service before breakfast."

It was only when he finally made it upstairs that Johnny's mind, spun up by the scare he'd had in the staircase or by the escalating civil war in his heart, quieted down. The bishop was at the front, but Johnny sat in the very back pew, even when Michael returned and told him that if everyone showed up for service, which wasn't likely, there'd still be plenty of space for him to sit at the front. It was only when Liz and Izzy came into the church, and his daughter insisted they move forward, that he reluctantly got up and followed them.

Until that time, though, Johnny sat quietly at the back and looked around the church. The cloud of witnesses, St. Paul had called them. People who had suffered great things—ridicules, exiles, beatings, tortures, violent deaths. And as his gaze swept toward the front, toward the iconostasis, it seemed the suffering increased: St. John the Baptist, imprisoned and beheaded; Mary, the Mother of God, through whose soul a sword had pierced; Jesus Himself, the Son of God, who was rejected by those He wished to redeem, sentenced to death by those He came to save, nailed to a cross like a criminal by those creatures He had made with His own hands.

Pain, suffering, and death were not alien to God's people; and the amazing truth with Christ is that pain, suffering, and death were now not alien to God Himself. Johnny felt His presence very distinctly as he sat in that back pew. Whatever else was true, it was true that God was there. Whatever Johnny went through, he knew, God would accompany him through it all. They didn't have to part ways at that moment when Johnny needed Him most, because He too had suffered; He too had prayed to the Father; He too had felt abandoned; He too had known there was only one way forward, and it was right *through* suffering and out the other side.

As he moved up to the very front pew because that's where Izzy wanted to sit, he forced himself to stop the gentle whir of those thoughts. Instead, he listened carefully to every word the bishop spoke with a strong and steady voice; and allowed himself to ride the waves, as if with his heart, of the subdeacon's chanting.

From the moment he'd entered the church that morning and throughout the matins service, Johnny felt a sense of deep peace, the like of which he hadn't experienced since the night he'd realized things had gotten really bad and decided that he and his family would lock themselves up in their house and ride it out. Actually, if he was being honest with himself, it was a stranger, more unique sensation than that. It was a quietness of mind and stillness of spirit that, perhaps, he'd never really felt before in his entire life.

He recognized it as a gift from God, and was grateful, and thanked

God for it. But he had the equally strong conviction that this was a moment of peace granted to him before a terrible battle; a period of rest before a grueling race; a temporary stop at an oasis on a hard journey, but a journey that would have to continue sooner than later. This very welcome period of peace and stillness, he felt, was an opportunity to restore his mind and spirit and prepare himself for a great and difficult trial ahead.

Chapter 19

THE feeling of peace didn't survive that morning's breakfast.

The children's excitement was infectious as they talked about the soccer game, but it also rekindled in Johnny the fear that this was the moment the demons would choose to attack—to maximize their efforts by spoiling a joyous occasion, or because they couldn't bear all that cheerfulness.

Osama, Ahmed, and Mahmoud were so animated that they hardly touched their food; they negotiated teams among themselves, trading players with as much seriousness as the most dedicated general managers of the most professional teams of a bygone era. The seriousness never got nasty, though, and the brothers seemed to be getting along better than he'd ever seen them, which was why, he supposed, Fatima didn't yell at them to stop talking and start eating.

Izzy listened to the boys talk with rapt attention. Liz glanced over at him more than once with a bemused but also genuinely pleased look—even a grateful look. Uncomfortable, he shifted his gaze away from her and to Wassim. The old man seemed to be surveying him with a curious if not calculating look. It wasn't any more comfortable than Liz's.

Johnny returned his attention to the boys. "And what about me?"

Osama looked up, as if startled that their negotiations were being interrupted by an outsider.

"Which team am I on?"

Osama shrugged. "We're just splitting up the kids. But if you want to play, you can be goalie." He turned to Liz. "You too."

The interruption was perhaps the opportunity Fatima had been waiting for. "All right, that's enough talking," she said. "Eat your eggs or there won't be a game at all."

They wolfed down their food, then helped clean up their own and other tables with so much enthusiasm that Johnny wondered if they shouldn't hold a game every day after breakfast.

185

He mentioned the idea to Liz, who laughed. Then he shared his suspicion with her that they were being asked to play goalie because the kids didn't feel that adults could keep up with them. She thought he was probably right, but felt that it was for the best.

There wasn't much to transforming the basement into a soccer field. Chairs for the spectators were placed in two lines just outside the long edges of the rectangle formed by the columns, with each pair of columns forming natural goalposts. Along the southern line of chairs, a gap was allowed for a small table and two chairs for Fatima and Izzy. Izzy was so excited that she stood on top of her chair, and glanced repeatedly at Johnny with a goofy, mirthful smile.

Miles directed the setting-up with incredible efficiency. Then, while those who wanted to spectate took their seats, he brought the players and Wassim off to the half-moon alcove in the eastern side of the basement, to split them up into teams and make sure they all understood the rules. He handed Wassim a referee's shirt he'd found somewhere, a golf shirt striped in black and white. Johnny would've put money down on Wassim never wearing something like that, but he would've lost the bet: Wassim immediately took off his brown cotton sweater, tossed it to the side, and pulled the referee's shirt over his head with a joy he didn't try to mask.

Miles returned to the field and announced the start of the game. He called out the names of the two team captains, Osama and Ahmed, to applause and hurrahs from the audience. Then he called out the other players, and Johnny was impressed that he knew each of them by name. Johnny and Theresa were next announced as the goalies for the first team, followed by Liz and Isaac for the second. Somehow the audience had naturally divided itself by this point so that it seemed the eastern side was cheering for his team and the western side for Liz's.

Finally Miles called out Wassim's name, who walked through the midst of players proudly but with a reserved dignity commensurate with his position.

So much laughter, happiness, and merriment filled the basement, and his own spirit was so lifted, that Johnny forgot all about his fear of the demons choosing this moment to interrupt, this period of joy to snatch away; forgot that fear to such an extent that when dark shadows began to play across the basement walls, for an instant he had no idea what they meant. He looked up at the windows with mild curiosity.

Silent and still, the bodies of the possessed surrounded the church.

Anger and resentment began to flare up within Johnny, but was checked by the reaction from those around him. Rather, the lack of a reaction. No panic, which perhaps he could explain by the fact that the possessed weren't kicking the windows and banging on the doors of the church, or raising up their voices in angry shrieks, as they had the previous time. But he sensed no fear from these people either, as he scanned their faces and saw an unnatural number looking back at him. Osama and Ahmed and some of the other kids looked annoyed that the game couldn't start yet; some of the adults looked apprehensive. But none of the faces expressed fear—in fact, many expressed hope and expectation.

With a shock, he realized why: they waited for him to do something about this. They weren't afraid of what the dark shadows meant because they were putting their trust in him.

The bishop had risen to his feet and, Johnny could tell from the focused but distant look in his eyes and his crinkled brow, he was praying with great fervor.

Before Johnny could do or say anything, he heard a voice. A familiar one, the voice of the old man who'd stood half-naked in soiled underwear outside his house, the voice of Father Gord.

"This is your last chance," he said; it sounded like a whisper at his ear, so much so that Johnny turned around quickly, causing those who were looking at him to raise their eyebrows. "This is what happens if you don't come outside immediately: we invade your church, destroy your altar, kill all of those within. All of them die. Your daughter dies. But only give yourself to us and they will be saved; and we will release your wife."

The voice kept speaking, entreating and threatening Johnny. Like a drowning man reaching for a lifeline, he whispered the Jesus prayer to himself repeatedly and, slowly, the voice quieted down.

Michael and Miles had been speaking with the bishop, and it seemed that they now reached the end of their quick huddle of a conversation. Bishop Joseph pushed his chair aside and headed for the staircase; Michael walked over to Liz and Isaac and whispered to them in turn. Then Michael met Johnny's gaze and indicated with a flick of his head that he should follow as well.

Miles returned to the middle of their makeshift soccer field and said, in a voice shaken but determined, that they would go ahead and play their game—and made a joke about simply having a few more spectators than expected. The joke elicited a few nervous laughs.

Johnny glanced over at Izzy, shot her a reassuring smile, then a grateful nod to Fatima, who nodded back. He walked toward the staircase.

Miles was gathering the players, many of whom had run off to their parents or guardians when the darkness descended.

As he moved past Wassim, Johnny felt the old man's hand descend on him and pull him close with surprising strength.

"You're Mr. Big Shot, yes?" Wassim said, the gleefulness replaced by the more familiar sternness and surliness. "Everybody is thinking you have great power. Everybody is hearing of things you do, things you are capable to do. Everybody is believing that you and your God will protect us. But I remember something everybody forget; I remember that this place was safe before you; I remember that those things outside never bother us until you come."

He finally relaxed the vice-like grip and Johnny continued on his way, without a single word, without a glance at Wassim, as if the interruption had never happened. He wanted to catch up to Bishop Joseph, but most of all he didn't trust himself to respond.

The narthex was lit by candlelight. The bishop, Michael, Liz, and Isaac stood talking together. As Johnny opened the stairwell door, all of them turned to look at him.

"They're not trying to get in," Michael said, as if bringing Johnny up to speed on the conversation he'd missed. "They're nowhere near the doors, just the windows along the basement it seems."

"They're not trying to get in for now," Johnny said, closing the door gently behind him. "Because they're waiting for me to go outside."

The features on the bishop's face, which had been pulled together with concentration or concern or both, tightened even further. "What makes you say that?"

"They told me. Same deal as before—if I go outside and give myself to them, you'll be safe. And they'll release Rebekah too."

"Come with me," Bishop Joseph said, crossing himself as he stepped into the nave. He led Johnny to the other end of the long church, perhaps trying to put enough distance between them and the others that they could speak in private.

Johnny sat beside him in the front pew.

The bishop seemed to be gathering his words very carefully. When he finally turned to face Johnny, hesitation made his voice sound even softer than usual. "John—the demons will say anything to make you do what they want."

"I know. I don't believe them."

The bishop looked surprised.

"When they first captured her, they kept Rebekah alive as bait; now they need to keep her alive as a bargaining chip. They have no reason to keep me alive, though. Maybe they'll release Rebekah if I give myself over; probably not. Probably they'll just kill me first, then her, then storm this church anyway."

The surprised look on the bishop's face hadn't vanished, but had slowly been morphing into one of confusion. "I hear the words you're saying, and I agree with them. But I don't think you're telling me everything, John. You sound to me like a man who has his mind set on a course of action."

"I still think I need to go outside. Just not to give myself up to them."

"Then why?"

"You said it yourself: we have to fight back. They've grown brave; perhaps because they think we've grown weak. I think it's time to let them know that we're not scared of them; that we're not going to give in; that we'll fight them with every ounce of energy we have. Maybe that will buy us some time, enough to figure out a real plan."

The bishop looked away. He seemed to be considering Johnny's words. But Johnny also sensed that he was looking for a way to turn down Johnny's proposal without discouraging him further.

"You said you'd trust me," Johnny said. *When the Son of Man comes,* he thought but didn't say, *He expects to find you ready. Working, not hiding; watching, not sleeping; praying, not trembling in fear.* And although he recognized that what the bishop had said about him was true—he was too impetuous, too eager to act and to move—it was also true that too much waiting would embolden the demons outside, while eroding their own people's courage. Not to mention his own.

"I don't like it," the bishop said, and seemed to be speaking to himself more than to Johnny. "We have to be so careful, John. This isn't just people's lives at stake—it would be bad enough if it were. This war is not over lives but over souls. Fear can do things to people. It can crush your mind; it can make your faith grow cold; it can make you do things from which your soul may never recover."

"That's why we have to fight back," Johnny said. "Enough hiding. 'The Lord is my light and my salvation; whom shall I fear? The Lord is the strength of my life; of whom shall I be afraid?' Right? So let's show the demons—let's show each other—what true fear is. Let's remind them of the fear of Christ." He paused, took a deep breath. "And if it's our time to die," Johnny continued, "let's die with 'Christ!' on our lips."

"All right," the bishop said, nodding, his eyes never leaving Johnny's. "We'll go outside—but we stay on the staircase, agreed? Baby steps, John, I'm trying to meet you halfway here."

Johnny smiled, then nodded in turn. "We should get going," he said. "I don't know how long their patience will last."

He started to get up, but the bishop reached out and gripped his arm. "I know you've gone through a lot. I pray for you. I pray God will grant you the strength to accomplish what's ahead. But God can't reach heavy hearts, John. I would like to hear what's troubling you if you'll allow me. I believe there's time."

You wouldn't say that if you knew everything weighing down my heart, Johnny thought. And where would he even begin? He hadn't attended confession since his early teenage years. Should he start there, with all the rebellion, anger, and lust that had colored so many of those days? Or with his dad, and the petty anger that had choked his heart to such an extent that nothing could make him forgive or speak to his father again? Or with Rebekah, and the casual, small sins that peppered their marriage, the thousand thoughtless words or acts that failed to honor the woman he'd chosen to grow in eternity with? Or with everything that had happened since the demons invaded the earth in full-force, the bad planning that had endangered his daughter and allowed his wife to be captured? Should he talk about all the people—not zombies, people—he'd killed since then? Or should he talk about Liz, whom he couldn't seem to keep out of his mind?

"I wouldn't know where to start," Johnny finally settled on. "To be honest, I've never been big on confession, probably because I'm too proud to admit my failures and weakness in front of another human being. But I hope one day to be able to tell you things, to confess my sins honestly and openly. I just don't think today is that day."

"As you wish," the bishop said, releasing him.

Together they walked back to the narthex. The others were speaking in low tones, but their conversation died off as they became aware of the bishop's presence.

"John, Michael, and I will go outside," he said. "We will try to send away those who've come to our church with ill intent."

"You're not going without me," Isaac said, then, perhaps suddenly realizing to whom he spoke, he turned the statement into a question by appending "are you?"

Bishop Joseph nodded. "You and Liz will let us out and close the doors behind us. You will open them for us only if we ask you to do so in the name of Christ."

Liz looked at Johnny as if for an explanation of what was happening, then returned her gaze quickly to the bishop. "Your Grace, we will do whatever you ask, you know that. But we don't want to abandon you out there. Where will we be without you? Are you sure about this?"

"I did not mean to scare you," he said, speaking more softly than usual. Johnny had been looking into his eyes, and what he saw there terrified him; the bishop himself seemed scared, or at least apprehensive. Why then was he going through with it? Why not talk Johnny out of it, if he believed it was such a bad idea? "We will stay close to the church, and I believe we will be safe. John is right—the demons are not making any noise right now because they are waiting for him to give himself up to them. Once they become convinced that's not going to happen, who knows what our timidity will inspire them to do? They have already grown bolder than I ever expected.

"Who knows if they won't try to break through the windows or the doors and set foot even in the church itself? Before that happens"—he couldn't help but glance at Johnny—"I have come to believe that we must give them reason to fear this place again, and those within it."

Liz seemed about to say something else, but the bishop held up his hand gently. "We will simply command them in Christ's name to leave this holy place. Then we will return. My previous request to you is just a bit of extra caution; however, it is one I wish you to honor."

Michael had left the narthex the moment the bishop had said what would happen; he now returned with five crosses, which he handed out to everyone.

"O Christ Our God," the bishop said, "cleanse us from every stain. Let those outside find nothing pleasing to themselves in us, but let Your presence in our hearts repulse them."

When he was done praying, the bishop asked Johnny and Michael if they were ready. They both indicated they were. Liz and Isaac stood at each end of the double door. They threw open the latches, but kept the doors closed, looking back at the bishop for the signal.

The three of them were lined up in front of the doors, the bishop in the middle, Michael on his left, Johnny on his right. Johnny could hear nothing outside—or even inside the narthex itself. Shadows cast by the candlelight danced on the walls.

He hadn't been paying attention, but the bishop must have given the nod, because suddenly Liz and Isaac took some steps back, swinging open the doors, flooding the narthex with bright, almost blinding sunlight.

Chapter 20

THE bishop moved forward. Johnny took a deep breath, gripped the cross tighter, and followed him outside. He forced himself to keep walking even as he saw the scene before him, the sea of faces that stared up at them, the bloodied and broken bodies that filled the space in front of and around the church as far as he could see, stretching out to the road and beyond it to the grassy field that led to the river.

Even though just the day before he'd been taken aback by their number around his house, he was still stunned by how many of them were gathered outside the church. How many *zombies* were gathered. Because in sight of them—in sight of this mob of monstrous beings with missing ears and eyes and hair, sometimes with missing limbs or oddly angled ones—in sight of their blank and vacant faces that, he knew, could so quickly become twisted by rage—it was hard to think of them as anything else.

They were pressing in on each other, swaying in place in that slight rocking motion that seemed characteristic of them. And yet, he thought, there they stood on the paved driveway in front of the church, and there they stood on the road. All in plain sight of the crosses, which was so uncharacteristic of them.

They did, however, keep about a foot's radius away from the half-moon steps of the porch, as if afraid to get too close to the church. *For now.* Those at the front seemed to be trying to put even more distance between themselves and the bishop, Michael, and Johnny, perhaps because of the crosses they carried, which Johnny believed he saw some of them glance at uneasily. *For now.*

Because the bishop is right, Johnny thought, *they're growing bolder and bolder, and who knows how bold they'll grow still.* And why not? They were so many, and those within the church so few. How much longer could they hold out, really? Another day? Another year? And what was the point? What was the point of fighting? What was the point of all of this struggle?

Give up! he yelled in his own mind. *There's no winning here. Give up!*

Suddenly he had the strange but very powerful compulsion to toss aside the cross. Instead, and quickly as if sneaking an action under his own watch, he forced himself to bring the cross up to his lips and kiss it.

The sense of despair began to clear, like a retreating fog. The compulsion, this voice yelling at him in his own mind to give up, had quieted instantly.

He looked over at the bishop for instructions or direction. The older man glanced back at him but shook his head slightly. This was Johnny's idea, Bishop Joseph seemed to say, and he would follow his lead. Past the bishop, Johnny saw Michael staring at all of those who stood against them, a stunned if not terrified expression on his face.

Johnny opened his mouth, but before he could say anything, he heard the familiar, hoarse voice. He looked quickly to his left and could tell that the bishop and Michael heard it too, though the old man—he couldn't think of him as Father Gord—was nowhere to be seen.

"This is your last chance," the old man said. "Choose to be selfish, and those with you will die. Your bishop will die. Subdeacon Michael will die. Liz, whom you lust after; she will die. Your daughter. All of the children hiding now in the basement, and all of those with them.

"Or choose to give yourself up for them, as Jesus Christ gave Himself up. Choose to imitate Him and they will live."

Johnny couldn't help but laugh out loud. "You invoke the Name of Jesus Christ, you who should fear that Name above all others?" Even as he said it, he saw the zombies at the front try to squirm further away. "And do you even know what you're saying? Christ gave Himself up that we might have eternal life, not that our days in this world would be long and prosperous. Christ withstood you and suffered, and our glory is to suffer with Him.

"Don't you understand?" he said, stepping forward and holding up the cross subconsciously. The front line of zombies couldn't stand it anymore; some squeezed their way backwards and others literally tripped over and fell to the ground.

"Careful, John," the bishop said.

Johnny didn't know what he had to be careful about and, carried away with his own sense of contempt for the demons and their pathetic temptations, he moved forward and raised his voice even louder, his tone steeped in ridicule. "Do you really not understand? Your time is almost up. That's not a guess; it's a fact. You know it. Christ will appear in glory, and when He does, we mere human beings will judge you for everything you've done to us."

The zombies had begun to yell at him, cursing him and cursing God and trying to drown out his voice with their own cries. It only served to embolden Johnny.

"We who love God will live in eternal bliss with Him; you who hate Him will suffer in agony from His presence forever. You expect us to fear you? Why? You've already lost the battle. You tell us to give up. That the struggle is useless? Say it to yourselves!"

"We have heard that Christ is coming for a long time now," the old man said. "Maybe it's so. But right now, where is He? It's just you and us. You speak of our eternal suffering. But right now, right here, in this moment and in this place, I have the power to pierce your heart with suffering."

The crowd of zombies in front of them began to split in two. For a moment, Johnny expected them to reveal the source of the voice, the half-naked old man at their center, and wondered how the bishop and Michael might react to seeing Father Gord standing there, if they recognized him. But after that initial reaction, he could've guessed what they wanted to show him even if he hadn't heard the yell for help that pierced through the air and into his heart. Another moment and enough of the zombies had cleared that he saw Rebekah in the middle of the street, on her knees. Two zombies stood at either side of her, each one holding an arm, and clearly holding her up to keep her from collapsing onto the pavement.

He was frozen in place with shock at how broken her body looked, how tired and pathetic her voice sounded, the blood that dripped onto the pavement from some unseen cut.

"Let her go!" he yelled.

From behind him, the bishop said in a warning tone, "John—"

They didn't let her go. Instead, the zombies began to pull in opposite directions as if intending to rip her arms from their sockets. She cried out, then yelled Johnny's name—and that was all he needed to set him into instant motion.

The bishop called out after him, but Johnny barely heard the words. He flew toward his wife, knocking aside everyone in his way. But he was too late. With horror he saw one of the zombies finally succeed and heard Rebekah cry out in unbelievable pain as one of her arms came away from her body and she fell forward and across onto the other zombie.

"No!" Johnny yelled, almost launching himself past the zombies who got in his way as he grabbed them and tossed them aside.

At the periphery of his consciousness, he was half-aware that the blurring line of angry faces seemed to be laughing at him.

His feet hit the road's pavement before he realized why. Rebekah wasn't on the ground with a severed arm; there was no blood on the pavement; his wife wasn't there at all. As he came to a sudden, confused stop, he felt hands descend on him, grab him, drag him down.

Too shocked to fight back, he allowed them to rip the cross from his hand. Was it a hallucination? The bishop's tone as he had called out Johnny's name came back to him—it wasn't a warning telling him not to go after his wife, he now realized. The bishop sounded concerned and his tone was questioning. He hadn't seen what Johnny had seen.

Johnny finally began to struggle, but the demons held him down firmly. It occurred to him that they weren't really trying to kill him or even hurt him, just to hold him in place for now. But why? They weren't even looking at him; they seemed to be waiting for something. Waiting for what?

The answer flashed into his mind with the force of lightning. "No!" he yelled at the top of his voice, trying to make himself heard over the noise of the zombies. "Stay back, please! Don't—"

A dirty, bloodied hand was shoved into his mouth. The zombie sat on his chest, making it hard to breathe. Johnny bit the hand hard, repeatedly, but the zombie never flinched.

He tried thrashing around, tried pushing the zombie off, tried kicking his feet or moving his arms, but there were too many of them holding him down.

"Save your bishop," the old man's voice said in his ear. "Let us in. This is your only chance."

Yes! Johnny thought. It was his fault; he'd brought the bishop outside; he'd fallen for their trap. He couldn't bear the thought of being used as bait, to catch and kill the bishop. *Yes, take me but leave him alone!*

But he heard something else, something from deep within his own heart, something too non-verbal to be called a voice. If he had to attach words to something that was more like a feeling or a conviction, they would've been simply: *No, John. No.*

Arise, O Lord, he prayed, *let them not triumph. Judge them, and put them in fear. Stir yourself up, my Lord and my God, and awake to my defense. Arise, O Lord. Save me, my God.*

The zombies who'd been content to hold him down and wait for the bishop to try to rescue him began to howl in displeasure as soon as he started to pray. The one who'd held his hand over Johnny's mouth removed it so he could grab Johnny's head with both hands and pound it against the pavement. Others were twisting his legs and striking him with rocks and fists.

Despite the pain, Johnny bit his tongue to stop himself from crying out. He didn't want his own cries to motivate the bishop to leave the church steps. He freed his hands enough that he was able to throw off the zombie sitting on top of him and trying to use Johnny's head as a gavel, but already he felt something warm flow down his neck and knew he had started to bleed.

A blur of angry faces swept into his vision as they tried to bite him; a blur of hands with long, uncut fingernails tried to scratch him. He pushed their faces and arms away as best he could, but there were so many of them. Right now they were mostly distracted by whatever they expected the bishop to do, but what would happen when they realized the bishop wasn't coming? What would happen when the dozens of feet he saw all around him began to stomp on his body and head?

He'd struggle and fight with every breath he had left, but he felt certain that those breaths could be easily numbered now.

Into Your hands, Father, he prayed, readying himself to twist and squirm so he could fight them on his feet, *I commend my spirit.*

The same non-verbal voice spoke to him again. *No, John. No.*

Johnny twisted and squirmed and rose to his feet, pushing back the zombies who were focused on him. He realized now that the other zombies weren't distracted by what they expected or were waiting for the bishop to do, but by what he was actually doing.

At the top of the church's stairs, Bishop Joseph held up the cross in his right hand, his eyes focused on the sky. He spoke words that were washed out by the reaction they provoked in the demons, whose zombies cried out with deafening yells.

Those around him were now so captivated by the bishop that no one paid Johnny any attention.

In a daze, caused by the recent trauma to his head or by the shocking scene around him, he watched the zombies, whose number so greatly exceeded their own, retreat from the bishop, pushing back against themselves. As Johnny moved out of the way himself to avoid being trampled again, he saw zombies at the edge of the crowd fleeing down the street.

A zombie near him seemed to summon enough focus to swing back her arm. She held a rock. Johnny leapt at her and knocked it out of her hand.

"Stop him!" she said, her pimpled face shoved into his own. "He stinks! Stinks! Stinks! I can't bear it."

"Then leave this holy place," Johnny said. "In the name of Christ, depart!"

The young woman collapsed, so that he had to reach out his arms to catch her and lay her down on the ground gently. The crowd of legs pressed in on them; he tried to pick the young woman up to move her out of the way, but someone jostled him and he fell over.

Beside him, another zombie had picked up a rock and was about to throw it. Before Johnny could stand, the zombie swung back his arm and released.

Johnny scrambled to his feet, and saw that Michael had stepped in front of the bishop, arms raised to protect his head from the rain of rocks and stones.

Torn between helping the young woman and running to the staircase to help protect the bishop, he looked at her and saw that she herself was providing the solution to his dilemma: she had begun to stir and rise to her feet, her hand holding her head as if after a splitting headache. He also saw that other zombies all around him had either collapsed or were confused-looking and silent enough that he was sure the demons had fled from them.

Even as a victorious, euphoric feeling swept through him, though, he turned back to the church and saw that Michael had collapsed and the bishop was being pelted with rocks and stones from every side.

He broke into a run, gaze fixed on Bishop Joseph, who seemed not to notice the hailstorm assaulting his body and still managed to keep his arm held high. His features were still except for his moving mouth, but sweat and blood had broken out all over his face and neck. Somehow many of the rocks and stones missed him, but he barely flinched at the ones that connected.

Johnny raced up the stairs. "Open the doors! In Christ's name, open the doors!"

Immediately they flew open, and Liz and Isaac stormed out.

"Thank God!" Isaac said, looking around. "I was dying in there." He stepped in front of the bishop, swatting at the rocks as if they were flies, then rushed down and into the crowd of yelling zombies, knocking them back and to the ground.

"Can you get Michael inside?" Johnny said.

Liz nodded.

Now that he was close to the bishop, Johnny saw that the sweat and blood were mixed with tears that flowed out of his eyes. The arm holding the cross trembled.

Johnny grabbed his hand with his own, and felt the energy go out of the bishop as he finally allowed himself to release the tension in his arm.

"What can I do?" Johnny said.

"I can't," the bishop said, the words coming out of him as thin and slow as air out of a punctured balloon, "hold them—much longer. Hold them—back."

"Can you hold on just a little longer?" Johnny said.

The bishop nodded, a slight smile forming on his lips. Perhaps he intended it to be reassuring, but the weakness of the smile, the heaviness of the bishop's eyelids, which seemed to shut of their own accord and only come open again by great effort, intensified Johnny's concern.

He turned at a touch on his shoulder. "Liz, help the bishop," he said. "Just help him stand for now."

Scanning the crowd of zombies for Isaac, he saw him buried underneath a small group of four or five, struggling to push them off but failing. And yet as many as were yelling and throwing rocks were looking at the chaos around them in confusion and fear.

"Listen to me!" Johnny yelled. "You are afraid, but there is no need to be. Christ Almighty, the Son of the Living God, the One Who Is, Who Was, and Who Is Coming—He has delivered you from the power of the evil ones. You were captives, but He has set you free. Pray to Him now—thank Him in your hearts for what He has done for you today, praise Him, glorify Him! Let the name of Jesus be on your lips and in your minds and in your hearts."

He knew how effective his words were not only by the way in which some of the confusion and fear cleared from the faces of those who'd been cured, but also because the enraged zombies had turned on him as one. He had to duck to avoid being pelted by the rocks.

"Take the bishop inside," he whispered to Liz. "Leave me his cross."

She pressed it into his hand.

Johnny raised up the cross in the air triumphantly. "The Son of Man is lifted up," he said, "that all who look up at Him and believe shall be saved!"

Isaac finally managed to throw off the zombies on top of him, some of whom had turned their attention on Johnny.

"Help me, Lord!" someone yelled, a cry that would've been pathetic if not for its intense depth of feeling.

It was more than the demons could take. Their agony was driving them into a frenzy; they almost shook in anger where they stood, as if they desired more than anything to rush at Johnny and shut him up, but were held at bay by an even greater fear of touching the staircase.

Others, who seemed to have returned to themselves, stumbled toward him and up the stairs. Liz ushered them into the church.

"Those of you who love the light are welcome in this holy house," Johnny said, almost in a frenzy himself. "As for you who work in darkness, the night has been long, but the sun is about to rise." Then, feeling like John the Baptist in the desert, he cried out with John's words, and in a voice perhaps as loud and certainly as sincere and heart-felt as that which belonged to the greatest prophet born of a woman: "Repent, for the Kingdom of God is at hand!"

Returning to awareness of himself, he saw a wave of zombies rushing forward, then felt himself tackled and picked up and thrown into the church, and heard the doors slam shut just as the zombies crashed into them. Isaac helped Johnny stand while Michael locked the doors.

A dozen or so men and women and children stood in the narthex, looking in the candlelight like refugees who'd been beaten and starved.

"You're safe now," Johnny said, ignoring how silly the banging on the doors and the barely-muffled howls made his words sound. He turned to Liz. "Where's the bishop?"

"Inside," she said, and spoke apologetically as if she expected Johnny to chide her. "In the front pew. That's where he asked me to take him."

Because that's where he wants to die, Johnny thought; surrounded by God and His holy saints and angels, and in view of the altar in the sanctuary.

"Bring these people downstairs," he said. "Give them some water and a little bit of food, as much as they can take for now. Dress their wounds."

"What about—?" Isaac began. The attack on the doors, which shook with the force of the assault, made finishing the sentence unnecessary.

"Just help these people downstairs for now," Johnny said. "The bishop and I will join you soon, and then we'll figure out what to do."

He walked over to the basement door and held it open for them. When everyone was in the staircase, he closed it gently, then turned to face the nave. He took a deep breath and crossed himself as he walked through the doorway. His heart pounded with every measured step he took down the aisle. Each beat sounded deafeningly in his ear, an unnecessarily loud reminder of the extent of the fear he felt of what he'd find when he reached the front of the church.

Chapter 21

THE bishop's breathing was shallow but present. Johnny finally let out his own breath at the sight of the bishop's stomach rising slightly but consistently.

Until that moment, he was sure Bishop Joseph had died or was mere moments from death. His bushy eyebrows and beard were stained red, the cuts along his forehead and cheek still bleeding. His left hand cradled his right arm over his chest, the way a child or animal will protect a hurting limb.

Not wishing to disturb the bishop now that he'd confirmed he was alive, Johnny turned away quietly.

"John."

The bishop's left eye was looking up at him; the other struggled to open, but now Johnny saw the bruise that had formed over it, and it seemed that eye was swollen shut. The bishop's voice was a whisper barely audible over the knocking and howling.

"I didn't want to bother you," Johnny said. "I'll go get a first aid kit and clean you up a little. You should rest for now. Are you comfortable?"

Bishop Joseph squirmed, tried to sit up. Johnny went to help, but the moment his hand touched the bishop's back, the old man winced.

"Don't sit up," Johnny said, drawing back his hand. "What do you need?"

"I don't need anything," the bishop said, the thin voice betraying some humor. His right eye was still closed, and the quick and energetic light so characteristic of them had dimmed even in the left one. "How is everyone? How is Michael?"

"Everybody's fine," Johnny lied, forcing a smile as he kneeled beside the bishop. "They're all safe inside. You're the one everyone is worried about." Johnny straightened his legs. "Let me go get that kit."

"The subdeacon tells me you used to worship at this church."

Johnny had to kneel again as soon as the bishop spoke, to make out his words.

"Yes, that's right. A long time ago."

"What made you stop?"

Johnny laughed in spite of himself. The words were barely escaping the bishop's tired mouth. "There'll be plenty of time for you to hear my confession later," he said. "Right now we need to get that blood off your face."

The light, once so bright and which now had to power only a single eye but seemed incapable of doing even that, mustered its energy as the bishop lifted his gaze to meet Johnny's.

"There's not much to tell," Johnny said, shrugging. "I stopped coming because Father Gord refused to commune me. I'd lined up with everyone else that morning. When my turn came, I leaned forward and opened my mouth; nothing happened, so when I opened my eyes, I saw Father Gord's face in mine and he said, softly, 'I'm sorry, Johnny. I can't.' I pretended to walk back to my seat, but I continued down the aisle and out the church. And didn't come back for years; and even then, I didn't approach the chalice."

With a strange but mild shock of realization, Johnny saw that the place where he now leaned, just to the left of the front central pew, was the same place where, all those years ago, he had leaned forward in expectation of receiving the Body and Blood.

"Do you know why he didn't want to commune you?" the bishop said.

"Because I wasn't speaking to my father. He was a big supporter of the church. Throw a rock in here," he said, looking around, "and you'll probably hit an icon he donated." Too late, he realized the image wasn't a very sensitive one under the circumstances.

Bishop Joseph didn't seem to notice. "Are you sure Father Gord was denying you communion to appease your father?"

"I don't know. I guess it's always been easier to think that was the reason, rather than admit to myself that I was at fault and needed to make things right with my father before I could approach again."

"Then you were wrong?"

"Oh yes," Johnny said, sitting down on the marble step and stretching out his legs because his knees were starting to hurt. "The disagreement itself was stupid, one of those things where each person can only see the situation from their perspective. But my dad—and then my mom on his behalf—tried to reach out to me afterward. I was too upset, though—I didn't want anything to do with either of them. If they weren't going to help me, I figured, I didn't want them as part of my life."

"Do you know where they are now?"

"They passed away. Years ago, in a plane crash. A business trip. My dad spent half his life on planes, but I guess it only has to happen once, right? My mother chose to accompany him on this one."

God forgive me, he thought. *Forgive me.*

"I'm sorry," the bishop said.

Johnny stared down the empty nave, this church where his parents used to bring him on Sunday mornings, dressed in a suit and standing on the pew in between the two of them, carried away by the liturgy and the chanting. Then, on the ride home, he remembered pumping his father for all the answers to his rapid-fire theological questions, before his mom finally had enough, turned around, and pelted him with questions of her own, without waiting to hear any answers, and reaching back to tickle his stomach. How could that kind of a relationship, so happy and so loving for so long, deteriorate to such an extent?

Then again, how could his wife be a demon-possessed zombie?

The bishop's cycloptic eye was watching him, narrowed as if Bishop Joseph could read his mind.

Before Johnny could say anything, though, loud footsteps sounded in the nave.

"Everyone's being taken care of," Isaac said to Johnny as he approached. He looked over the back of the pew to the bishop. "Liz sent me up to see if you need anything." He spoke the words mechanically, as if these were the ones he'd prepared, but with the realization that they now seemed inadequate in the face of the bishop's wounds.

Johnny began to ask if they could spare a first aid kit, but the bishop spoke over him, if his weak voice could be said to speak over anyone's. "We're fine," he said, trying by an effort of will to raise his voice so that Isaac could hear him. "We just need a few more minutes alone. Then we'll join you."

Isaac looked back at Johnny, perhaps waiting for him to finish the sentence he'd started. Johnny refused to make eye contact with the big man, who finally turned around and walked away.

"If you plan to hear my confession," Johnny said, "it's going to take a lot more than a few minutes. I've got a whole lifetime of sin."

"That doesn't make you special," the bishop said, and Johnny realized after a moment that he was making a joke. "Something specific is bothering you right now, though."

Normally Johnny might not have answered; but the bishop seemed intent on getting this information out of him, and now that the bishop's voice was sounding even hoarser and weaker, Johnny was anxious to end their conversation and get Bishop Joseph some help or at least some rest.

"I love my wife," he said. "But ever since all of this happened, I've had thoughts that are"—he tried to think of the right word—"disloyal. Dishonorable. I had a dream about another woman. Not a sexual dream," he added quickly. "A—domestic one, I guess."

"Is that all?" the bishop said. "Dreams are just dreams. They don't have any power unless you give it to them."

"But don't you—"

Again the bishop tried to speak over him, so that Johnny cut himself off. "Are you planning to act on these thoughts, John?"

Not in a million years, Johnny thought. Rebekah was his wife into eternity, and he wouldn't do anything that was within his power to cast even the slightest shadow on their relationship.

"No," he said. "Never."

"There you go," the bishop said, as if he'd solved a seemingly difficult riddle for a small child. "John—come closer."

Johnny sat forward on his knees.

"You have such spiritual power," the bishop said, reaching out his right hand with effort to rest on Johnny's forehead. "Yet you lack spiritual discipline. Promise me you'll work on that."

"I promise," Johnny said.

The bishop didn't remove his hand. "I wish we'd had more time," he said, softly, his voice finally seeming to fail him.

Johnny didn't know what was happening. The bishop began to move his lips; he was praying softly. Johnny overheard enough words to finally glimpse the bishop's plan.

"I don't want this," he said, almost in panic, but didn't dare pull away.

The bishop didn't reply; perhaps couldn't reply. The response, though, was written in his soft features and gentle one-eyed gaze: *I know, John.*

Johnny could see now how much effort it was taking the bishop to hold up his arm, how much energy it had robbed of him to speak to

Johnny, how much even now he struggled to stay conscious.

He didn't dare interrupt again. As Bishop Joseph prayed over him, his hand on Johnny's head, Johnny felt the sense of despair and panic slowly being replaced by peace and calmness, as of a candle being lit and chasing away the shadows from a dark room.

After a while, the bishop's hand dropped to Johnny's cheek. Johnny opened his eyes. Isaac and Liz were standing by the pew, staring at him and Bishop Joseph in silent bewilderment.

"Father John," the bishop said weakly, though his lips broke into a smile at the name, the way an artist might step back from a fresh painting and look at it with satisfaction.

Although Johnny didn't think the bishop was aware that Liz and Isaac had returned, his eye rolled up to meet theirs and dropped down again. They both leaned in to hear him. "This is your father in Christ," he said. "Follow him."

The bishop's gaze met Johnny's again. "This is your flock, Father John. Care for them."

He leaned his head back slightly, closing the eye he'd kept open by such an effort of will. A moment later, the shaking hand he'd held on Johnny's face dropped to his chest again.

For the rest of that afternoon, Liz, Isaac, and Johnny sat on the marble steps, watching the bishop as he lay stretched out on the pew, his breathing slow and shallow.

Later Johnny realized that others had joined them in the nave, and had come to take a seat beside and behind them on the higher steps. They'd come up quietly, figured out what was happening, and sat down without disturbing at least Johnny's thoughts. It was then he noticed that the loud banging sounds from outside had ceased as well.

Michael came up a short while after that, holding an ice pack to his head. He sat beside the bishop. Another moment and Izzy's tiny frame appeared at the back of the nave, dwarfed by the large background that Miles constituted. She ran down the aisle toward Johnny, her loud cry to him a piercing of the silence, but she stopped short at the front and looked at the bishop. She seemed to size up the situation herself, then struggled to rise to her tippy toes, and kissed the bishop on the forehead. She sat on the ground between Johnny's legs.

Izzy was silent until Steven and Theresa appeared, to whom she cried out loudly as soon as she saw them that they should be quiet because the bishop was resting.

More people joined throughout the rest of the day, so that soon there wasn't any room on the steps and people filled in the pews behind the bishop. Among those faces were familiar ones—Fatima's and Wassim's and their grandchildren's, for instance—and unfamiliar ones. From the latter group's emaciated and gaunt features, and from their combed but dirty hair, and from the obvious wounds that had just been cleaned up and bandaged, and from the shirts that didn't fit well for the most part, Johnny figured these were people who even this morning were standing outside, swaying from a compulsion to attack the church and a fear of approaching it. People who didn't know the bishop, who had perhaps heard or figured out what was happening and had come upstairs to pay their respects.

When the light in the nave began to grow dim, the bishop's left eye opened slightly. Johnny had been watching his face, and his own heart leapt at this sign of life. The bishop's eye roved over those gathered in the church to watch over him. Hardly daring to breathe from joy, Johnny prayed with all of his heart, *Yes, Lord, let him live.* In the hours he'd watched over the bishop, he'd resigned himself to the fact that Bishop Joseph was dying, and wondered what he would do without him, especially since the bishop, in the last significant act of his life, had laid a tremendous burden on Johnny. *Yes, Lord! Let him live to serve You. I need him, Lord; I can't do this alone.*

The bishop's gaze returned to Johnny. A small smile played at the corner of his lips—a smile of gratitude, Johnny felt, or perhaps one of encouragement. Certainly, though, it was a farewell smile.

Johnny grabbed Izzy and gently moved her out of the way, but when he looked up again, the bishop had closed his eye. A moment later, and his body was still.

Chapter 22

"No," Johnny whispered, and dashed forward. "Please no." He held his fingers to the side of the bishop's neck. No pulse. He lifted his arm, checked there. No pulse. No breathing. No movement. Just a bruised, broken, dead body.

From behind him, he heard Izzy begin to cry. He turned his head, saw Liz slide over to comfort her, then she met his gaze and mouthed to him, "You should say something."

He didn't want to say anything, didn't want to console or lead this group of people; mostly he just wanted to be left alone. But whether they wanted him or not, Bishop Joseph had made Johnny their priest; and whether he wanted them or not, Bishop Joseph had put this flock under Johnny's care and responsibility.

He stood. Those in the pews looked up at him expectantly. He turned around; those on the staircase seemed to be waiting for him to speak as well. "He was a nice man," he heard Izzy say to Liz, who responded in soft tones, "I know, darling. I know."

"For those of you who don't know him," Johnny began, "this is Bishop Joseph. He and I didn't always get along, but I don't for a second doubt that he lived every day in the service of his Lord. Even at the end, his faith and resolve never wavered; he gave his life to save us, even as Christ gave His life. We are poorer for his loss. The whole world is darker for his loss, but he has run the race and fought the good fight and now he enters into his rest and reward. As for us, though, we must continue to run, to fight, to struggle.

"Most of you have figured this out by now," he continued. "Our war is not a physical one, but a spiritual one, like St. Paul said. The truth is that those outside did not become infected with a virus; their bodies became possessed by demons."

He turned around as he spoke, uncomfortable that half the time he had his back to half of them. This time he caught Wassim's arched-eyebrow gaze. "You don't believe me? There are some among us today who were once possessed, who were healed by the power of God."

Michael rose suddenly, went into the sanctuary.

"But it doesn't matter if you believe me or not. We are under assault, we can all agree on that. The good news is that we can fight back. We will fight back. And we won't destroy life, but save it. We can help those people outside, redeeming the time we have left in this world. When the Son of Man returns in glory, He will find us struggling, His co-workers, trying to save as many as possible until the end."

Michael emerged and began to light the candles in front of the iconostasis.

"Now, I know that not all of you are Christians," Johnny said. "And some of you don't believe in any God whatsoever. That's fine. I'm not asking you to change your beliefs. In fact, our Lord tells us that in the age to come, those who inherit life in His Eternal Kingdom are not the ones who can call on Him by name, but those who worked good for others, those who helped their fellow human beings."

He paused. "I never liked that, to be honest. It's easier to pay Him lip-service and move on with your life, but that won't work.

"Anyway, whether or not you believe in Him, I am asking you to be like Him. To overcome evil with good. To fight back against the darkness, and bring a little more of His light into the world.

"If you believe, do all things in His name and He will strengthen you. Pray with your heart, mind, and soul, and His Spirit will fill you and enable you to do things you never dreamed possible; it will enable you to become like Him who gave His life for the world. If you don't believe in Him or in any God at all, do good, and your good works will pray to Him for you."

"That's a really fine speech," Theresa said. She sat with Steven in the pew just behind the bishop's body. Her voice was laced with so much antagonism, and the look on her face so distrustful, that he felt certain someone had told her what had happened in his basement. "You make it all sound so very noble and easy."

"There's nothing easy about this."

"He's lying to you," Theresa said, speaking over her husband, who tried to quiet her down, and looking around for support from the others. "He's making it sound easy. But it's dangerous, really dangerous. Bishop Joseph understood that." She turned back to Johnny. "But you don't care, do you? You're like a little boy playing cops and robbers, and you don't care who gets hurt. Do you?"

"I'm not suggesting everyone engage the demons directly," he said, not taken aback by her words though he might've expected himself to be. "In fact, I won't be responsible for anyone engaging them at all who doesn't believe in the power of the Cross. But there are other ways to help—you know that better than anyone, you've been doing it.

"But let me be clear, Theresa—everyone is going to be hurt. Most of us already have been hurt deeply. We've lost people we care about; we've done things to survive that we wish we'd never had to do; we've discovered depths to our sin we never suspected."

He wondered then if he should send Izzy and the other children downstairs, but he realized that his words applied to them as much as to any of the adults. It was too late to shield them now. Too late to allow them time to grow up before discovering that the world was in reality much uglier and messier than the one their parents had constructed for them, if they were lucky enough that circumstances allowed them to live that existence for a little while. None of these children were that lucky.

"This is not the first time that Christians have thought the world was ending," he continued. "We've thought it anytime the Church has undergone great tribulation or persecutions—and we've had more than our fair share. So maybe I'm wrong, maybe this isn't the end of the world—but boy does it feel like it. Boy does it feel like the devil has been let loose upon the earth.

"No, I don't believe there's a happy ending here. There wasn't a happy ending to Christ's life, either. Just suffering and death on the Cross. But then there came the Resurrection. And that's what we're promised, not a happy ending but a happy new beginning. We have that hope to sustain us; but in the meantime, we live in a world that is passing away.

"Yes, what I'm proposing is very dangerous," he continued. "But what option isn't dangerous anymore? The demons are just outside; any minute now, they can start banging their fists and heads against the doors again. Maybe they'll break through this time."

Wassim sat behind Theresa; Johnny saw his mouth working away quietly, as if he were building up the courage to speak out against him.

I'm losing these people, Johnny thought. *They don't believe what I'm saying, like Wassim; or they believe me, but don't trust me, like Theresa. Or they believe me and trust me way too much, like Liz and Isaac and Miles—and what if I'm wrong and let them down?*

"Look, nothing needs to be decided right away," he said. "We can continue this conversation later. I don't know why I started down this path. If it's all right with you, I'd like to hold a funeral service for Bishop Joseph tonight after dinner."

"Is it the fault of the people?" Wassim said, suddenly, explosively.

Johnny ran the words through his mind again and again, trying to understand them. "Which people?"

"The people. The ones you say were taken by the *Sheitan*. Are they the ones who are at fault?"

"I don't know," Johnny said, shrugging. "For some, I'm sure it was, even before all of this started. They allowed hatred, bitterness, envy—all kinds of evil things—to take root in their hearts. They allowed the demons to shape their thoughts and their lives. For others, I don't think it was their fault. Maybe they became possessed because of fear that overwhelmed them. My wife is possessed by demons, but I believe she gave herself over to them to save our daughter. Does it matter, though? We have a commandment from the lips of our Lord: 'Judge not, lest you be judged.'"

"My son, he become one of them," Wassim said. "His wife too, my daughter-in-law. I don't think it was their fault."

"I'm sorry," Johnny said. "It's a horrible thing. But I can tell you—whether it was their fault or not, God loves them and wants to heal them. I believe that's our calling right now, to spread His light throughout the world until the night wears out its time and the Light is revealed for good."

Wassim leaned back in the pew. "So you are the boss now?"

"Bishop Joseph ordained me before his death. It's not something I wanted, but the bishop had much greater discernment than I do, and he felt it was God's will that I become a priest. I'll be honest with you all, the thought scares me even more than those demons outside. It's a heavy and terrifying cross he put on my shoulders. But I plan to carry it as best I can, for as long as I can."

"You will make good priest," Wassim said. "Father John, yes?"

"Yes," Johnny said, smiling. He looked around for Miles. "Stand up, Miles. That's the man right there, that's our innkeeper." Miles shook his head humbly, but Johnny saw the sudden but subtle pleasure that seemed to beam from his face. "None of us is in the mood to eat tonight, I'm sure, but it's important that we do so. Miles, will you get us organized for dinner?"

Miles nodded and led most of the people back downstairs. Johnny sent Izzy down with Fatima, telling them both that he'd join soon. A small group stayed behind to congratulate Johnny. When all but a few were left, a young man with broken teeth and a deep cut across his face said to him, "Father John, will you baptize me?"

What do I know about baptizing anyone? Johnny hoped the thought wasn't visible on his face. "You weren't baptized before?"

The young man shook his head. "My parents didn't believe in infant baptism. And by the time I was old enough... I'd lost all interest in that kind of thing."

"Let me think about it," Johnny said.

"I can recite the Nicene Creed," the young man said. "I believe it."

"That's good. Give me tonight to think things through, all right? We'll talk about it tomorrow."

He nodded, though he was unable to hide his dejection. He turned around and began to walk away.

Johnny called out after him. "What's your name?"

His name was Tom.

"All right, Tom. Go see if you can help Miles set up for dinner." He faced the others. "You guys go ahead as well. Let Michael and I speak for a little while."

"What about the bishop?" Isaac said. "Should we move him?"

"That's where he wanted to be," Johnny said, looking back at the old man's still features. "We can leave him there until morning." *And then what?* he thought. They couldn't risk burying him outside, although a proper and decent burial was what he deserved. But they couldn't keep a dead body in the church with them either. He pushed the problem out of his mind for the moment.

When the others had left, Johnny sat with Michael in the pew on the other side of the aisle from the bishop's. He asked him how his head felt.

Michael still carried the ice pack, now melted, in his hand. "Fine," he said.

They stared together at the iconostasis for a long time in silence.

"I don't know if I'm ready for this, Michael."

"Bishop Joseph told me this was his plan. I don't think he ever thought it would happen so quickly, though."

"You're not making me feel better."

"I don't know what to tell you, Father. Just this, I guess—I'll serve you to the best of my ability. I'll serve you as well as I tried to serve the bishop. I agree with him that God is calling you to do this. I agree with you that it would be better to go out into the world and help those who want to be helped, while there's still time."

Johnny nodded. "Thank you," he said, simply. "I'll join you downstairs in a moment, all right?" At first he'd wanted to be alone with Michael; but now he simply wanted to be alone.

Before he left, Michael stared down the nave toward the outside doors. "They're being quiet. That's a good sign, right?"

"Right," Johnny said, although he didn't know.

Michael left, but it didn't take long for Johnny to feel the same antsy desire that compelled him to change—something. He'd wanted to be left alone, but now he felt the impulse to go back downstairs and be with others. It was only a few minutes later that, unable to sit still any longer, he stood.

The bishop was sitting up in the pew, staring forward.

"You're—" Johnny began.

"You're making a mistake," the bishop said, turning his face toward Johnny. His right eye was whole and there were no signs of the wounds he'd received that morning. "You're endangering all of their lives."

"What should I do?"

"You have to do the right thing. You have to give your life to save them. And you have to do it tonight." The bishop turned away from him, looked forward again. "While I lived, my prayers were able to protect this church. But now that I'm dead...." He let the thought trail off. "They're showing clemency. But their patience won't last forever. Give yourself to them right now, Johnny Salibi. This very moment."

"Yes, you are dead," Johnny said. "But Bishop Joseph is not dead. He's alive in Christ."

The bishop didn't look at him but a smile had formed on his face: an ugly, and unnaturally wide smile that stretched out his lips.

Johnny closed his eyes and said in his heart, *Lord Jesus Christ, Son of God, have mercy on me a sinner.* When he opened them again, the bishop was lying as still as ever on the pew, the bruise over his right eye visible.

Making the sign of the cross over the bishop's body, Johnny prayed for peace for Bishop Joseph's spirit. He walked down the darkened nave, saw a small figure outlined in candlelight in the narthex.

"Izzy?"

She stood at the doors, facing away from him.

"Honey?" he said, stepping into the narthex.

"Mommy's outside," she said, still staring at the locked handle too high for her to reach.

He grabbed her and turned her around. "I know, munchkin," he said. "We're going to find her and help her—I promise."

"No," she said, and there was something strangely unfamiliar about her voice. "You don't understand. She's outside right now. Just behind this door."

"How could you possibly—" he began, but a sudden, loud *knock-knock-knock* cut him off.

"Daddy, open the door," Izzy said. "Let mommy in."

Knock-knock-knock.

"Open it!" Izzy yelled.

He grabbed her quickly and ran back into the nave, down the aisle and toward the altar, praying, pleading, begging God to spare his child. The knocking on the door grew louder and more insistent.

He put Izzy down in front of the icon of the Theotokos.

"Holy Mother," he prayed out loud. "You know what it's like to love a child, flesh of your flesh and blood of your blood. Do not let any foul or evil thing dwell inside of her; do not let evil spirits take possession of her. Protect her, Holy Theotokos; protect her with the love of a mother; protect this little one as you protected the Holy Child born to you."

He'd kneeled down and held Izzy by the shoulders as he prayed; she'd begun to convulse violently right away, but he'd forced himself to continue.

"What's going on?" Isaac yelled from the middle of the church. Others had come up behind him. They held flashlights, and Johnny saw more beams in the narthex.

Izzy's convulsions were getting worse; he pulled her in close to him.

"In the name of Christ," he said, "leave this precious child."

Izzy shook so violently he thought she might snap her neck; he brought his arm up to cradle her head and hugged her even more tightly.

"I will not leave quietly," she said, her voice muffled. Johnny loosened his hold on her. "Cast me out, and I will kill her."

"Johnny?" Liz stood at the edge of the marble staircase, Michael and Isaac beside her and more people behind them—Steven, Theresa, Tom, and others he didn't know by name but recognized from earlier that day.

"It'll be all right," Johnny said, speaking to her and to the others. "The doors will hold."

As if to contradict him, the sounds of the assault reverberated throughout the church, louder than ever before.

"This is it," Izzy said. "We're coming in."

"Oh God, Izzy, no," Liz said, leaping forward and dropping down beside her. She stared into Izzy's placid face. "What do we do?" she said to Johnny.

"Take everyone back downstairs," he whispered. "Keep them calm. Everything will be all right." She didn't budge. "Please," he said.

"Here we come," Izzy said, as a loud screeching erupted from the narthex.

Isaac broke into a run, cutting through the small crowd, with Michael at his heels, but they were too late: mangled, snarling bodies appeared at both doorways to the nave and streamed into the church.

"Come back!" Johnny yelled. He suddenly remembered the vision he'd seen and was filled with the conviction that above all else, nothing could happen to the altar.

He wrapped his arms around Izzy and picked her up, then stepped in front of the royal doors. Izzy yelled so much, and squirmed so much, that he couldn't help but let her go. She scurried away backwards.

The nave was in chaos; Isaac and Michael tried to stand their ground near the back of the church, fighting and pushing away the screeching zombies, but they were outnumbered. They fell back, Isaac literally pushed into the back of a pew, which he tumbled over. A woman Johnny didn't recognize was cowering near the bishop's body. Theresa was yelling at him to help them, to do something.

"Come up here, all of you," he said, speaking firmly. "Stand beside me."

A few of the others had dashed toward the narthex after Isaac and Michael, and were locked in their own struggles. The screams, yells, and cries of pain from both sides were indistinguishable.

He raised his voice. "Come back here! We must protect the altar!"

Although there were far more zombies than there were of them, it seemed to Johnny that this wasn't even a tenth of those who'd stood outside. And he felt certain that if once these present zombies could destroy the altar, nothing would stop all the others from coming in, and from destroying the rest of the church too, pulling down its walls even.

Liz stood on one side of him, Steven on the other.

"Stay beside me," he said. "They won't touch us."

Then he raised his voice ever louder to be heard over the screaming. "Isaac! Michael! Come back here right now!"

They fought their way back, as did the others, and by slow degrees, all of his people—or at least, all of those who were left alive and conscious, he thought morbidly—were standing along the iconostasis, in solidarity with Christ and His saints and angels behind them.

The zombies in the church were like frenzied monkeys, destroying or trying to destroy everything around them. They pulled down the icons within their reach, used them to break the glass of the windows, then tossed them outside. They threw themselves into walls so that the higher-placed icons shook, and kept doing so until the icons fell. Johnny saw a red and orange blaze in the narthex, and realized they were now trying to destroy the church by setting fire to it.

"Do something or we're all dead," Liz said to him. "Cast them out of here—you've done it before."

Johnny glanced down at Izzy, who stared unseeing over his shoulder. Instead of answering Liz, he said, loudly, "Hold your ground."

"There she is," Izzy said to him, without looking behind her.

But behind her was where she was referring to. Rebekah had walked into the nave like a bride entering the church, as he like the expectant groom waited for her in front of the altar, just as he had five years before. She was not the happy, glowing bride dressed in white and bathed in sunlight that he remembered, though; she looked rather like a dark, nightmare bride, the flickering light of the fire outlining her figure in a hellish glow.

Chapter 23

SHE walked up the aisle.

He felt his heart shatter within him when her twisted features came into view. Her steps were small and deliberate as she made slow progress toward him, but the internal struggle played out on her gaunt, dirty face. Hers was a concentrated, pained, confused expression, as if one part of her was trying to stop her while another pushed her forward.

"Daddy," Izzy said. "You don't have to give yourself up anymore. There's a sledgehammer by the door over there. Take it and destroy the altar and we'll all be together again. Mommy and me and you. They'll leave this church once the altar is destroyed. Do that and you save everyone! Do that or you will watch me and mommy die, and everyone else here."

He felt the strength going out of him. His heart beat irregularly. He felt himself about to collapse. He couldn't bring himself to cast out the demons from the church—not if it meant he'd be responsible for his daughter's death. *God forgive me*, he thought, *I don't have that strength. I don't.*

I'm sorry, he continued, closing his eyes and speaking to the bishop. *You gave me this beautiful church to care for, you handed your flock into my care, and less than a day later it's all over. Half the icons are destroyed, windows are shattered, pews have been tossed around the nave, and your narthex is on fire. Your sheep will be slaughtered, and I with them, because I just don't have the strength to do what's required to save them.*

"Daddy," Izzy said, but her voice was different and it was coming from behind him.

He opened his eyes as he turned around.

A young woman, perhaps in her early thirties, sat on top of the altar as naturally as she might sit on the edge of her bed. She wore a dress of pure white, a dress so bright as to be made of light itself, and her golden hair fell around her shoulders. Her blue-green eyes sparkled with peace and calmness, but the look on her face was one of pure joy, as of seeing a close friend after a long absence.

"It's okay, Daddy. It's okay. Don't you remember? This was my dream. I give my life but you and mom are together again. No, no, just listen—you have to be strong, okay? Our Lord still has a lot of work for you to do before this is over and we can all be together again."

"I—" he said, tears forming in his eyes.

"You have to be strong, Daddy."

"Johnny," Rebekah said from behind him. He turned around again; she stood at the edge of the marble staircase, not daring to touch it, an army of zombies beside and behind her. "You have to be smart." Her voice was hoarse and thin. "Do what's right."

"Yes," he said, nodding and taking a step forward. He spoke loudly, "Blessed is the Kingdom of the Father, and of the Son, and of the Holy Spirit, both now and ever and unto ages of ages."

Without a pause, those behind him responded as if with one voice, "Amen."

Izzy had fallen and was shaking with her whole body on the ground, almost at Rebekah's feet.

Johnny walked down the steps and said, "In peace let us pray to the Lord."

Rebekah stepped away from him; some of the zombies, he saw, were fleeing out of the church in terror, right into the burning narthex.

As he asked for God's peace and the people asked for His mercy, Johnny picked up his daughter, held her tightly in his arms.

They prayed together, Johnny at least ignoring the chaos in the nave as zombies fled or dropped as if dead to the ground, and ignoring except for squeezing her tighter the violent shakes Izzy produced in his arms. When Rebekah and a few others tried to shout him down, he spoke even louder. When with a great and violent yell Rebekah fell to the ground herself, he kept going.

Only after the final *Amen* did he allow himself to look down at Izzy. Her body was still. The look on her face was peaceful.

"My poor baby," he said, kissing her forehead. "My poor, poor baby." Tears streamed down his face onto hers.

Liz put her hand on his shoulder. She was crying too.

Isaac stepped down the stairs, looked toward the narthex, then back up at Johnny. "We need to get everyone out of here," he said. "This place is burning down. We can go out the side doors."

"No," Johnny said. "Use the fire extinguishers to put it out."

"There aren't any fire extinguishers up here."

"Get the ones from downstairs." Johnny examined the line of people behind him. "Take Steven, Theresa, and Tom with you."

"But the fire is all over the narthex. We'll be burned."

"The fire will not harm you," Johnny said, making the sign of the cross over each of them in turn.

Something led them to obey—the tone of his voice, or the way their prayers had scattered the demons, or perhaps just desperation.

"Father, what can I do?" Michael said, stepping forward as well.

"Pull the bodies away from the narthex, bring them here. See if any are alive. All of you, help him. And do the same with the icons."

When they were off, he handed Izzy's body to Liz, then walked down the three steps toward his wife. He bent down beside her. *Your will be done*, he thought. *Your will be done.*

Her pulse was faint but present. Burying his face in her chest, he wept in relief until someone pulled him away from her gently.

"The fire?" he said to Isaac, in response to the deep look of concern on the big man's face.

"That's under control. But you need to go downstairs."

The doors leading outside were open in the narthex, and a cool breeze blew into the church.

He walked down the dark staircase, Isaac shining a flashlight behind him. The door to the basement had been torn off its hinges.

Johnny turned and took Isaac's flashlight. The beam revealed a scene of devastation. It seemed that Miles had led a defense of those who had stayed downstairs and armed themselves with skillets, pots, knives, chairs, and whatever else they could find. The defense had worked for a while; shattered bodies in shabby, torn clothes lay strewn throughout the entrance, so that Johnny and Isaac had to step over them. But ultimately the zombie's numbers proved too great. Other bodies lay scattered throughout the basement, the floor sticky with their blood.

"My God," Johnny said.

His search beam had returned to focus on Miles, a pool of dark blood around his head, the large skillet still in his hand, blood and hair on its sharp edge.

"My God," Johnny said. "My God."

He felt like collapsing to the ground, but forced himself to keep walking. Further up, his beam caught Osama. He'd tried to step in front of his brothers and grandparents to protect them, but Johnny's flashlight revealed he'd failed: Wassim and Fatima and Ahmed and Mahmoud, all dead, their necks broken or heads bashed in.

"Did anyone survive?" he said finally, turning to Isaac.

The big man shook his head, the haunted look in his eyes gleaming in the flashlight's beam.

How, Lord? he thought. *How do we keep going? How do we keep from despair? It's too much for anyone to bear, Father. You see into everyone's heart. Can't You can see that mine has been shattered? Can't You see I can't take anymore?*

"Go back upstairs," he said to Isaac in a weak voice. "We need help to move the bodies."

By the time Isaac returned with others, Johnny had decided to turn the main, central section of the basement into a hospital and the eastern alcove into a morgue. There were a lot more dead than injured, but they packed them in closer together.

"We'll keep the bodies here for now," Johnny said to Michael, when they were done, working late into the night by the light of candles and propane-powered lanterns they'd set throughout the basement. "To give our people and anyone else we find and heal a chance to search for their relatives. Then we bury them."

"Bury them?"

"In the ground, behind the church. All of them."

"Do you think that's wise?"

Johnny didn't care if it was wise. "It's what they deserve."

"I know that, Father. You've chased them away from the church for now; but they're still out there and it seems they grow bolder each time they return."

Instead of responding—what response could he give?—Johnny placed his hand on Michael's shoulder and gave it a squeeze.

In the middle of the basement, Liz stood by Rebekah, who lay stretched out on a cot. Liz had cleaned and dressed his wife's wounds and wiped away the mud and dried blood from her face and hair and body, then given her fresh clothes to change into.

"How is she?" he said, coming up to them quietly to not disturb the other patients.

"Resting. I gave her a bit of water."

"Thank you again," he said. "You've been wonderful with her—with all of them."

He wiped Rebekah's hair away from her forehead, then bent over to kiss her.

"She'll be all right," Liz said. "She's tough."

"Yes," he said, nodding. "She is that." Then he drew himself up and said, "You should go get some rest yourself. It's the middle of the night."

She shook her head, seemed to hesitate. Then, after a long pause, she said, still whispering, "Have you decided what you're going to do?"

"What do you mean?"

"Isaac told me that someone let them into the church, upstairs. They didn't break through. Someone from inside unlocked the doors and let them in. The locks were singed, but they weren't broken."

"I see," he said.

"Forgive me," she said. "That terrifies me. How do we sleep? How can we ever feel safe again?"

"We can't," he said. "We won't be safe, not until Christ comes in His glory."

"So what do we do?"

He wanted to answer and calm the desperation in her voice, but he had no more response for her than he had for Michael. He squeezed her shoulder as well, then left before she could say anything else to him.

His heart feeling as heavy as his tired legs, he climbed the staircase wearily. The damage to the narthex was substantial but not extensive: the fire had consumed the candle stand and the icons, but only darkened the walls. Someone had closed the heavy doors leading outside, against the cold of the night or whatever else was out there. In the nave, the broken windows had been boarded up with plywood.

He sat down at the front pew, where the bishop had lain. His intention was to pray, to seek guidance or at least comfort from God. But as soon as he sat, the exhaustion caused by the morning and day's and evening and night's events and efforts caught up with him. He felt the tiredness overwhelm him like a blanket; he tried to fight it back, but his eyes closed as if on their own, and he fell asleep.

Chapter 24

"THE form of this world is passing away," the bishop says. He sits beside Johnny in the pew, but is staring straight ahead at the iconostasis.

"When?" Johnny says, his unease giving a sharp edge to his tone. "How much longer?"

"No one knows the hour, not even the Son, but only the Father."

"It's been so long." Although the bishop is sitting next to him—close enough to touch, if that wouldn't be weird—there seems to be a great distance between them, as of an uncrossable chasm. Nevertheless, even if the bishop isn't looking at him, his presence is a comfort, and Johnny feels the edge of his unease softening.

"With the Lord," the bishop begins, "a day is like a thousand years —"

"—and a thousand years is like a day," Johnny finishes for him. "I knew you were going to say that."

The bishop finally turns his head to face Johnny. He smiles kindly, his eyes full of compassion. And full of sympathy for Johnny's pain, too, though Johnny feels he doesn't deserve it.

"I've let them slaughter your flock, Father," he says. "I'm so sorry."

"The world has come to its judgment," the bishop says. "And when it does, every one shall stand before the Throne of Christ and give an account of what he has done—and what he has failed to do. And the angels themselves will be judged by men."

"So what do I do?"

"Redeem the time, for the days are evil. Bear good fruit, that you're not cut down and thrown into the fire like a diseased tree."

Johnny's pride is pricked by the bishop's words. "I've tried," he says. He is about to add, *I've done more than you!* but he has enough sense to stop the words in his throat.

"On that day," the bishop says, "many will say to Him, 'Lord, Lord.' And many will say, 'We cast out demons in Your Name.' But He won't know them."

Johnny's heart, which had started to feel freer at the sight of the bishop, now feels heavier than ever. "I don't know what you're saying. What else can I do?"

The bishop doesn't answer.

Johnny hears his name being called from far away, but his gaze never leaves the bishop. "I feel empty inside," he says, weakly but insistently. "I don't know that I have any more to give."

The bishop shakes his head in reproach, his soft, compassionate eyes narrowing. "When you are weak, then you are strong."

Someone keeps calling Johnny's name. With a sudden rush of awareness, he realizes that he is dreaming and is about to wake up.

"I believe," he says, and feels that these words he's about to say encapsulate everything he's feeling. "Help my unbelief."

The reproving look drops from the bishop's face, and is replaced by one of pure joy. "Father John," he says, "you are full of the Holy Spirit."

L IZ stood over him; he'd stretched himself out on the pew without realizing it. Her hand was on his shoulder. She shook him gently and called out his name again, a concerned if not haunted expression on her face.

He sat up slowly. The dull orange glow of the rising sun filtered through the windows.

Liz had taken a step back, was looking at him as he stood up with a mixture of relief and fear; rather, looking past him, her sunken eyes focusing on something very distant, the purple flesh under her eyes looking darker and more pronounced. "Seeing you like that," she said, in a distracted, almost internal voice, "stretched out—there."

"Liz," he said, and after a moment her eyes focused on him again. "I'm fine. I just came up here to pray, and I guess I fell asleep. It's an old story: the spirit is willing but the flesh is weak."

"Lucky you," she said, shrugging playfully. "I have the opposite problem."

"Don't sound so superior," he said. "That's a sign of a guilty conscience."

She raised her eyebrows but laughed when he stuck out his tongue at her. A moment passed, and she seemed to remember what had brought her upstairs. "Rebekah is asking for you," she said, the levity dropping from her voice. "And—for Izzy."

He began to walk quickly with Liz back toward the narthex. "What did you tell her?"

"That I'd go get you; I couldn't bring myself to say anything else. There was so much hope and joy in her eyes, and in her voice. I almost burst into tears. I'm not sure if she noticed."

They went through the doorway and down the staircase to the basement.

"How is she right now?"

"She's tired. Her body is very weak, malnourished—you don't need me to tell you. But she's in good spirits."

At the bottom of the stairs, before opening the door, Johnny stopped, looked back up at Liz in the relative darkness illuminated only by her flashlight, and said, "You wouldn't be able to tell the difference, actually. Rebekah in bad humor is better than the rest of us in good spirits." But as always lately, whenever he had a happy thought, a dark cloud swept in to mar it: *you're about to test that theory*, he thought.

Rebekah's bed was in front of the eastern column closest to the kitchen. As he approached, she turned her head on the pillow and saw him. A smile spread over her face.

"All this work to get done," he said, speaking softly, "and you're laying about, huh?"

"I'm not supposed to move too much," she said, and Johnny tried not to wince at her weak and hoarse voice. "Nurse's orders."

"She's a tough one," Johnny said, looking over his shoulder at Liz, who'd gone into the kitchen. "I wouldn't cross her."

Rebekah shook her head *no*.

He bent down to kiss her, but Rebekah turned her face away.

"I have bad breath," she said.

"I don't care," he said, chasing her mouth with his own. He kissed her lips, then proceeded to kiss her cheeks and her neck, then buried his face in the crook of her shoulder.

She gave him a moment, then kissed his cheek. "Johnny," she said, after another pause, "what do you need to tell me?"

He pulled his head back. *Don't lie to me*, the look on her face said; *and don't play dumb*. Still he couldn't bring himself to speak.

"Did something happen to Izzy?" He didn't need to reply with words. Rebekah's features tightened. "Is she hurt?" Her voice, so hoarse already, managed to sound even weaker.

"I'm so sorry," he said.

Rebekah's features collapsed on themselves and, in small, painful shudders, her body began to shake. Johnny put his arms underneath her back and hugged her, and together they wept for their little girl, Johnny apologizing to his wife every few minutes until she told him to stop.

After a long time, Rebekah pulled away from him and asked Johnny how it happened. He told her about finding Izzy in the narthex, possessed; of how he'd tried to cure her but stopped when the demon said that she'd die if he continued; of how the demons had overrun the church, while he stood helpless; of how he'd seen Izzy as a beautiful young woman, sitting on the altar and giving him the strength to cleanse the church and save those within it; of how Izzy had given her life to save her mother's, as her mother had once given up her body to save Izzy's life.

He kept speaking even as fresh tears poured out of Rebekah's eyes. When he was finished, she closed them and wept.

"Can I see her?" she said, finally.

"Later," he whispered. "When you're stronger. Please." Then, without knowing what he was doing, he added, "I—I brought this from our house."

He pulled out the picture and gave it to his wife. Rebekah held it in front of her for only a second, then she placed it over her heart and tried to keep the picture steady even as her body shook.

"We'll go back to our house," he said, and felt almost as if he were speaking to himself. He sat down in the chair next to the bed, held Rebekah's hand in his as the tears flowed from his own eyes. "Soon we'll go back to our house, honey. We'll get the rest of our pictures, all of them. We'll reclaim all of our memories."

After their grief had exhausted itself for the moment and they had sat together quietly for some time, Johnny became aware that Liz stood beside him, holding two bowls.

"I'm sorry, Father," she said. "I didn't want to disturb you." She saw his gaze go to the bowls in her hands, and said, "You should eat. This is yours. It has frosted flakes in it, I hope you like those. This one's just milk for Rebekah."

"How did you get milk?" he said, accepting the bowls and placing his on the floor by his chair.

"It was evaporated," she said. "We have lots."

He nodded gratefully, then said, "Are others eating?"

"Isaac made eggs for people," she said. "I'll track down the rest and make sure they have something to eat too." She paused as if a sudden thought had grasped her mind, then laughed softly to herself. "I was just thinking—Miles would be so upset with us right now. He thought we should always eat together, that every meal should be a sit-down meal."

"He's right," Johnny said. "We'll get back to that habit soon."

When she left, he helped Rebekah sit up against the column and tried to spoon-feed her some milk, but she insisted that she was strong enough to manage on her own.

They ate breakfast together mostly in silence; Rebekah stared off into the distance and he was unwilling to disturb her thoughts. When she was finished, he took the empty bowl from her and stacked it on top of his. She looked at him with a strange expression on her face.

"What?" he said, making a duck-like sound that used to playfully annoy her.

She shook her head, as if to say she wouldn't speak of the thoughts on her mind. Then, with a smile, she said, "So it's Father now?"

"Oh, yes," he said. "I've become a priest since last we spoke. Did I forget to mention that?"

She waited for him to explain, and he told her about Bishop Joseph, a man Johnny was convinced didn't like him all that much, but who'd ordained him a priest and put him in charge of the community.

"Probably he did it *because* he didn't like you," Rebekah said. "It's not such a plush gig these days."

"Glad you still have your sense of humor." Even Rebekah's little joke was tinged with sadness, though. *Will it ever be otherwise?* Then, answering himself, he thought of the words of Christ: *I have come that you may have life, and have it more abundantly.*

"He gave his life for me," he said.

"There seems to be a lot of that going around." Rebekah brought her hand to his cheek, rubbed her fingers against his stubble.

"We'll see her again," he said.

Rebekah nodded slowly.

"You don't believe that?"

"Of course I do." He opened his mouth, but she cut him off. "Johnny, I know. But I also know that the world is dying. And as bad as things have been, the worst is still ahead of us."

Although he thought the same, it was still shocking to hear someone else describe things so starkly. And not just someone else, but his wife. With everything that had happened, he felt that if she had given up, he'd give up too; he didn't think he could summon enough optimism to lift her up. He felt himself barely keeping his head above water, and that the weight of her despair would drag him down.

"Maybe it's a mercy that Izzy doesn't have to live through it," she continued. "If we're lucky, the time will be short. But if it's not, if Christ doesn't come in His glory right away, then it must be because there are still those for whom such a delay is profitable. There's still a chance for those people to repent, to be saved, to turn their hearts back to the Kingdom of God before His Light floods the world and its burning glow blinds and torments those who hate Him."

She smiled knowingly at the relief he knew was written all over his face. "You're a priest now, right?"

It's a strange non sequitur. "Yes," he said.

"Well doesn't that make me a *khouria*?"

"Yes, it does."

"Have I ever let you down before?"

"No," he said. "Never."

"For as long as it's in my power, John," she said, grabbing his face with both her hands and staring into his eyes, her voice stronger and surer than it had been so far, "I'll run the race with you, to the end, and by God's grace we'll enter into His Kingdom together, and make our little girl proud."

THAT evening around dinnertime, while Rebekah was sleeping, Johnny went looking for Michael. Isaac and Liz hadn't seen him since the night before when Michael was helping move the bodies of the dead into the basement. Johnny found him in Father Gord's office. Michael sat on the couch, reading from a Psalter he held in both hands by the waning sunlight coming through the second-story window, from which the curtain had been pulled back.

Johnny knocked on the open door to get his attention. When he looked up, Johnny said, "You look as tired as I feel."

"Trust me," Michael said, smiling, "you look as tired as you feel. How's your wife?"

"She's resting," Johnny said, stepping into the room. "She was able to eat some solid food at lunch. Nothing spectacular—we thawed and mashed up bananas and mixed it with nuts. But it's something."

"I'm glad. You helped her, just like you said you would."

But I lost our daughter, Johnny thought. *That wasn't part of the plan.* "My wife wants to see her," he said, and only after he'd spoken did he realize that his words must have sounded nonsensical to Michael. "My daughter," he explained.

Michael nodded slowly.

"Listen, I know you spent last night carrying all the bodies downstairs. How upset would you be if we moved them all back upstairs again?"

"To the church? Why?"

"I'd like to have a funeral service for them, first thing tomorrow morning. If you'll help me."

"Of course. I think it's a great idea. But—I'm sorry if this is insensitive—have you decided what we're going to do afterward? We can't keep them in the church or in the basement forever."

"I haven't changed my mind," Johnny said. "I'd still like to bury them, after the funeral."

"Bury them in the ground?"

Instead of answering, Johnny said, "You pulled back the curtain from the window."

"I didn't feel like lighting a candle," Michael said, a little defensively.

"What did you see?"

"I didn't look."

"Look now," Johnny said, although it was simply a hunch.

Michael stood and walked over to the window.

"What do you see?"

After a long pause, Michael said, "They're out there. There's a group of them standing behind the trees near the river."

"But why aren't they any closer? Why have they retreated so far when we're so vulnerable right now? Why not swoop in for the kill?"

"I don't know."

"Come and have dinner with us and we'll talk about it," Johnny said.

Isaac and Liz had the same reservations as Michael. The four of them stood in the kitchen, eating slices of pepperoni pizza with their hands. A stack of discarded boxes lay on the countertop; Tom had taken it upon himself to make dinner for everyone, but that consisted of removing pizzas from the freezer and putting them in the oven. Tom and the others had already eaten.

"We won't survive another attack," Isaac said. "We're too tired and our nerves are too shot. We should take the time to recuperate, maybe check out some of the new people, to see who can be relied on."

"They deserve to be buried," Liz said. "But I agree with Michael and Isaac—can we risk being attacked right now?"

Johnny put down his slice of pizza. "My feeling is that if we're not safe on the grounds of the church, in full view of the crosses on top, then we're not safe inside the church either. We saw that. I agree that we have to recoup our energies, I just don't see us doing it while we're living in fear. Some of us aren't sleeping," he continued, scanning their faces and trying not to linger on anyone's too long. "Some of us are eating only by forcing ourselves."

He paused, then settled his gaze on Isaac. "We have shovels, right?" he said.

Isaac nodded, a little reluctantly.

"You three go get them, then meet me upstairs."

"Where are you going?" Isaac said, but Johnny was already moving away and didn't stop to answer him.

He went upstairs to the narthex to wait for them.

Stop me if this is just my own arrogance. He continued to pray until the others joined him.

Michael and Liz carried a shovel and flashlight each; Isaac two pairs. He handed the second shovel to Johnny, who took it and leaned it against the wall near the door.

"I don't believe we're in danger," he said, "and I'm going outside to prove it."

"And if you're wrong?" Michael said.

"You're the ones with the shovels. You come out and rescue me."

Michael handed his flashlight to Liz, then fished something out of his cassock's pockets. "It was the bishop's," he said, approaching Johnny. "I believe he'd want you to have it."

Johnny bent his neck and Michael slipped the large golden cross over his head.

"Thank you," Johnny said, holding it up to examine it, then letting it fall back into place on his chest. Liz tried to give him Michael's flashlight, but he waved it away.

Isaac stood ready, both hands gripping the door handle. Johnny took a deep breath, then nodded. The big man swung open the door.

Chapter 25

JOHNNY stepped outside. The sun had sunk further into the horizon and a diffuse orange glow illuminated the trees and the river ahead. He peered around in all directions, but couldn't see anyone. It was eerily quiet. Too quiet, unnaturally so. They were still out there, he sensed, watching him.

"I know you can hear me," he said in a loud voice. "And I know the night has been long. But haven't you read, 'the night is far spent, the day is at hand'? And in another place, 'the end of all things is at hand'? Or again, 'the darkness is passing away, the true light is already shining'?

"You have thrived in the shadows, yes—but the ax is laid at the root of the tree. Don't you know that you will be cut down, and that the Light of Christ will be revealed? It will shine forth into the world, and it will destroy you like the sun melts away the cold morning dew."

He saw something finally, movement near the river. He walked down the staircase and peered into the growing darkness.

"You have become very bold, I know," he continued. "But what do you think you're doing? What is the purpose of all your manic activity? It's maniacal. It's pointless—you will be destroyed, you know that. Your sentence is certain. He is already on His throne at the right hand of God, and you will be made His footstool."

Below the tree where he'd first seen his wife when she was in the power of the demons, he caught sight of the old man half-illuminated by the fading light.

But isn't it written, "Don't worry about tomorrow," Johnny Salibi? For whatever is to come—today we will feast on your pain and desolation. We will separate you from the One you think loves you, that you may feel His wrath as we feel it.

Instead of responding, Johnny broke into a run toward him, the large golden cross clattering against his chest. As the old man had been speaking to him across that unnatural distance, and Johnny felt anger rising up inside of him, it was quickly overwhelmed by a different kind of feeling: a righteous anger under-girded by deep sadness. Father Gord, pitiful in his soiled underwear and his starving body, didn't deserve what was happening to him; didn't deserve to be the personification of the demon possessing him; didn't deserve to be the visible target of Johnny's fear and hatred. Whatever he'd done in this life, God knew—and God alone could judge.

In the faint light, he didn't know what the old man's reaction was to his sudden and rapid approach. But Father Gord hadn't moved, and that was all Johnny cared about: he headed straight for him, his heart full to bursting with pity for everything his old priest had been forced to suffer; and with compassion, because Johnny too had suffered at the hands of these demons, though in different ways; and with love, because he suddenly saw that this man he'd once despised was, if nothing else, his own flesh and blood. Father Gord was his fellow human being, and they shared the same Father in heaven.

All of the natural affection one feels for one's closest friends and family, and all of the forgiveness one so easily offers to oneself, Johnny felt going out from him with the force of a windstorm bursting out of his heart.

As he'd approached, Johnny saw that a small smile had formed on Father Gord's parched and broken lips, a knowing and victorious smile. But it had begun to fade as Johnny got closer, to be slowly replaced by confusion and wariness.

Johnny stopped short only so he wouldn't knock Father Gord to the ground, then grabbed him and pulled him into an embrace, ignoring the old man's attempts to fight him off except to hold him tighter.

"Why do you torment this son of Adam?" he said, whispering into his ear. "Leave him be, by the power of the new Adam who has broken the bonds of death. In the name of Christ, I tell you, leave him be."

The life went out of the old man, to such an extent that he would've dropped to the ground if Johnny didn't hold on to him. But right before he died, there was a moment when Father Gord stopped trying to push Johnny away and instead tried to return his embrace; the movement was slight and feeble, but Johnny felt Father Gord's arms close around his back before the old man's arms fell away. As he laid him on the ground, Johnny saw that the sneer had fallen away from Father Gord's face as well.

After a few moments, he picked him up again, which wasn't difficult because the old man's body weighed almost nothing, and carried him back to the church.

"It's all right," he called out. "You can come outside."

The door opened, and Isaac stepped out first, holding the shovel over his right shoulder, gripping it tightly with both hands as if it were a baseball bat he was ready to swing. He looked at Johnny with a mixture of suspicion and fear, Michael and Liz coming out behind him and standing at the top of the staircase with shovels in one hand and flashlights in the other. The beams of light were fixed suspiciously on Johnny's face.

He squinted from the light but smiled. "The grace of our Lord Jesus Christ, and the love of God the Father, and the communion of the Holy Spirit, be with you all."

Reflexively, Michael said, "And with your spirit." Isaac's face split into a grin as hearty and wide as any Johnny had ever seen, which turned congratulatory at the sight of their fallen foe, whom Johnny cradled in his arms like a baby. Liz thanked God repeatedly that Johnny was safe in a soft voice that she probably didn't expect to carry to him.

It didn't take long for both of them to realize that something was wrong, however. Michael had glanced down at the body, then quickly back up at Johnny and down again. "My God," he said. "My God, forgive me."

"This man was my priest as a child," Johnny said to Liz and Isaac. "He was taken by the demons, but Christ has set him free. I loved him. The subdeacon did too. Michael," he continued, "will you carry him into the church?"

Michael nodded, handed his shovel to Isaac, and took the body from Johnny.

"Father Gord wasn't perfect," Johnny said, when Michael returned. "None of us is. Whatever he did, though, I feel I owe him the honor of a decent burial; I believe he may have saved my soul. Unless you object, Subdeacon, I would like to bury him with the others."

"I'd like that very much," Michael said. "Thank you, Father."

They dug throughout the night in the stretch of grass to the side of the parking lot. At first they worked only by the faint moonlight and then, as people from inside the church joined them, by the light of the candles they brought. Tom had been the first to come looking for them, shining his flashlight for a while and then saying, decisively, "You're digging a grave. I'd like to help."

Throughout the night, they took turns digging, napping or resting on some chairs that were brought up, or holding candles in the spontaneous vigil. By the time they'd finished carving out the large hole, inclined on one side, there wasn't a living soul left in the church, as even those who couldn't walk were carried out. Rebekah had come outside by leaning on the shoulder of an older woman.

As the sun rose, they returned to the church and brought the bodies to the nave, placing them in front of the altar. With Michael's help, Johnny held a funeral service for them. Throughout, Johnny noticed, Rebekah's gaze never left Izzy's body.

At the end of the service, they wrapped the bodies in linens and took them outside. Johnny carried the bishop; Rebekah carried Izzy; Michael carried Father Gord; Isaac and Steven together carried Miles. Behind them came those who carried the bodies of Wassim and Fatima, and their grandchildren, and the others who'd died in the church basement or on its porch.

Outside, each person walked down the incline and placed the body they bore in the earth, saying with a loud voice as they came back up, "Into Your hands, Father, we commend the spirit of our beloved" and adding their names for those of whom it was known, and "brother" or "sister" otherwise.

Johnny's heart broke as he heard his wife say their daughter's name.

INSIDE they had breakfast together. Johnny blessed the food and said that they ate it in memory of those who had departed this life, both known and unknown, in the faith and out of it, and he called on God to shine His mercy and His love on all of them.

Although he sat next to his wife, he didn't get any real chance to talk to Rebekah since it seemed everyone else wanted to talk to him. After dinner, and after he and Steven and Theresa had finished washing and drying the dishes, he went looking for her.

He found Rebekah arguing with Liz, who turned gratefully at his approach. "She's been running around, cleaning wounds and replacing bandages and feeding people, as if she's a doctor and not one of the patients. Can you please tell her she needs to take a break?"

"I feel fine," Rebekah said, not without some exasperation.

"Leave her to me," he said to Liz, then took Rebekah by the hand. He led her to her bed by the column.

"Johnny—" she began.

"Just sit down, please? There's something I need to tell you."

She sat down on the bed and waited.

"I'm sorry, honey." She tried to stop him. "Rebekah, listen to me," he said, speaking over her. "I'm sorry about what happened to Izzy. I'm sorry about what happened to you, honey, and everything you've had to go through. And I'm sorry that I didn't listen to you and come to this church in the first place. Maybe none of this"—he cut off his own thought with a shake of his head and, after a brief pause, started again: "I needed you to hear that, and I'm begging for your forgiveness."

"You have it," she said. "I'm sorry too." Johnny tried to interrupt her, to say she had nothing to apologize for, but she spoke over him this time and said, "I tried to kill myself, John. The night I gave Izzy to you. I saw what they were doing—I saw they were going to use me to get to you, and maybe even to Izzy. So I forced my body to the river and tried to drown myself. But the demon inside of me was too strong, and he wouldn't let me."

"Wait," he said, gripping her shoulders almost in anger. "Are you apologizing for failing to kill yourself?"

She didn't look him in the eyes, and he saw tears forming in hers. "I caused you a lot of suffering. I—"

"Listen to me, thank God that demon wouldn't let you drown. Thank God, you understand?"

She nodded.

He hugged her closer to him, and held her in his arms. After a while, he climbed up beside her, lay his back against the column, and Rebekah rested her head on his lap.

She'd been so quiet for so long that he thought she'd fallen asleep, but presently she asked him what he was thinking about.

"Some people want me to baptize them," he said. "It started with a young man named Tom, but he spoke to some others and now there's a handful who've come to talk to me."

"What are you going to do?"

"That's what I've been thinking about. I've decided to baptize them. Tomorrow, in the river."

He couldn't see her face; she didn't say anything.

"The demons won't bother us," he said.

He felt certain she would question him, or at least express concern or doubt—and given everything that she'd gone through, he wouldn't have blamed her.

Instead, though, she turned her head to look up at him and smiled. "What can I do to help?" she said.

Chapter 26

THE next morning, Father John, in his priestly vestments and carrying a golden cross around his neck and a wooden cross in his right hand, led a group out of the church and to the river. There he baptized them in the name of the Father, and of the Son, and of the Holy Spirit. He baptized all who wanted to be baptized who'd never been baptized before; the others he blessed with the sign of the cross.

With him were his coworkers: first, his wife Rebekah, from whom he had cast out a demon; then his subdeacon Michael, and Liz, and Isaac, and Steven, and Theresa. These brought to him more people to bless or baptize, for the demons did not attack them but fled from them, so that many who were held captive in that area were set free.

By the time he was finished, dark, pregnant clouds had formed. Spears of rain began to pierce the surface of the water. A crack of thunder tore across the sky.

He raised his eyes. A beam of sunlight had managed to break through the dark clouds in the distance.

In Father John's ears, the thunder spoke as if with a voice, a deep and terrifying voice, the voice of the Alpha and the Omega, crying out the words He'd spoken to the Beloved Disciple: "Behold, I am coming quickly."

Even so, come, Lord Jesus, he prayed in his heart. *Even so, come.*

ABOUT THE AUTHOR

An Orthodox Christian, Karl El-Koura lives with his family in Ottawa, Canada's capital city, and works a regular job by day while writing fiction at night. In 2012, he independently published the present work, his debut novel. He published the sequel, *Bishop John vs the Antichrist*, in 2015, and the final novel in the trilogy, *St. John vs Death*, in 2024.

Karl maintains an online home at http://www.ootersplace.com, where you can discover more work by him and keep up-to-date with his latest news. He can be reached at karl@ootersplace.com.

Did you love *Father John vs the Zombies?* You should read the sequels!

Bishop John vs the Antichrist:
Book Two of the Father John Trilogy

They've barely survived a worldwide plague—will they survive what comes next?

Beset by violent nightmares and feeling abandoned by the God whose presence he'd felt so keenly only a short while ago, Father John Salibi is distracted, irritable, and completely devoid of spiritual power.

But then he meets an enigmatic old man who tells him that all will be well. In contrast to John, the old man commands staggering power: he travels great distances in moments, he multiplies food in his hands; and he performs wonderful miracles of healing in a world desperately in need of healing.

The old man even claims to have defeated the antichrist, the mysterious figure haunting John's dreams and whose activity in the world allowed the plague John had once thought of, in his ignorance, as the "zombie apocalypse." Is the old man real, or a figment of John's troubled imagination? If real, where does his power come from—from God or from somewhere else?

A story of good and evil, of faith and love, of defeat and death and resurrection, and of the one thing necessary.

In this epic sequel to *Father John vs the Zombies*, the story of the end of the world continues...

Visit <u>www.ootersplace.com/BishopJohn</u> for more information.

Saint John vs Death:
Book Three of the Father John Trilogy

A man who has survived a world overrun by demons, and who has withstood the temptations and assaults of the antichrist, must now face the ultimate test. He enters the undiscovered country of death, where he must choose between darkness and light, between deceit and truth, between accepting an easy, false paradise or clinging to the One who is the true paradise of human hearts.

In this captivating conclusion to the Father John trilogy, John Salibi's death is only the beginning of a fearsome but wondrous adventure.

Visit www.ootersplace.com/StJohn for more information.

www.ingramcontent.com/pod-product-compliance
Lightning Source LLC
Chambersburg PA
CBHW010730250626
47155CB00011B/3628